OVER HER HEAD

In the Shadow Book 3

JL CROSSWHITE

Tandem Services Press
SOUTHERN CALIFORNIA

Praise for JL Crosswhite

"This is a very suspenseful story and I'm looking forward to the next book in this series."—Ginny, Amazon reviewer

"I was impressed with the suspense in this book as well as the romance. Great storyline. Morality issues were great. An overall great read."—Kindle customer

"Absolutely loved it. Fast paced and kept me guessing concerning the outcome. I highly recommend it to all who like a good mystery or suspense."—Linda Reville

"Very well written, with interwoven stories and well developed characters"—Mary L. Sarrault

Other books by JL Crosswhite

Hometown Heroes series

Promise Me, prequel novella
Protective Custody, book 1
Flash Point, book 2
Special Assignment, book 3

In the Shadow series

Off the Map, book 1
Out of Range, book 2
Over Her Head, book 3

The Route Home series, writing as Jennifer Crosswhite

Be Mine, prequel novella
Coming Home, book 1
The Road Home, book 2
Finally Home, book 3

Contemporary romance, writing as Jennifer Crosswhite

The Inn at Cherry Blossom Lane

Eat the Elephant: How to Write (and Finish!) Your Book One Bite at a Time, writing as Jen Crosswhite

Devotional, writing as Jennifer Crosswhite

Worthy to Write: Blank pages tying your stomach in knots? 30 prayers to tackle that fear!

Published by Tandem Services Press

Post Office Box 220

Yucaipa, California

www.TandemServicesInk.com

Ebook ISBN 978-1-954986-01-5

Print ISBN 978-1-954986-02-2

Library of Congress Control Number: 2021910117

Cover design credit: Alexander von Ness of Nessgraphica

To my Bible study ladies from Sermon on the Mount. I loved digging into Jesus's words with you. Thank you for your prayers and encouragement on my journey.

Behold, I am doing a new thing: now it springs forth, do you not perceive it? I will make a way in the wilderness and rivers in the desert.

Isaiah 43:19

Chapter One

Jessica Blake swept the last of the client's platinum blonde hair into the dustpan at the end of the first day of her job at Salon Moritz as she tried to tune out the chatter about clubbing from the girls around her. Not her. Not anymore. She was headed straight home after this. There was still a pint of mint chip in the freezer, if Mom hadn't eaten it yet. That was celebration enough. She was lucky to get this job right out of cosmetology school.

Madison Rubio, the stylist Jessica was working under, seemed pleased with her work. Though it had been a long day, her heart was light at the praise she received. She hadn't realized how much her parched heart needed the watering of encouraging words. It had been a long time.

Lyric Madden came bounding over, neatly side-stepping the pile of clippings Jessica had made. "The girls invited us to go for drinks with them to celebrate our first day on the job. Sounds fun." Lyric had gone to Jessica's school, and they'd both started here today.

But the salon owner, Crystal Moritz, had made it clear there was only one permanent position. And that she was watching. Of course, she'd left about two hours ago. Still, given the amount of gossip that went around a salon, Jessica wouldn't be surprised if every bit of what went on here made its way back to Crystal.

"I can't. Sorry." Jessica put away the broom and dustpan and grabbed the glass cleaning spray. She wiped down the mirror then looked around. Anything else that needed to be done? Otherwise, she'd better to get out of here before she got questioned further.

Lyric tugged on Jessica's arm. "Come on. You can't say no." She leaned in and lowered her voice. "It's a great way for us to make friends with them outside of work, get some face time in so we both can keep our jobs. You know they'll report back to Crystal. You don't want to give off a vibe that you're too good for them."

Jessica shook her head. "That's not it at all. I just have other plans." With nothing else to do, she headed to the break room and grabbed her bag out of her locker.

Lyric stayed on her heels. "It can't be that important. Whatever it is, change it."

Jessica rolled her shoulders. She hadn't expected this. She should have had a ready excuse, something unassailable. Mother's birthday? Already passed. Grandma's funeral? Not funny. The way Gran was going, she'd outlive them all.

Near the stations, Erika—the stylist Lyric was working with—and Madison stood with designer bags over their shoulders. Erika touched up her lipstick in the mirror and adjusted her sleek blonde bob that swished below her jawline. "We're thinking of drinks in Newport. I'll buy the first round. And then maybe see where we want to go for dinner. And whatever else sounds fun." She laughed. "We don't have any early appointments tomorrow. So no need to worry about a curfew, girls."

Jessica swallowed. How was she going to get out of this? She'd been sober eight months, and she wasn't about to risk it. If it came down to her sobriety and her job, she'd of course choose sobriety. But did it have to come down to that? How could she keep her promises to herself without losing this job that had been hard won? Especially since Madison liked her work. She could imagine the disappointment in her parents' eyes if they found out she lost her job the first day. Or maybe they wouldn't be surprised.

Madison frowned. "No. Don't tell me you have a hot date already?"

"Uh, well, actually…" Jessica bit her lip.

Madison grinned and tucked a dark, long curl behind her ear. "Spill it. Who is he? Do you have a picture?"

Jessica dug in her bag to buy herself time. Madison had handed her an excuse. Yet who could she say was her date? Joe or Kyle, her brother's friends and practically her big brothers, would likely cover for her. She probably had some pictures from the wedding. Well, Kyle had been the groom, so he was off this list. Her fingers closed over her phone, and she brought it out, swiping it on.

"Of course she does. At least we can go on his social media profile." Lyric hovered over Jessica.

No time to type out a quick rescue message with Lyric watching her every move. She opened her photos. One of her and Austin came up in the grid of recent images. Memories of their slow dance at the wedding washed over her. Austin was one thing in her life she didn't want to mess up. Her dating track record was nothing to be proud of. Even if she wasn't exactly dating Austin. They were…friends. He was about as opposite of her as you could get: solid, logical, steady. And yet since he was new in town, she felt like she could actually help him with something: navigating a new social environment by introducing him to friends and inviting him places.

The phone slipped out of her hand as Lyric snatched it away. "Ooh, he's cute. What's his name?"

"Austin. And yes, he's cute. Now I've got to go." She stuck out her hand and wiggled her fingers. What kind of person took someone else's phone? They barely knew each other.

Lyric spun away, tapping on Jessica's phone and giggling. What was she doing?

"Lyric, give it back, please."

Lyric flashed Austin's picture at Erika and Madison, who giggled.

"Yep, he's a hottie. Worth spending time with him for sure," Madison said.

Lyric handed the phone back to Jessica.

"What did you do?"

Lyric shrugged. "We want to meet him. I just said you needed to be picked up."

Jessica saw the last sent text message on her screen. **Hey babe. Come pick me up at the salon? I promise I'll make it worth your while.** Followed by heart and kiss emojis.

Jessica's face heated. How was she going to explain this to Austin? She'd have to call him. It was more than she could say in a text.

To her horror, three dots flashed across the screen. He was texting her back. Oh no! She couldn't call him right now, not with these three listening.

Be there in a few.

Lyric peeked over Jessica's shoulder. "Ooh, it worked. We'll get to meet him." She squeezed Jessica's arm. "You made a good choice."

Austin Montgomery didn't know how anyone got any work done in this open-office concept with all the noise and distraction. In the two hours since most people had cleared out, he'd reveled in the quiet and gotten more work done and made more progress than he had all day. Finally, he was able to feel good about the work he was doing. This program had real potential to help businesses overcome their marketing challenges in a simple and elegant way. If he ever had time to work on it.

It didn't help that Randy Dalton, their acting group leader, kept pulling him into meetings. It was enough to make him yank out his hair.

Footsteps muffled by the carpet caused him to peer over his computer monitor. Who was still in the building? Max Harmon's glossy, slicked-back head of hair appeared over a divider a minute before his lanky body materialized around the corner, messenger bag slung over his shoulder. His boss, the VP of Operations.

"You still here?" Max set his travel mug on Austin's desk and let the bag drop into the chair.

"It's the only time I can get any work done." He waved a hand at their surroundings. "This open-office concept might be great for collaboration, but it's terrible for concentration."

Max nodded. "I know. I've been talking to Edward about making some changes. But he wants to hire the Software Engineering Director first." Edward was the Chief of Operations, Max's boss. He'd had a heart attack a few months ago but seemed to be ramped up to full-time work again. Because they didn't have a director for Austin's department, Randy had been named the temporary group lead. And Austin's biggest headache.

"Which is why I'm glad you're still here. I wanted to talk to you about something."

Austin glanced at his monitor one more time. He wasn't going to get any more work done tonight. Plus, he was hungry. He saved everything and began shutting his system down. "What's that?"

"I think you should apply for the director position."

"What?" Was Max crazy? Austin was an engineer, not a boss.

"Hear me out. How well do you think Randy's doing at leading the group?"

Austin shook his head. "He's a micromanager. We have so many meetings and status updates that we can't get anything done."

Max met his gaze for a minute. "Edward's leaning toward

letting him have the position. They'll recruit from outside, but Randy has the inside track since he knows the staff and the projects."

No. No, no, no. If Randy was his boss, he'd have to seriously consider leaving. It was one thing to put up with temporary frustration. It was another to live that way. It was almost enough to make him consider applying for the job. Almost.

"Look, I know he's not ideal. Or even preferable. I personally think you could do a much better job. You may not think you have much in the way of leadership experience, but the team looks up to you. They would respect you. You know what needs to get done and the best way to do it. We could get you whatever support staff you need. Just do me a favor. Consider it, seriously. Okay?"

Austin stared at the man for a moment. Then he let out a breath. "Okay. I'll think about it. But no promises."

Max grabbed his cup and bag. "That's all I ask."

Austin's phone buzzed on his desk. He normally kept it shut in a drawer, but ever since Dad had been diagnosed with dementia, he tried to be more available. His gaze slid to the screen. A text message, but he couldn't see from whom.

Max pointed at the phone. "I'll let you get that. Hope it's your dinner plans." He winked then headed out.

Ha! Dinner plans. He hadn't even thought about which drive-thru he'd hit up on the way home. He snatched up the phone.

Hey babe. Come pick me up at the salon? I promise I'll make it worth your while. Love and kisses emojis ended the text from Jessica.

He read it twice. Had she drunk texted him? She'd confided her struggle to him at Heather and Kyle's wedding when she avoided using sparkling wine for the toast, opting instead for sparkling water. He'd joined her. He didn't care for the taste of alcohol and never wanted to be out of control, so it was no loss for him. She'd been sober for eight months, and he knew how committed she was to it. But he didn't know what to make of this text.

And wasn't this her first day at her new job? Maybe it was a joke. He'd admit he didn't always get humor, especially over something like text. Why couldn't people just be straight forward?

He blew out a breath. The first line was the kicker. Babe? She'd never called him that. But heat rushed through him at the idea. No, he and Jessica were too different. They were just friends. Even if they'd escaped a fire together and survived the singles' table at Kyle and Heather's wedding. And she'd been a good friend to him, introducing him, carrying the conversation in that easy way she had with people. He admired her passion and boldness, her lack of concern about what others thought. She let out all the things he kept locked up inside.

Grabbing his keys and his backpack, he knew there was only one way to find out what was going on. He'd go pick her up. He texted her back.

Be there in a few.

His mind spun out scenarios. If she was drunk, then he could take her to her sponsor or one of their mutual friends. How did he help her and not mess it up? He didn't have the capacity for someone struggling with a problem as big as this. He could barely help his family with their issues. No, he couldn't help her. But he could get her to someone who could.

He'd just climbed into his car, grateful that he'd driven today —planning to grocery shop after work—instead of riding his bike like he usually did, when another text came through.

Sorry! One of the girls took my phone and texted you. Could you do me a huge favor and pretend we have a dinner date tonight? I'll explain later.

Relief flooded through him. Now there was a logical explanation. He was curious as to why someone would take Jessica's phone and text him. But ever since he'd moved to Orange

County, California, to work with DataCorp, life had been a little more strange than he'd expected.

Sure. On my way.

It was just late enough that much of the rush-hour traffic had dissipated. And it helped that the salon wasn't too far from his office. Jessica's text mentioned pretending they had a date tonight. He wasn't good at pretending. Not at all. So, if they had dinner together, it wouldn't be pretending. Where could they go? A few options were close by. He'd give her a choice.

As he turned into the parking lot, he considered if he would have to go inside the salon to get Jessica. He didn't want to, but at least he could honestly say they were going to dinner.

But she stood out front and waved to him, hopping in the car the moment he pulled close. "Thanks for rescuing me."

"Don't you want to get your car?"

"Maybe later. Could we just leave before they come bombard you with questions?"

Three women exited the salon, smiling and waving.

Jessica waved back. "Let's go."

Austin pulled out of the parking lot and onto the street. "Do you feel like seafood or hamburgers?"

Jessica glanced back. "Um, hadn't really thought about it. Why?"

"We're going to dinner. That way it won't be a lie."

She laughed. "Austin, you're amazing. Thank you." She pushed her blonde hair still sporting the hot-pink streak back from her face.

She looked great, as usual. Dinner with her was no hardship.

"California Fish Grill is close. Why don't we eat there? Then you can bring me back for my car after."

"Sounds good. So what happened? I was worried you had drunk texted me and needed me to take you to your sponsor."

She pinned him with a glare, her jaw firm. "What? Why would you think that? I'm committed to my sobriety. That's the last thing I'd do."

He shrugged. "I didn't know what to think. It wasn't like you."

"Because it wasn't me." She explained about Lyric and the girls' offer for drinks and dinner and her scramble to find a way out. Her tone was more strident than he'd ever heard it.

He parked in front of the restaurant. "That's mean. What kind of person does that?"

She got out and shrugged. "Some people think it's funny. Maybe it was. Just a little."

He opened the restaurant door for her, bumping his shoulder into hers. "I'm just glad I got to be the rescue hero for once."

She rolled her eyes at him.

They placed their orders then found a table.

Austin put the blinking pager between them. "Other than that, how was your first day?"

"Busy. It's a high-end clientele, very demanding. I didn't even have time for lunch. But Madison seemed happy with my work. We'll see. Lyric—the girl who took my phone—she and I are basically competing for the same permanent position."

"Sounds vicious."

She opened her mouth just as their pager buzzed and blinked.

He snatched it. "I'll go get our order." Hopping up to grab their tray of food, Max's words rattled in his head. He hadn't had time to process them. Maybe he'd talk about it with Matthew when he got home. But his roommate had been spending every spare moment with his girlfriend, Kim. If only he had Matthew's charisma and way with people, he'd take the job in a minute. But Austin didn't have those kinds of skills. He brought the tray back to their table and set it down. After he asked the blessing on their food, they dug in.

The silence stretched a bit as they ate. Jessica had done a brave thing, reaching out to him for help so she could keep something important to her: her sobriety. Maybe he could learn from her.

"My boss stopped by my office on his way out tonight." He gave her a quick rundown of their problems and Max's offer.

"You should totally do it."

He shook his head. "I'm not a leader. I'm not good with people. I'm good with numbers, machines, code, logic. Things that make sense. People don't make sense."

She laughed. "True. But Austin, Max is right. People do look to you. You could make the work situation so much better, not only for yourself, but for your whole team. You could advocate for them. You know what they need. Matthew can help you with people skills. But honestly, most people just want someone to listen to them."

Warmth flooded him for the second time that evening. Unusual, but not uncomfortable. She believed in him. Huh. He'd have to think about that.

They finished up their meals, and he dropped Jessica back at her car. She leaned over and gave him a quick hug. "Thanks for bailing me out." She opened her door.

He touched her arm. "I'm glad you called me. And I'm glad you had a good first day, ending not withstanding. You're going to kill it at this job."

She smiled and held his gaze a moment. "Thanks. That means a lot." Then she left the car, leaving a swirl of her scent in her wake.

He made sure she got in her car and started it before he pulled out. As usual, he'd misread the situation. Why did women have to be so complicated? And while he thought he was rescuing her, she was also rescuing him.

Mia Latham cranked up the volume on the Cardi B song she was listening to over her computer. Her stupid parents had taken her phone away. Just because she'd come home after curfew. They didn't understand. She'd seen Isaac at the beach with another chick. No wonder he'd been ghosting her. They'd gone to prom together and talked about how great this summer was going to be before their senior year. Then he'd just grown distant.

Thank goodness Vanessa and Olivia were with her. They'd gone to Olivia's house and hung out, talking trash about him. It made her feel better, but she lost track of time and missed curfew. Which was stupid and too early for summer. It wasn't like she had to get up for school. Plus, she was almost eighteen.

She pulled up Instagram on her computer. There was a message waiting for her from Nicholas. She smiled. His messages always made her feel better. He told her how beautiful she was, how she deserved so much better. He really understood her. Even if he was older. Her parents would freak if they knew. But he was a friend of her cousin's. She told him what was going on.

You don't deserve that. He's an idiot for breaking up with you. Sneak out after your parents are asleep. I'll come get you. We'll have fun. Then I'll introduce you to a friend of mine who has modeling contacts. I showed him your picture and he said you'd be perfect. He wants to meet you. He can get you work.

Wow. Really? She always thought she was too short to be a model. But maybe that didn't matter as much anymore. Her parents would worry if she was gone tomorrow. But maybe it would serve them right. Soon enough she'd be on her own, and they'd never know what she was doing. And since they'd taken her phone, she wouldn't be able to contact them to let them know where she was. Maybe if they worried about her for a day or two, they'd be more reasonable when she came back.

I'm not sure. I kinda want to make my folks worry for being so mean, but it might just make things worse when I come back.

There was a long gap before Nicholas replied. Maybe she'd been too much of a baby. Maybe he didn't think she was grown-up enough. She was just about to reply when his message came through.

If you change your mind, I'll bring you back home. You could be back before they woke up.

She smiled. That just proved what a great guy he was. Always thinking about her and her feelings.

I'll see you in an hour.

She gave him her address.

Chapter Two

Jessica sat in Kim's car as they looked for parking in Sarah's condo complex. Kim had given Jessica a ride after she'd gotten off work for this very reason —parking was difficult. Luckily Saturdays ended earlier than most days. But battling the parking was worth it to get together with the girls. It would be one of their last ones before everything changed. Heather and Kyle were already married. Sarah was marrying Joe at the end of August. Scott and Melissa were sure to be married soon, and Melissa would move up to Washington State with him. Kim and Matthew were serious.

Jessica's support system was shifting. And she wasn't sure how she felt about that. In the past, she would have numbed her feelings with alcohol. But that wasn't an option. And since she didn't think drowning her feelings in mint chip was the healthiest plan, she had to come up with some better options.

Austin's face flashed through her mind. She hadn't heard from him since he'd rescued her earlier this week. She'd sent him a thank you text the next day and had gotten a terse text back. Which she knew now was just his way. Face it, they were just friends of convenience. They'd gotten thrown together when everyone else was paired off. He'd been in Laguna Vista for two months now. Pretty soon he'd know everyone well enough himself and wouldn't need her to help him make the connections. A heaviness settled over her.

"You must be in deep thought." Kim's voice broke through Jessica's contemplations. "Work going okay?"

Jessica realized they had parked. She pulled down the visor and checked her appearance in the mirror. Should she do something different with her hair? Get rid of the pink streak. "Yeah. Madison is happy with my work. It's a lot of hours, but I think today I finally figured out where everything was and how I could be most useful. It's the kind of salon I've always dreamed about working in. It still seems a bit surreal that I got the job." She and Kim climbed out and headed toward Sarah's condo. They'd parked fairly far away.

"How's Austin?" Kim grinned.

"You know as much as I do. I haven't seen him since he rescued me Tuesday." She'd told Kim the story that night on the phone when she'd gotten home.

"Matthew said there's a lot going on at work in Austin's department."

"Yeah, he mentioned that. I'm sure I'll see him tomorrow at church."

"Let's plan on lunch after per usual." Kim knocked on Sarah's door.

Sarah opened up and hugged them both. "Come on in. I thought we'd sit on the back deck since the sun is behind the trees and is heading down. It won't be too hot."

They crossed the living area of the small condo and exited the French doors to Sarah's wooden deck. Heather, Melissa, and Allie were already seated with icy drinks.

"Help yourself to refreshments." Sarah gestured to the teak table set with frosty pitchers of iced tea and fruit-spiked water along with platters of fruit.

Jessica grabbed a drink and a snack then found a seat. Sarah's garden was so peaceful. The weight of the world fell away, as if she'd stepped into another world. She tuned out the chatter of the women around her, letting rest wash over her. She didn't realize how weary she'd become until she had a moment to check in with herself. In the past, she would have pressed on, seeking some adventure in unhealthy ways to keep the adrenaline flowing. But now? Peace had developed its own allure. She clung to that, and trusted that God would make his path forward visible to her as she needed it.

Melissa leaned forward. "Tell us about your wedding plans. Do you need help with anything?"

Sarah grinned. "I should ask you the same thing. Anything you want to tell us?"

Melissa shrugged. "We haven't made any firm decisions yet. Whatever we do, it will be small and simple. Neither of us wants a big fuss."

"Boy, do I hear you on that." Sarah blew out a breath. "Honestly, if I could have my way, I'd get married right here." She glanced around her fully blooming garden surrounding them. "It's my happy place. But it's not real practical. Still, I see why people elope. I love Joe's sisters, but… They're a bit overwhelming."

Kim nudged Heather. "You got off easy in the sister-in-law department."

"Don't I know it." Heather wrapped her arm around Kim's shoulders and gave them a squeeze.

Sarah talked for a bit about her plans to find something similar to her back patio, a garden-like setting. "We found a beautiful place in Dove Canyon. It's a courtyard on a hill surrounded by flowers. It's got a gazebo and a waterfall. It's just perfect. And it holds two hundred people. Plenty for us. But then Sophia, Joe's oldest sister, kept suggesting other places with bigger capacity. She even called around and made appointments for us to see different venues, including the Hacienda, where she got married. I appreciate her wanting to help, it's just that I feel she's working at cross purposes with me. I got a guest list from their side of the family that's nearly two hundred people itself. I'm constantly getting texts from her with all these ideas of what we should do. She even made her own Pinterest board of our wedding."

"What does Joe say about it?" Heather asked.

"He's talked to her, but she still sees him as the little brother she practically raised after their dad died. She acts like he doesn't know what he wants."

Melissa pointed a strawberry at her. "It's your wedding. You should have what you want."

"I know. And Joe will back me one hundred percent with whatever I want. I just hate to make waves. His family has a part in this too. Besides, some things I don't have strong feelings about."

"Sarah, I love you like a sister. But I also know you can't stand conflict. And I'm sure that's what's flowing under the surface of all of this. You don't want to start out your life with Joe in conflict with his family. But your opinion matters. You matter. Especially on your wedding day."

Tears welled in Sarah's eyes as she nodded. "I know. Thank you for reminding me of that. I just want everyone to be happy."

Melissa laughed. "An impossible task. Just focus on the kind of day you and Joe want. Everyone else will come around. You can't control what other people do, think, or feel."

Sarah ran a finger under each eye.

"On that happy note, let's talk about the bachelorette party," Heather said. She was Sarah's matron of honor.

Jessica slid a look at Kim. She seemed to have shrunk a bit, sliding down into the ice-blue chair cushions. She had planned Heather's bachelorette party that had been rudely interrupted by a forest fire that sent them to the middle of Holcomb Lake until they could be rescued. Memorable, but not in a good way. Kim still blamed herself, for some weird reason.

Though Jessica knew plenty about misplaced guilt. She still struggled with guilt for failing to live up to the ideal that her big brother Christopher had set, even though he had died before she was born. Competing with a ghost was a losing battle, she had to remind herself.

The women talked about a spa day. Melissa and Allie had great things to say about the place Heather had chosen.

Jessica spun the glass in her hand and listened. She was on the periphery of this group, invited because of her brother Scott and his relationship with these women and their significant others more than her own merits. Still, they were kind enough to include her. Melissa was already treating her like a sister, even before she and Scott married. And Kim had gladly resurrected their old friendship.

All of their phones buzzed nearly at the same time. An Amber Alert for a missing seventeen-year-old girl. Jessica swiped through and read the details. She could remember being seventeen and mad at the world, dumb enough to make stupid choices. She prayed this girl was found quickly.

Heather spoke up. "I hope she's not a human trafficking victim. Kyle said there's a ring that's getting more active in this area. Often they offer young girls the promise of a job or a modeling career. So please keep your eyes open and be aware. If something doesn't look right, call the police."

A shudder ran through Jessica. God had kept his eye on her. She'd done some stupid things when she was drunk. It was amazing nothing like that had happened to her. It made her grateful for his loving care of her, even when she didn't care about herself.

As the group broke up and women began leaving, Melissa pulled Jessica and Kim off to the side. "Hey, do you two have to run off? Or do you have time to talk tomorrow? I have something I want to run by you."

Kim glanced at her phone. "Matthew and I have a date tonight, but tomorrow after church?"

Jessica thought of the mint chip in the freezer. Her date for the night. What was Austin doing if Matthew was going to be gone? Probably playing video games or working.

Melissa nodded. "We usually all go to lunch anyway. Maybe we could stay after."

Jessica didn't have any plans, and anything that kept her time filled was a good thing. But why would Melissa need to talk to her and Kim both? Well, she'd find out tomorrow.

She and Kim headed to Kim's car and left. Once they were driving down the road, Kim glanced at Jessica. "Actually, tomorrow we should talk about the camping trip, figure out what to bring, and all that."

"What camping trip?" Jessica was lost.

"The singles' group from church. You didn't know about it?"

"Between school and the new job, I haven't been able to get to the singles' group in over a month."

"Yeah, but there's been emails and Instagram posts."

"Haven't been on social media much, and I skimmed the emails. It's just the usual weekly update stuff, and I knew I wouldn't have time to attend. I never know how late Madison is going to keep me. I'm getting a better idea of her schedule and preferences now."

"Well the camping trip is in two weeks. It's in Holcomb Springs. We head up Friday night and return Sunday around noon." At a stoplight, Kim turned and looked at Jessica. "It'll be fun. We have to redeem our Holcomb Springs experience after what happened last time." Kim grasped Jessica's arm, her eyes pleading.

"I don't know that I can get it off. I work most every Saturday. Let me talk to Madison. But no promises. I need this job. It's important."

Kim smiled and moved through the green light. "That's all I ask. I'm going to get Matthew to pry Austin away from his computer and get him to come too. It will be what last time was supposed to be."

"Without the nice accommodations." Jessica grinned.

"And no forest fire chasing us." Kim dropped Jessica off at home. "I'll see you tomorrow. Want me to pick you up for church?"

"Sure. Thanks." Jessica exited the car and waved as Kim drove off. She entered her house. The sounds of the TV floated to her from the family room. Sounded like Dad was watching a game.

She headed down the hall toward her room, stopping at the shadow box commemorating her brother Christopher. His high school football jersey was pinned to the background, along with photos, awards, and a newspaper clipping highlighting his accomplishments. She passed by it many times a day but never stopped to look at it as she did at this moment. Weird to think he was younger than she was now. She always thought of him as older than her. But he would never be older than seventeen. The reflection of her face in the glass covered his smiling face in the photo. They had the same eyes. How would her life have been different if he'd lived? The irony that he had been killed by a drunk driver and she was a recovering alcoholic wasn't lost on her. She gave the glass two taps with her finger and headed to her room.

Dropping her purse on the floor, she flopped on her bed. This room hadn't changed much since she was a teenager. Purple walls, black-and-purple swirled curtains and matching lampshade. A fuzzy rug. It was her teenage self frozen in time. She hadn't thought she'd still be living at home at twenty-four. Then again, she'd wasted a lot of time and money on stupid things. If she was going to stay here much longer, maybe she should make some changes: new paint, new curtains, new comforter.

She still had an old bulletin board covered in sparkling fabric pinned with old high school photos, tacked-up dried corsages from prom and homecoming, and concert ticket stubs. She should take all that old stuff down. It'd been there so long she didn't really see it anymore. But even the good memories were tainted.

Pulling out her phone, she searched for the story of the missing girl. Mia. Her name was Mia Latham. She held the girl's photo up next to one of herself at the same age. There was a resemblance for sure. *God, please be with that poor girl. Give her a way to get back home. Keep her safe.*

God had protected Jessica and given her a second chance. Now, how to best use it? She didn't plan on staying at her parents' house forever. However, she could barely figure out how to keep a job. And until that was more of a sure thing, she still had to live at home. Right now it felt like every aspect of her life was shifting, and she wasn't sure she could keep her balance.

She rolled to her side and picked up her phone and swiped to the Inspiration for Today app that her sponsor, Chelle, had recommended. "It's never too late to be what you might have been." --George Elliot. Huh. The question was, what might she have been? Or still be? She didn't know.

If Kim still felt guilty over Heather's bachelorette weekend, and Sarah—a woman who was marrying the man who was like a brother to Jessica—felt overwhelmed by family obligations, what hope was there for her?

AUSTIN WAITED UNTIL HE HEARD THE SHOWER SHUT OFF IN Matthew's bathroom. The double suites in this apartment meant they no longer had to share a bathroom like they had when they had stayed in the hotel before they'd gotten this place. He shut his laptop and headed out to the kitchen, grabbing a soda and a bag of chips before sitting on the couch.

Matthew emerged from his room a few minutes later. "Is that your dinner?"

"It's early yet. I haven't decided what I'm going to eat. What are you and Kim doing?"

"We're headed down to Laguna Beach. After dinner, we can walk along the beachfront and watch the sunset."

"Do you have a minute before you go? I've got a work thing to run by you."

"Sure." Matthew flopped in the recliner. "What's up?"

Austin told him about Max's suggestion that he apply for the director position.

"You should do it. You'd be good at it."

Austin shrugged. "I can run the projects, figure out what needs to be done, and make assignments. That part doesn't worry me. It's the leadership part, the soft skills dealing with people that I'm more unsure about." What he didn't say was that if he could be more like Matthew—confident and able to charm people—he'd have no reservations. But all he could see was the potential for failure. Why couldn't there be a logical, linear process for this? Wasn't there a path somewhere that would guarantee he wouldn't fail? Guess not.

Matthew leaned his elbows on his knees. "Look, I hear what you're saying. But you'd be leading a team that is wired a lot like you. It's not like you'd be on the sales team, having to deal with a variety of people. You know what your team needs. You can advocate for them. And what I've learned about being a leader is that it involves a lot of listening. And you're a good listener."

"I could figure out how to make it work. The idea of having autonomy over how the department runs is very attractive to me. Randy is about to drive me nuts with his constant meetings and need for project updates."

"See? I bet others on the team feel the same way. You'd be able to give them the support they need. Max wouldn't have asked you if he didn't think you could do it. I'm sure he'd be happy to mentor you through the process. And you can always bounce things off me."

Austin nodded, considering Matthew's words. "Maybe you're right." It wasn't a guarantee of success. But how would he feel if he continued to let Randy run the department into the ground when he could have stood up, taken a risk, and made a difference?

Matthew got to his feet. "Of course I am. Hey, why don't you come with us? See if Jessica wants to come. Make it a double date."

Austin leaned back into the couch cushions, shaking his head. "Oh, no. We're not like that. We're just friends. We just happened to get paired off because we were the leftovers."

"I've seen the two of you together. I watched you slow dancing at Heather and Kyle's wedding. There's some chemistry there." He narrowed his eyes.

Austin shook his head. "A woman like that would never be interested in a guy like me. She's bold and outgoing, vivacious, makes people laugh." She made him laugh. He couldn't help but remember the feel of her in his arms at the wedding. How she fit so naturally, and for once, he didn't even think about how his dancing might appear to others. It was just the two of them. "No, we're just friends."

"Friends can still have dinner together with other friends."

"Nah. If I'm going to get that director job, then I need to do some work tonight. You go have fun. Tell Kim I said hi."

Matthew stared at him a moment longer. "All right. Don't wait up." Then he grabbed his keys off the hook by the door and left.

Austin laid his head back on the couch. He'd made the right decision. Hadn't he? An evening with Jessica seemed a lot more fun than eating fast food while working on his laptop. Why hadn't he gone? Because Jessica was kind to everyone. She would have showed up. He didn't want a pity date from her.

He touched the shark's tooth that hung on a leather string around his neck, hidden below his T-shirt. Maybe he should call his folks, see how Dad was doing. The shark's tooth always reminded him of Dad. They'd gotten it when they'd visited Dad's family in Hawaii. His sister lived there now. It always reminded him how strong his dad was. He hated that dementia was stealing the strong man that was the father he knew.

He could still catch up with Matthew and Kim. Or he could

call Jessica and see what she was doing. They could eat pizza and watch a movie. Friends did that, didn't they?

She'd seemed to be having a good time at dinner last Tuesday when he'd rescued her. Then again, maybe she was just grateful and relieved.

But what if she didn't want to come over tonight? Or worse, she came over out of pity? He drummed his fingers on his thigh. He'd see her tomorrow at church, and they all usually went to lunch afterward. Maybe he'd be better able to scope out the situation then.

He touched the shark tooth one more time and picked up the phone. "Hey, Mom."

Chapter Three

Jessica sucked down the last of her Diet Coke as she sat at Chili's with the rest of the group after church.

Melissa sat next to her, eyeing the folks around them. By the way she kept arranging the silverware on her finished salad plate, it was obvious she was waiting for everyone to leave so she could talk to Kim sitting across from her. When Joe and Sarah said their goodbyes, Melissa leaned her elbows on the table, glancing at Matthew and Austin. "I guess you guys can stay and hear this. You might even come in handy. But you have to keep it a secret."

Matthew glanced at Austin, who had somehow ended up on the other side of Jessica. She'd spent the whole lunch trying not to bump into him at the crowded table. "Of course," Matthew said. "What's up?"

Melissa looked around the room, apparently making sure no one was listening. "Scott and I want to have a surprise wedding."

Matthew frowned. "What's a surprise wedding?"

"It's when people get invited to a party and don't know that they are actually coming to a wedding."

"Why would you want to do that?" This from Austin.

"Scott and I don't want a big fuss. We don't want to horn in on Sarah and Joe's celebration, but we also don't want to wait until Scott can get more time off. He's coming down for the week of their wedding, so we thought we'd do it then. Also, I put my townhouse up for sale, thinking it might take awhile. But I already have an offer. If we wait to get married, I have to find someplace to live in the meantime."

"I think it's a great idea." Jessica scooted her chair back a bit so she could see both Melissa and Austin on either side of her without feeling like she was at a tennis match, swinging her head back and forth between them. "Do you have a specific day in mind?"

"I want to keep it as far from Sarah and Joe's events as possible. Scott's coming down Friday night, August eighteenth so he can go to Joe's bachelor party the next day. I think they're all going fishing at Irvine Lake. I thought I could ask everyone to meet somewhere on Sunday evening to welcome him back and have the surprise wedding there. That would give us a few days for a honeymoon, and we'd be back in time for the wedding rehearsal. Then I could fly back to Washington with him after the wedding."

Matthew leaned his arms on the table. "I've never heard of a surprise wedding, but it sounds like a great idea. Saves a lot of hassle."

Kim smacked him on the arm. "Weddings aren't a hassle, they're romantic."

"Yeah, but we saw what Sarah's going through," Melissa said. "Though in my case, it's my family that would be difficult."

"Hey, I'm your family," Matthew protested.

"I know. And I'll talk to Allie too. But I'd rather present it to Mom as a done deal. Then if she and Larry want to come, great. I don't know if Daniel and Nikki and Brittany can get off work, but someone can FaceTime them during the wedding if they can't. I just don't want it to be a big ordeal trying to take everyone's schedules and preferences into account. Look what happened trying to organize the road trip. Scott and I have been separated for eight months now, and I'm tired of it."

Jessica touched Melissa's arm. "We'll do everything we can to make it a special day for you." She glanced at Kim, expecting to see confirmation. Instead, her lips were pursed. "What's the problem?"

"I was just thinking. The weekend before is the singles' camping trip. But it's not a problem. We should be able to do both."

Melissa finished her drink. "It shouldn't be that complicated. I don't want anyone having to change anything on my account."

Kim pointed at Austin and Jessica. "That means I expect both of you to go on this trip. No excuses."

Austin raised an eyebrow and looked at Jessica. "Did you know about this?"

"I just found out yesterday. But I didn't think I'd committed to anything."

Austin turned to Matthew. "You didn't say anything."

"I'd forgotten about it, actually." He glanced at Kim. "But it'll be fun."

Jessica wasn't so sure about that, but she could use the time to fill her weekend. If Madison would let her take the time off. She did want to help her brother and Melissa with their wedding. "What all have you thought about in regards to the wedding?" she asked Melissa. The camping discussion could wait.

Melissa mentioned a few restaurants that had large enough rooms to host a wedding and dinner but wouldn't raise any suspicions among the guests.

"What about Collins's house?" Kim asked. "He's going to end up being your brother-in-law soon enough. It's big enough and has a great backyard for the wedding."

"I need to talk to Allie anyway. I'll ask her what she thinks. But that's a good idea."

"You'll need a dress," Kim added. "Have you thought about that?"

"I was thinking we could go to Lynnae's boutique and see what might work. Dressy but not overly formal." The two continued rattling off ideas.

A sliver of sadness wedged in Jessica's heart as she thought about Melissa leaving them. She had been a good friend, already like a sister, to Jessica. She was going to miss her. Once again, her support was rocking a bit.

She glanced at Austin, who was looking at her. Heat filled her face. She scrambled for something to say. "So, up to taking on the mountains again?" She smiled.

"It might be a good break from all that's going on at work."

"Did you decide to go for the job?"

"I did. I talked to Matthew about it and decided that it was the best way I could control the future of the department."

"You'll do great." Without thinking, she touched his arm.

He glanced at her hand and then at her.

She snatched her hand back, certain her face was flaming now. How had things gotten so awkward between them?

"Uh, how was work? Did the rest of the week go okay? Did they give you a hard time about, well, you know." Was pink crawling up his neck or was it her imagination?

"It was fine. I actually started to feel like I knew what I was doing by the end of the week. They, uh, asked how our 'date' was." She made air quotes around the word and grinned. "Thanks for bailing me out. I appreciate it."

"Anytime. I hardly ever have dinner plans, so we could always eat together sometime." He picked up his straw and began playing with it.

Was he trying to ask her out? Or was he just being nice? "Yeah, we should do that sometime."

The sound of chairs scooting over tile pulled her attention away from him. Matthew and Kim were standing. She jumped to her feet.

Melissa leaned over and gave her a hug. "Thanks for everything. I'll call you later this week and we can make some plans."

"Sounds good."

They left the restaurant, and there was an awkward moment standing by Kim's car while Matthew kissed Kim goodbye. She caught Austin's gaze. He rolled his eyes, and she laughed. Maybe they were back on even footing again.

Kim drove her home, chattering about Melissa's plans and how fun it was going to be. "We never did plan the food for the camping trip. Do you have some time? We can head to my condo and make some menus and lists."

She had nothing but time. And while she wasn't thrilled with the idea of camping, today just proved she needed to reach out and make more friends, create her own network, since her current one was changing.

She could do that. Right?

MIA SAT ON A DIRTY COUCH IN THE DARKENED APARTMENT. Her stomach growled. She didn't know when Nicholas would be back. She wasn't even sure what time it was. He'd been disappearing for longer periods of time. First, it had been fun. He'd treated her like a grown-up. They'd gone dancing; he'd brought her fruity drinks that made her head fuzzy and light. She'd gone home with him.

The next morning, she couldn't find her purse. When she asked him about it, he said she didn't need it. He would provide everything she needed. And he'd taken her shopping and bought her clothes. The clothes he'd picked out were a little more daring than she normally wore, but he said they were for her new modeling career. He'd also paid for a designer purse she'd been eyeing.

"I can't wait to show this to Vanessa and Olivia. They'll be so jealous when they see it," she'd told him, throwing her arms around his neck and kissing him.

He'd pulled her tightly to him. "You don't need them. They're not helping you; I am. I'm all you need."

Her heart dropped a bit. Surely he didn't mean she could never see her friends. Maybe he just wanted to spend more time with her. He'd told her that he wanted to keep her to himself. And since he'd just bought her such an expensive purse, she really couldn't complain.

That night they'd gone to another party. This one had plenty of drugs in addition to alcohol. The vibe wasn't as fun, and people paired off in dark corners. More than once she'd seen something she wished she hadn't. But Nicholas had kept his word, and at the party he'd introduced her to Ron, the photographer.

The next day he'd brought her here, to Ron's place. He had a studio in one of the back rooms. He was older than Nicholas, almost her dad's age. Which gave her the creeps. Ron had taken pictures of her, even some that made her uncomfortable. When she'd asked Nicholas about it, he'd encouraged her to go along with whatever Ron wanted. "He's a professional. He knows what he's doing. Plus, this is how it works. The casting couch isn't a myth. You should feel flattered he thinks you're pretty. There are plenty of other girls who'd give anything for this opportunity."

So she did.

Nicholas had left her here but had said he'd return. That was yesterday.

Right now, she just wanted to go home. She didn't even care about the modeling portfolio at this point. But her parents had taken her phone, and she didn't know where she was. She stood and rummaged through the kitchen, looking for something to eat. Dirty dishes and empty fast-food containers covered the countertops. The cupboards revealed some half-empty boxes of rice and oatmeal, a bag of clumped-up sugar, and a little coffee. The refrigerator held some bottles of ketchup and mustard, a few beers, and a dried-up lemon. Something green and furry was growing in one of the drawers.

She could make some oatmeal if she could find a pan. She was searching through the bottom cupboards when Ron entered the room.

"What are you doing?"

"I'm hungry."

"Later." He reached for her arm. "I have a modeling assignment for you." He grinned at her.

"Where's Nicholas?"

"He'll be back soon. Just do this quick job, and then you'll be free to be with lover boy when he gets back."

"Okay." She shoved her hands in the pockets of her ripped skinny jeans and followed him to the back room.

He showed her where to stand and where to look. It was at a computer with a lit-up web camera.

"The computer's camera is on." She pointed.

He grinned. "That's the point. Just put on a little show."

When she hesitated, he said, "You have to pay for those modeling pictures some way. They don't come cheap."

She hoped Nicholas returned soon. Were her parents worried about her? Had they reported her missing? She wanted to cry. She'd made a big mistake.

Chapter Four

Austin stared at the computer screen at work, not actually seeing the code. His mind couldn't get away from Jessica and their post-church lunch. Austin did want to ask Jessica out, and when he'd floated the idea to her, she seemed enthusiastic. He kind of regretted not grabbing the opportunity Matthew had offered Saturday to go on the double date. But he needed time to weigh the pros and cons of things. He was about as opposite of Matthew when it came to spontaneity.

Now, he was ready. Jessica had been a good friend to him, but there was a spark of something more. He wanted to explore what could be between them. He liked being her rescuer, the solution to her problem. And he was flattered that she'd thought of him. Even if one of her coworkers did the actual texting. Being her pretend date hadn't felt very pretend. Now it was time to take the next step.

But would a group date be better—with Matthew and Kim easing some of the conversational pressure? Or should they do something by themselves—fewer witnesses if he embarrassed himself?

An alert scrolled across his screen. He hated the internal

messaging system that interrupted his work. Randy was calling another meeting. He had to be kidding. It was Monday morning. How much progress could they report?

He leaned back in his chair with a sigh, just as Zach passed by his cubicle. He stopped and walked back a few steps. "Hey, did you see Randy's meeting request?"

"Yep." Austin wanted to roll his eyes, but he needed to be professional. "Have anything you want me to report?"

"Everything's on track. Same as it was Friday."

Austin nodded. "Guess those coding fairies didn't come in this weekend and do our work for us."

Zach chuckled. "Yeah, let me know if you find one of those. I could use the help."

"You and me both."

Zach took a step away and leaned back. "Hey, want me to take that meeting for you? I can, then you could still work. I know meetings aren't your favorite."

"How do you know that?"

"The perpetual scowl on your face during them." Zach leaned against the cubicle. "It's not a problem."

"No. Thanks, I appreciate it. But I'll do it."

"Okay." Zach straightened. "Let me know if you need anything."

"Sure." But they both knew he'd never ask for help. He never did.

An hour later, after another mind-numbing meeting with Randy, Austin almost wished he'd taken Zach up on his offer. Instead, he shot an email to Max Harmon, asking for a meeting to discuss the director position. If Randy continued to run this group, Austin was going to have to find another job. He hadn't been this scrutinized at his first job out of college. And it wasn't just him. Randy was alienating the whole team with his micromanagement.

Austin was going to have to step out in faith that he could do this job. If Matthew and Max—two men he respected and he didn't think would steer him wrong—thought he could do the job, then he'd have to trust their words. *Lord, please don't let me be making a mistake. Make it clear what direction I should go.*

Because the other alternative was to find a job somewhere else. Like back home in Phoenix close to his folks. There was some merit to that idea. But he and Matthew had burned the bridge of their previous employer, who was none too happy when they left to go to DataCorp. So there wasn't an easy alternative. Did he want to waste time and energy looking for another job, supporting his folks, and still try to do this job? Plus, Jessica was here.

Like Occam's Razor—his guiding principle for coding—the simplest solution was usually the best one. And the simplest solution was going for the director position.

Just because it was the simplest didn't mean it was the easiest.

Jessica's phone buzzed in her capris pocket as she threw in a load of wash. She started the cycle then tugged her phone out. A text from Sarah.

I have a favor to ask. I got called into an important meeting but I'm getting a delivery today. It's expensive enough that I don't want to let it sit on the doorstep. Since you're the only one I can think of who's available, could you run over and get it when it's delivered? I can text you when I get a closer time estimate.

Mondays were her days off, and she had very little planned today. It would be one more thing to take up her time.

No problem. I don't have much going on.

Thanks a ton! I'll let you know when it'll be there.

She sat on her bed and folded the load of laundry she'd already done. After she put it away and tidied her room, she glanced at her Inspiration for Today app. "Winning is doing better today than you've done before."

Depending on what they meant by *before*, that could be a pretty low bar. Every day she stayed sober was a winning day. But it made her think. What could she do today that was better than before, even in some small way? And what could she do on Mondays to keep herself busy?

"Whatcha doing?" Mom leaned in Jessica's doorway.

"Laundry. And I'm going to help Sarah out with a delivery later."

Mom nodded and looked around Jessica's room. "You haven't changed anything in here in a long time. Maybe we should pick out some paint and redo your room."

"Maybe. But if I do well at my job, I'll want to get my own place or move in with a roommate." It was pretty expensive to live on her own in Southern California.

"Even if you get your own place, you'll want a new comforter and curtains."

Mom was trying. Her parents never seemed to know what to do with her. They pretended not to notice when she was drunk. And when she told them she wanted to get sober, they were supportive in a pat-your-hand-and pray-for-you kind of way. She figured they were so paralyzed with fear over losing another child, they didn't know what to do. So they did nothing.

"I'll think about it."

Mom paced around Jessica's room, studying her bulletin board.

Maybe Mom was right. She really should take all that old stuff down. She needed a fresh start. And if she moved out and got her own place, this would likely become a guest room. It didn't need purple walls.

Mom leaned down and kissed her head. "Let me know what you decide."

She nodded then turned back to her phone, thinking of the Amber Alert girl, Mia, again. She thought about what Heather said. Putting down her phone, she opened her computer. Sitting on her bed, she went through the various websites and resources on human trafficking. When the alarm went off on her phone, she jumped. The laundry was ready to be put in the dryer.

She closed her laptop and went to the laundry room, burdened by what she'd read. And once again feeling the grace of God that she hadn't fallen into one of those traps. She so easily could have. She prayed again for Mia's safety.

Her phone buzzed again. Another text from Sarah. **It's supposed to be there in the next two hours.**

On my way.

Thanks so much!

She grabbed her purse out of her room and slipped on her sandals. Mom was in the family room watching TV. "Hey, Mom. I'm heading over to Sarah's now. I might run a few errands, but I'll be back for dinner. I have clothes in the dryer. When it goes off, do you mind laying them on my bed so they don't wrinkle?"

"Sure. Have a good time."

She leaned over and gave Mom a quick hug then headed out to her car. The trip to Sarah's was a quick one, with little traffic during the middle of the day. Sarah had texted her the code to the garage, so Jessica parked in front of Sarah's condo then walked around the corner to the garage and entered the code. The door rolled up, and she stepped into the dark, single-stall garage. Neat as a pin, just like the rest of Sarah's place. She hit the garage door button to close it as she entered the house. Quiet surrounded her. The French doors beckoned her to the garden, and she stepped outside. If she kept them open, she'd be able to hear when the delivery arrived.

She eased into a lounge chair. She could see why Sarah loved this place. The garden exuded peace. Jessica needed something like this. Her parents had a yard services that mowed the lawn and trimmed the hedges. It was all very suburban and not terribly peaceful. Plus, she didn't want to spend a lot of time and energy making some sort of garden at her parents' house. Painting the walls in her room a neutral color was enough.

A terrarium. That would do it. A miniature garden she could keep in her room. It would give her something to do. She loved the idea. She studied Sarah's garden with new eyes. How could she translate that into something small that kept the peaceful feeling? She made notes on her phone and started a Pinterest board with ideas.

When the doorbell rang, she almost came out of her skin. She glanced at the time. Two hours already! She jumped up and headed for the door, opening it and waving at the departing delivery person. She hauled the box inside and locked the door then texted Sarah that it had arrived.

Her phone rang. Sarah.

"Jessica! Thank you so much. It's Joe's wedding gift, and I didn't want to risk anything happening to it. I appreciate you taking the time out of your day. Since the architectural firm is in rebuilding mode, I really needed to take this client meeting. You're a life saver."

"It's not a problem. I spent my time sitting in your garden and getting ideas. Oh, and apparently I got a bit of a sunburn." She touched her slightly pink forearm. "I think I'm going to make a terrarium, so I can have my own miniature garden."

"I love it. That's a great idea."

"We'll see how it actually plays out. But it gives me something to do. So is Joe moving in here after the wedding? I can't imagine leaving that garden."

"That's the plan for now. We haven't decided if we'll rent out his place or sell it. And we've talked about picking out a place together and making it our own. Eventually, that's what we'll probably do. But for now, I get to keep my garden."

"If you had a house, you could make a bigger garden."

"That thought has crossed my mind as well." Sarah laughed.

They chatted a bit more then hung up. Jessica made her way back out the garage and headed to the garden store. She was going to create her own little space of peace and serenity. And that would have to be her win for today.

As Austin was packing up to leave at the end of the day, he thought about Jessica. He let out a breath. He was prepared to call her and ask her to dinner some time this week. But now with work... The timing wasn't good. It'd take all his bandwidth to deal with Randy and apply for the director position. Max had told him there were some meetings he wanted him to attend and presentations to make so people would start seeing him as the director.

He pulled his bike out of the stairwell and buckled his helmet on. Pushing his bike outside, he climbed on, glad he'd ridden it today. It felt good to do something physical after being in front of a screen for hours. He let his mind wander as he swung into the bike lane and pedaled toward home.

They had a few weeks before the camping trip, but he and Matthew would need to talk about it, see what they would need to bring. They'd have to borrow a tent and sleeping bags, but that shouldn't be a problem. Perhaps the most redeeming thing about the whole trip would be a chance to spend time with Jessica. Though maybe that would make it harder to stay away from her when they came back and he needed to focus on work. Was there a way to explain that to her?

Maybe she wasn't even interested.

Could he apply Occam's Razor to Jessica? What was the simplest solution?

In the mirror attached to his helmet, he caught a glimpse of a white van coming too close to the bike lane. He pulled as near to the curb as possible. But the van was riding with two wheels in the bike lane. He risked a glance back and motioned to the driver to move over.

But the driver didn't. One of those idiots who thought the bike lane was a turn lane.

Austin had no room. He hopped his bike up onto the sidewalk just as the van flew by, the gust of wind blowing over him. He studied the retreating vehicle. No markings, the license plate partially obscured by mud. When had it even last rained?

With a deep breath and a glance back down the street, he maneuvered back into the bike lane and continued his journey home. Who would drive a full-size van if not some sort of service provider? Gas was too expensive and parking too hard down here for anyone to make that vehicle as a choice for regular commuting.

Austin counted on the stress relief provided by biking home. But his biggest danger came from distracted drivers. Any more close calls and he might have to reconsider his commuting choice.

Their apartment came into view. He pulled into the parking lot and coasted up to their door. Once he was inside with his helmet off and his bike on the rack, he said hi to Matthew lounging on their couch. Austin pulled a bottle of water out of the fridge and relayed his experience to Matthew.

"We could always carpool."

Austin shook his head. "I stay later than you. And it's ridiculous that I can't ride my bike safely to and from work. It's part of why we picked this apartment." He flopped in the recliner. "We need to talk about the camping trip."

"It'll be fun, but it's a few weeks away." He leaned forward. "More importantly, when are you asking Jessica out? I heard what you did yesterday at lunch. She's interested. Do you want to do a double date with Kim and me?"

Austin rolled the cold water bottle between his palms. "Not sure. I was trying to figure out what would be best."

"It doesn't matter. The point is to spend time with her. Don't overthink it."

"Yeah, about that. I told Max today I was going to put my

hat in for the director position. He's got some things he wants me to do so I come across as a strong candidate. I don't think I'll have enough bandwidth to deal with that and start something with Jessica."

"There's always going to be something. You just have to go for it."

Austin leaned back against the chair's headrest. "I wish I knew how she felt. I don't like open-ended solutions. I want to have a reasonable certainty of the result of a course of action. Women don't fit that scenario at all."

Matthew laughed. "No, they don't. But are any of the truly important things in life certain? In matters of the heart, you have to take a risk."

"That's easy for you. You're outgoing, and girls like you. I'm a computer geek. I could barely get through lunch Sunday with Jessica without it feeling weird and awkward the moment I stopped thinking of her as just a friend."

"What's that thing you're always quoting? Occam's Razor?"

"Yeah. The simplest solution is usually the best."

"Right. Well, the simplest solution here is to ask her out. You're never going to know how things will turn out unless you spend some time with her. Let's make it a double date, if you're worried about things being awkward."

Austin let out a long breath. "Fine. But work still has to take priority. I'm going to take a shower." He levered out of the chair and headed toward his room. If it was meant to be with Jessica, she'd be there when things settled down. Wouldn't she? *Lord, why did you have to make women so complicated? I'm going to need your help to figure this out.*

Mia shifted as the hard metal of the side of the van pressed into her spine. She and six other girls were seated on the smelly rubber floor in the cargo area, handcuffed to cleats in the floor. No seats. The August heat made the windowless area feel like an oven. She blinked to force back the tears that welled in her eyes.

Nicholas had come back, but there was a hardness in his eyes when she told him she wanted to leave. "You wanted to be a model. I bought you all those things. You asked for this." He pulled her close and kissed her hard. "You'll be fine once the money starts rolling in."

She didn't know how long she'd been in this van. When Ron had snapped the handcuffs on her, she thought it was another one of his "performances." But then she'd been put in a van with another girl, Brianna, whose glossy black hair fell halfway down her back. And others had followed at their various stops, climbing in or being hauled into the van, all handcuffed. Some girls had a defiant attitude, like this was nothing. Others wept openly. Some, like Mia, sat there numb.

How was she going to get out of this? She wanted to go home. But there was never an opportunity. Ron had another big guy working with him. He had two full sleeves of ink and must have weighed 250 pounds. He'd snap her in two and looked like he'd enjoy it. She shuddered.

The van pulled in somewhere and parked. Big Dude turned around. "Don't even think about getting out of this van or showing your face. You'll regret it." He grinned and climbed out, slamming the door shut.

Wherever they were, it was quiet. No traffic noise.

Brianna raised up on her knees, attempting to peek out the front window.

"Don't! They'll see you!" Mia reached out to pull her back down.

"I'm just stretching. My legs are asleep." She leaned close to Mia where the other girls couldn't overhear. "Looks like we're at a park somewhere. A big one. Lots of green and trees. I didn't see either one of them."

"They could easily be just out of view," Mia whispered back.

She eased her legs into a different position, earning a scowl from the girl across from her. "Sorry."

Time stretched out, and the men didn't come back. Mia hadn't had anything to eat or drink since this morning. It had to be early evening, going by the decreasing light and heat. Maybe they'd left them here? Her hopes rose a bit. Maybe they were done, wanted to walk away and let the girls go in a way where it couldn't be traced back to them. Except the van would have to be registered to someone. Unless it was stolen.

She met Brianna's gaze and leaned forward. "Do you think they've just left us here?"

Brianna shrugged and rose up again, and her handcuffs slipped out of the anchor. Surprised, she looked down. One edge of the anchor had worked loose. It wasn't obvious until she'd pulled on it. Brianna shrugged and edged toward the front seats on her knees.

A few girls hissed at her, but she ignored them. When she reached the front, she lowered down below the window level before slowly rising up, scanning the area. She must not have seen anything, since she became bolder. "No door handles on the inside. They've been sawed off. Must need a screwdriver or something to pry them open." She rummaged around up front, tossing back a few water bottles, using a two-handed toss since her hands were cuffed together.

Mia eagerly grabbed one, took a few delicious swallows, then passed it to the girl next to her. Within minutes the bottles were empty. They might get a beating for it, but it was too hard to resist.

Brianna had opened the glove box and scanned the papers inside before closing it back up. She looked under the seats. "Nothing." She was scanning outside of the van when she froze, then scrambled back to her spot just as the driver's door unlocked and popped open.

Her panicked gaze met Mia's.

Ron stuck his head back in. "You girls being good?" His gaze traveled around the cargo area. He lifted his chin. "Just like I thought." He backed out and slammed the door shut. His footsteps retreated, and it was silent again.

Mia leaned forward. "What did you see? Where are we?"

Brianna shrugged. "The far end of some parking lot. There aren't any other cars around. I think it's a regional park or something. It's bigger than a typical park, and we're back pretty far. Can't even see any roads."

They couldn't get out of the van. And even if they could figure a way out, she didn't know where they were or how to find help. Was anyone even looking for her? Hope was about as scarce for her as water right now.

Chapter Five

Jessica was cleaning up the shampoo basin and putting away supplies after escorting a client back to Madison's chair. A clack of heels entered the room, and she looked up. "Oh, hi, Crystal." The salon owner and woman who'd hired her stood in the doorway, looking as elegant as many of the models on the magazines that graced the reception area.

"Jessica. I was looking for you. Madison says you've been doing good work. She's impressed." Crystal's gaze studied her.

Jessica dried out the basin then wiped her hands on the towel. "That's good to hear. I'm trying my best." She tossed the towel in the hamper.

"The permanent position could be yours. You're a strong contender. And there will be other opportunities as well to help with fashion shoots and even some TV and movie work. They often shoot down here. I have connections."

Jessica nodded. "Wow, that would be great." She'd helped Kim on one of her fashion shows, doing the models' makeup and hair. It had been fun. Kim would always use Jessica, but she couldn't keep her busy. More gigs like that would be even better. "I'm open to any opportunities." She thought of the camping trip. Would now be a good time to ask about time off? Or would it seem presumptuous?

Crystal's gaze traveled around the room, and she moved a few bottles around behind the shampoo bowls.

"Um, I know I haven't been here very long, but there's an event at our church. A camping trip. It's okay if you say no, but it's in a couple of weeks, and I was wondering if I could get that Saturday off." She regretted the words the moment they were out of her mouth and she saw the expression on Crystal's face, like something was moldy. She wanted to grab the words back. She was never going to get this thing right. Being loud and bold and different from her brothers had been a bad decision that had only brought her trouble. Now trying to do the right thing and build a new career and a new group of friends didn't seem to be going well either. She just couldn't get it right.

"A church thing?"

"Yeah, but I don't have to go. I know it's too soon."

Crystal studied her again. "It's fine, if Madison doesn't need you that day." She spun and headed out the door, pausing and turning back. "Go work the front desk as soon as you're done here." Then she was gone.

Jessica leaned against the shampoo bowl, not quite believing what she heard. She let out a breath then scanned the room. Everything was back in its place, and the area was spotless. She headed out to the front desk, where their receptionist, Kendra, was packing up her purse.

"Thanks for covering for me. I have to leave early for a doctor's appointment. Just answer the phone when it rings. 'Salon Moritz, Jessica speaking. How may I help you?' That's what Crystal likes." She pointed to the computer. "All of the girls' books are on here. Their names are on these buttons here. Click on it and then a drop-down menu will give you the various services you can book. This list here will tell you who does what."

"Seems simple enough." Jessica slid into the chair Kendra had vacated.

"Oh, and no personal calls. You have to use your own cell phone for those, and make them in the back where clients can't see."

Jessica nodded. Not that she'd have anyone to call. She waved at Kendra as she exited the front doors then ran through the computer program, making sure she understood how it all worked. Then, what was there for her to do?

She pulled a small book with an attached pencil out of her pocket. She had picked it up at the dollar store, thinking it would be great to have some way to record what she was learning from Madison. On the job was different than in the classroom.

Plus, she had heard a business magnate say that the key to his success was remembering personal details about people—like the names of their spouses and kids, birthdays and anniversaries, vacations and special occasions—and asking them about it. It made them feel special. She'd need every edge she could get, so she'd jumped on this idea. She'd been reading business books at night trying to learn as much as she could to give herself options.

Once she'd gotten her notes caught up, she flipped through the hairstyle magazine Kendra had left on her desk. She answered one call and successfully booked the appointment.

Pleased with herself, she checked Madison's schedule for the Saturday of the trip. Madison had blocked the whole day off. She wasn't working. Yay! Madison usually took one or two Saturdays a month off. Luckily, this was one of them.

Now what? Noticing a duster in a cubby under the desk, she picked it up and began dusting the display shelves in the waiting area. She could easily get to the phone if it rang. As she lifted up various hair products to dust around and under them, she thought about Crystal's words. Did she really mean it? Or had she told Lyric the same thing? Was she trying to pit the two of them against each other?

Why couldn't Jessica just believe the good news? Was this really what she wanted? Of course it was. She'd gone to school too long and spent too much money not to succeed at this career. She was going to be as useful and helpful as possible, putting her bold self aside and working hard. Even if that meant volunteering to stay late.

She thought about Austin. It'd been two days since their lunch after church, and she hadn't heard from him. Maybe he hadn't meant the dinner invitation to be anything more than a casual hangout some time. Why were guys so hard to read? Then again, Austin was a smart guy. Maybe he wanted to date smart women, like someone from his work. Not a girl like her who barely made it through high school.

She moved over to the floral display and began dusting the silk flowers. Not like the real ones in Sarah's garden or even the succulents she had used in her terrarium. But the sculptural silk flowers matched the hard-edged sheen of the marble and glass everywhere. Anything from Sarah's more natural garden would look out of place here.

The front door opened, and a girl with long, dark hair slipped in, looking around, her eyes shadowed.

Jessica stepped back toward the desk and hid the duster. "Can I help you? Who are you here to see?"

The girl's gaze darted out the door and back to Jessica. She bit her lip. "Can I use the phone? Please? It's important."

Jessica remembered Kendra's warning about personal calls. Since this person wasn't a client, she figured Crystal wouldn't want her using the phone.

But something about the way the girl's eyes pleaded, her hands twisting in front of her, tugged at Jessica's heart.

"Let me get my cell phone. You can use that."

"Thanks." The girl gave a quick, tentative smile.

Jessica headed back to the break room and her purse, pulling out her phone. But when she got back to the reception area, the girl was gone. The front door shimmied slightly as if someone had just exited. Hmm. Maybe the girl had solved her own problem. Perhaps she was waiting for a ride. But it was weird. This was not an area of town someone wandered through. This building contained the salon and a business office of some sort next door. They shared a parking lot. And all up and down the street were other professional offices.

She pushed open the front door and looked out, catching a glimpse of dark hair and a big man grasping the girl's arm, hustling her around the corner. That didn't look very friendly. Jessica glanced back at the phone, praying it didn't ring. She stepped all the way out and hurried down to the corner where the girl had disappeared. When she reached the corner, a van was pulling away from the curb. No sign of the girl anywhere. She scanned the area as long as she dared, then hustled back inside. Hopefully Crystal hadn't come out and seen the empty front desk.

But no one emerged from the back to scold her. She tucked her phone in her pocket, keeping it close by in case the girl came in again. The whole thing gave her a creepy feeling. Was the girl in trouble? Was there something else Jessica should have done?

She plopped into the desk chair. Why did she always feel like she was never quite doing the right thing? Just missing the mark somehow.

Crystal strode through the reception area, phone plastered to her ear, leaving the scent of expensive perfume in her wake. She shoved open the front door without sparing a glance at Jessica.

Jessica was still staring after her, wondering if she was coming back, when Madison came over. "You can do the blowout for this client."

"Oh." That put her in a quandary. "I'm covering for Kendra. Who will answer the phone?"

"There's a phone in the back by my station. You'll hear it ring and can pick it up there."

"Okay." Jessica stood. "Also, that Saturday in a few weeks that you have marked off? Crystal said I could have that day off. Just wanted you to know in case there was something you were planning on me doing."

"That's fine." Madison waved her hand over her shoulder as she moved off.

Jessica smiled as she reached Madison's station and met the client's gaze in the mirror. She couldn't remember this woman's name. Ugh. She should have checked the schedule again and her little book. She began the blowout, thankful that the noise of the blow-dryer made it harder to talk. She kept one ear tuned for the ringing phone.

Her mind replayed the interaction with the girl who wanted to use her cell. Maybe Jessica should have had her come with her to the back. That would have gotten her out of view of whoever she seemed to be avoiding. But what would Crystal have said if she'd seen?

Later, Crystal had found her in the break room. "I heard that a girl came in today who wasn't a customer. What did she want?" Her gaze was steady on Jessica, giving nothing away about the true meaning behind her question.

Great. Was she going to be in trouble? "Um, nothing. Well, she wanted to use the phone. She didn't say why, just that it was important. I didn't think you'd want her using the office phone, so I went to get my cell phone. When I came back out, she was gone." She left out the part about following her outside and what she saw.

Crystal studied her a moment.

Was she trying to decide if Jessica was lying or not? Nothing she could say would help. In fact, trying to defend herself might just make her look guilty of something. She didn't know what.

Finally, Crystal said, "You did the right thing. Our phones are for salon business only." She turned and left.

Had Lyric told Crystal that Jessica had let someone use the

phone or do something else? How would Crystal have known? And why was any of it a big deal?

It seemed like whatever she'd done today, it'd been the wrong choice.

AUSTIN SAW MOVEMENT OVER HIS MONITOR AND GLANCED up. Max was headed his way. He repressed a sigh. He liked Max, but these constant interruptions made it hard to get any work done. Hadn't any of these people heard of *Deep Work*? Perhaps he should gift everyone a copy of Cal Newport's book on knowledge workers and their needs to produce the best results.

Max tapped the top of Austin's monitor. "Got a minute?"

I do now. "Sure."

"Edward would like you to present on the state of the SHIELD project to the major stakeholders. This will be the kind of thing you'll do regularly as director, so he'd like to see how you handle it."

Austin nodded. He was fine with presentations. He liked sharing his knowledge. "That's fine. When?"

"Friday right after lunch."

It was Tuesday afternoon. That gave him two full days to prepare. On top of his regular work. Would it be enough time? It would have to be. He started thinking through what points he should cover, how he would need to get the audience up to speed.

"Austin?" Max still stood there. He'd almost forgotten. "You good?"

"Yeah, sure. I'll be ready by Friday."

"Great. Looking forward to it. I know you'll knock it out of the park. Edward just needs to see how well you know this project and can lead the team."

"Got it."

Max tapped his monitor again and then turned and left.

Austin's phone buzzed in the desk drawer. Since he was already not working... He pulled it out. Matthew.

Headed for lunch soon?

No I'll eat at my desk. Max just dropped a presentation on me for Friday.

That's a good sign.

I have to figure out how to do my regular work and get this presentation done.

You'll pull it off. You call Jessica yet?

Jessica? What was Matthew talking about? Jessica didn't have anything to do with— Oh, the double date Friday.

Not yet.

I told Kim about it so you'd better call Jessica before she hears it from Kim.

One more thing on his plate. He couldn't think about that now. He put his phone away and pulled up a blank doc to take notes on what he should include in his presentation. If he wanted the director position, he was going to have to figure out how to do the work as well as all the other responsibilities that came with the promotion. Was it going to be worth it?

He glanced up as Randy walked by on his way to lunch. Unfortunately, Randy stopped outside Austin's cubicle. "Hey, just wanted to let you know that I'm calling a status update meeting after lunch in the conference room."

"Can't make it."

Randy frowned. "It won't take long. I really need your updates."

"Everything's on track. Nothing's changed since the last status meeting."

Randy stared at him and swallowed. "Well, I'd still really like to see you there. In case anyone has any questions." Then he hurried off.

Yeah, well, that wasn't going to happen. He had too much to do for those stupid meetings. So, even if he didn't like all the extra work that would come along with the director position, it was better than working like this.

He turned back to his blank doc and started a brain dump on the SHIELD project.

Jessica had just pulled into the driveway at her parents' house when her phone rang. Kim. "Hey. I just got home. Long day."

"You sound tired. Do you need to get something to eat? You can call me back. I have a couple of things to talk to you about."

"No, I grabbed tacos on the way home. Taco Tuesday. If you don't mind me crunching in your ear, I can talk and eat. I've got something to talk to you about too."

Jessica exited her car, grabbing her bag and drink, and entered the house. Sounds from the TV floated to her, and she waved at her parents in the family room, pointing to the phone tucked between her ear and shoulder. Once in her room, she put the food and drink on her nightstand, dropped her purse on the floor, and set the phone to speaker. "Okay, I'm settled. What's up?"

"I got a call from Ryan Bradley from the church. You know, the cute worship pastor? Looks like Chris Evans."

"Oh, yeah. Why'd he call you? You don't sing. Do you? Some hidden talent I don't know about?" Jessica laughed and took a bite of her taco, careful to lean over the wrapper as the bright pico de gallo flavors mixed with the creamy cheese and spicy meat.

"No, but he's in charge of the camping trip now. Jerod's wife just got put on bedrest for the remainder of her pregnancy. I don't think she was too thrilled about camping while pregnant anyway. So Ryan's taking over, probably because he's single, on staff, and doesn't have any other plans to work around."

"No singing gigs?"

"Apparently not." Kim paused. "I don't think you know all that went on last year with Ryan and Sarah."

Last year? Jessica was still being stupid last year. "No, but wait. Ryan and Sarah? Sarah is with Joe."

"This was before that. She and Ryan dated briefly. He didn't take it too well when she broke up with him, and he kicked her off the worship team."

"Yikes. That sounds… real Christ-like."

"Yeah. I don't know what all went on, but I think Ryan got in some trouble over it. At some point he apologized to Sarah, but she was too busy rebuilding her architectural firm and dating Joe to want to go back on the worship team."

Jessica really had missed a lot. These people were like her family. She'd known Joe forever. How had she not been aware of this?

She knew why. Drinking. Just one more reason in an ever-growing list of reasons to stay sober.

She took a breath. "Okay, so Ryan is leading this trip. Sarah won't be on it. Neither will Joe. Do you foresee any problems?"

"Not really. He's not the most organized person, but Jerod had everything planned out. You and I are handling the food. Did you get the time off?"

"Yep. It's not a problem. Actually, Crystal said she's really pleased with my work."

"That's great! On both counts."

"Yeah." Jessica would mention the girl who'd come into the salon in a minute, once they were done talking about the camping trip. "So we're good to go? You know what food to bring, how many people are coming, who's going to help with the cooking and clean up?"

"Got lists for all of that. I don't expect Ryan to do too much on that front. He'll mostly lead the devotional, prayer, and singing time. He can be a fun guy. But, he did make one request."

"What's that?"

"There's this woman he's invited along. Macy Villenueva."

Jessica thought for a moment. "Why does that name sound familiar?" She finished the rest of her taco. It hit the spot.

"Because she went to high school with our brothers. I don't know all the details, but at one point she was dating Scott—"

"Oh yeah. I remember her now." Boy, did she. Macy seemed like the epitome of a hot high school girl when Jessica was in elementary school. Macy had curves, style, and boys falling all over themselves for her.

"Anyhow, she created some sort of drama between Scott and Joe. They almost lost their friendship over it. She's got a job working for a fundraising company, and last year she worked with the fire department on a project. I don't think Joe was too thrilled."

"I can't imagine why," Jessica said dryly. "So somehow she and Ryan have connected, and he's bringing her camping. She doesn't strike me as the camping type. Unless she's changed."

"Nope. I gather that Ryan had to do some promising or arm twisting to get her to come. I get the feeling he's interested in her. He wants us to befriend her and make sure she feels comfortable."

Jessica laughed. "Okay, I'm sorry, but I just can't picture it. How could Ryan be interested in someone like Sarah and then someone like Macy? They are so different."

"I don't know. But I said we'd be nice to her. I hope she's not a complete diva. Why on earth he'd want her to come, I have no idea."

"Well, it's going to be an interesting trip." How would Austin react to meeting a woman like Macy? She was definitely not his type, but Jessica hoped she didn't set her eyes on Matthew. She wouldn't want to see her friend's heart broken or watch Matthew do something stupid. Guys tended to do stupid things around women like Macy. Then again, high school was a long time ago. Maybe she'd grown up now that she was in her thirties.

Kim was talking again. "Okay, so that's all the camping news. I have something else to tell you. Unless you want to go first."

"No, go ahead."

"The guys want to go on a double date Friday after you get off work."

"You mean Matthew and Austin?"

Kim laughed. "Of course. Who else?"

"It's been kind of a weird conversation, so I wasn't sure where you were headed. But yeah, that sounds good. Is Austin letting you do the asking?" She would be disappointed if that was the case. He should care enough to ask her himself.

"Nope, he's going to call you. Hopefully tonight. I was supposed to wait to talk to you until he'd called. But I had the camping trip update to convey."

"Do you know what they have in mind?"

"Dinner and a movie, I think. But they're letting us pick the movie. So get some ideas."

"Okay, before I swipe up the movie theater app, I wanted to talk to you about something that happened at the salon today."

"You said you got the time off, right?"

"Yeah, but—" Her phone buzzed, and Austin's face and name popped up. "Austin's calling. Let me call you back."

"Ta ta!" Kim disconnected.

Jessica touched the screen. "Hey, Austin."

"Hi, Jessica. How was work?"

"It was good. My boss said I was doing well and that I have a real shot at a permanent position."

"That's really great news. I knew you could do it."

"Thanks. How about you? Did you decide to go for the director position?"

"I did. I talked to Matthew about it and decided it made a lot of sense. But my boss, Max, said he wants me to prepare a presentation for this week so people will start seeing me as the director. I don't love making presentations. I'd rather teach a class. A presentation has to be flashier, more eye catching. I'm just going to put something together that's straightforward with the information they need."

She swung her foot off the bed, impatient. She didn't want to exchange formal pleasantries with him, like they were strangers. Where had their easy friendliness gone? Then again, Austin had never asked her out before. And it was the first time he'd called her, though they'd texted. Perhaps they needed to be chased by a forest fire for them to feel comfortable with each other.

"I'm happy to be your test audience if you want. Or I'm sure Matthew would do it. When is your presentation?"

"Friday."

"Oh, that's coming up fast. Well, at least—" She started to say at least when they went out Friday they'd have something to celebrate, but he hadn't asked her yet. "Um, at least it'll be over soon, and you won't have to worry about it over the weekend."

"True. Anyhow, that's not even why I called."

The silence dragged. "So why did you call?"

"Would you want to go out Friday?"

"Yes, yes I would." Elation lifted Jessica's heart, surprising her with its intensity. She didn't realize how much she wanted to hear those words from him until he said them.

"Like a date?"

She worked to keep her voice even. "Yes, sounds like fun."

She heard him let out a breath. "Great. Um, dinner and a movie with Matthew and Kim?"

"Yeah, that would be great." She smiled, hoping he heard the warmth and reassurance in her voice. "I'm looking forward to it."

"Yeah, me too. Great. Okay, well, good. I'll pick you up, well, I guess probably Matthew and I will pick you up on Friday."

"Cool." Because they'd both said *great* about a million times. "And, Austin?"

"Yeah?"

"Thanks for calling instead of texting. It means a lot."

"Yeah, sure. Of course. See you Friday."

She hung up and stared at the phone a minute. Austin had actually asked her out. Good thing Kim had given her the heads-up so she could be encouraging to him instead of trying to figure out what he was doing.

She flopped back on her bed. Friday would be fun. If Austin could relax and enjoy it. What was she going to wear? Wait, she had to call Kim back.

She sat up and tapped the phone. Kim answered. "Well?"

"He actually asked me out for Friday."

"Yay!"

"I'm just glad he called instead of texting."

"Me too. Now, what was the other thing you wanted to tell me about work today?"

"Oh, it was weird. This girl came in asking to use the phone. Which is odd, right? Everyone has cell phones. I was covering the front desk, so I went back to grab mine, since Crystal doesn't like people to make personal calls on the office line. But when I came back out, the girl was gone. She had seemed nervous or scared, so I went outside and saw this big guy hustling her away by her arm. I think they drove off in a van. I couldn't tell for sure, since they had disappeared around the building corner before I caught up with them. Something about the whole situation didn't feel right."

Kim was silent for a moment. "That really is weird. But I don't know what you could have done differently."

"I don't know. I keep thinking that maybe I should have had her come to the back with me when I went to get my phone. Then when that guy came in, he wouldn't have seen her. Then again, if Crystal saw her, she might have been upset. So hard to know what the right thing is to do."

"I know. And you had no idea that the guy was following her. Maybe it wasn't even anything nefarious."

"Yeah." But she wasn't convinced. She'd seen the haunted look in the girl's eyes.

"Tell you what. I'll give Kyle a quick call and tell him what you told me. Then if there was anything reported in that area, he'll have more information."

"Thanks, Kim. That makes me feel better. And if he needs to ask me anything, he can call."

Jessica hung up with Kim and sighed. She should take her food wrappers to the trash and go say hi to her parents. But that girl's face haunted her. She didn't know if Kyle could do anything to help. But at least it was something.

Chapter Six

Austin carried his laptop to the conference room and connected to the overhead projector, getting his PowerPoint set up to be displayed, his heart beating a little faster than normal.

The other members of the executive team filed in—a few cast quizzical glances his direction—and found their seats. Bernie Wilkins, a member of the finance team and one of the older members of the singles' group at church, entered and gave Austin a nod and a smile as he sat.

Austin waited through the beginning part of the meeting, until Max introduced him to everyone as one of the team leads working on the SHIELD project who was there to give them an update. No mention was made of the director position, which was good. That would have added more pressure. How many, if any of them, knew that he was a contender? Max nodded for Austin to begin his presentation.

Austin touched the shark-tooth necklace under his button-down shirt, reminding himself of Dad's strength and courage. If Dad could fight dementia, Austin could find the courage to do this. Picking up the remote clicker, he stood at the front of the room and opened his presentation, beginning with a history of the SHIELD project, its purpose, goals, and methodology. There wasn't time to talk about each of the team members and their competencies and skill sets. The stakeholders would have to trust that the right people were working on this project.

He glanced over from the screen at the front. Around the room, some of the eyes were glazed over. A few people stared at their phones. Bernie gave him an encouraging nod. So this wasn't the most exciting part of the presentation, but it was necessary for understanding the pieces that would come. He continued until someone cleared their voice. He looked up.

Edward was making a rolling motion with his hand. "Hey, Austin, that's great. You've clearly done a lot of work here, and we trust that you guys have laid this foundation properly. Could you just hit the high points for us?"

"Yeah, sure. Just let me —" He clicked through a few more slides trying to find some that talked about where they currently were. "As you can see, we are on track with the metrics to meet our goal—"

"Austin." Edward again. "Why don't you forget the PowerPoint and tell us in your own words what's going on, where you are, what you've accomplished, that kind of thing? We don't need a whole presentation."

Austin swallowed. "Okay." He scrambled to get his thoughts together. Off the cuff wasn't his thing. He liked to have prepared notes and know what he was going to say. What were the high points, the most important things they need to know about this project? His mind started clicking through facts and figures. If he'd known that was what Edward wanted, he would've been able to prepare from that standpoint.

Edward glanced at his watch and looked around the room. Everyone else had checked out.

If this was going to be a regular part of his duties as a director, he'd have to do better. He glanced at Max, who gave him a sympathetic look.

Austin rambled through a bit what each of the team

members were doing and where they were in the project and reiterated again they were on track to accomplish their goals. His face was hot when he gathered up his laptop and left the conference room.

Maybe he should rethink this whole director thing. Maybe he should rethink this whole job, this whole move to Orange County and see this meeting as a sign from God that he needed to return to Phoenix, find a job there, and be closer to his parents. He didn't know. What he did know was this had not gone well.

He was still sitting in his cubicle when Max came up. It looked like he had come straight from the meeting.

"Hey, Austin." Max gave him a sympathetic smile. He looked a little disappointed. "I'm sorry, that was my fault. I should have prepared you better on what to expect. Edward likes a high-level view: where the project is right now, where it's going, are there any roadblocks. You were right in saying that everything is on track. He just wants to be able to keep an eye on everything without having a lot of background." Max slapped his shoulder. "You'll do better next time. Don't worry about it."

Austin nodded, and Max left.

He sat there for a moment, staring at his screen. If there was one thing he knew how to do, it was research. He pulled up windows for Google and YouTube and typed in various search terms for presentations, summary reports, and whatever other search terms he thought would be helpful. He spent his lunch hour queuing up articles and videos he hoped would be helpful in preparing his next presentation.

When his phone buzzed, he looked at the clock on his screen. He couldn't believe it was past quitting time. No wonder it had gotten so quiet. He pulled out his phone.

A text from Matthew. **You getting home soon? You're gonna want to shower before we pick up the women.**

Austin's mind spun for a minute, and he came back to the present. Oh yeah, today was Friday. They had a double date. He was half tempted to Google *what to talk about on a date* but figured he didn't have time for that. He shut everything down, ran to the stairwell, grabbed his bike, and headed for home.

Hopefully tonight would go better than today had. Though he had just as little dating experience as he did presentation experience.

JESSICA HAD COME INTO WORK EARLY AND LEFT LATE EACH night that week. She couldn't even really explain why, other than she hoped that girl might show back up. But on Thursday, Madison had left early and didn't have any evening clients. Jessica offered to help Erika, but Lyric gave her the side eye.

In the shampoo room, Lyric had grabbed her arm. "Hey, I don't know what your game plan is here, but Erika is my stylist. I can do everything she needs."

"I know. I'm not trying to horn in. Just trying to be helpful." Which was clearly backfiring.

"You don't need to. Crystal said she was happy with my work. I know we're both competing for the same permanent position. You stay in your lane."

"Fine. I'm heading home then." She'd called Kim for any updates from Kyle, but there hadn't been.

So now it was Friday. Date night. And she was glad she was able to leave on time to get home, change her clothes, and freshen up. It would be good to take her mind off things. That was the problem. She really didn't have anything else to occupy her thoughts. Maybe tonight that would change.

She had just walked in the door at home when a news alert dropped across her phone screen. She was ready to swipe it away when the headline caught her eye. She hurried to her room and dropped on her bed.

It was her. The girl who'd come into the salon three days ago. And they'd found her body today.

Tears welled. That poor girl. She had needed help. Jessica desperately wished she could have done something different.

She was torn. She wanted to read everything about this girl, find out who she was and what on earth had led her to the situation that resulted in her death. And yet she had plans with Austin, Kim, and Matthew. While Kim and Matthew would understand if she called off, she knew it had taken a lot of courage for Austin to ask her out. She couldn't cancel on him. Plus, she wanted to spend time with him, get to know him better. He was a bit of a mystery. So different than the type of guy she used to be attracted to.

She swiped up Kyle's number while she pulled clothes out of her closet. It wouldn't take her too long to change. She half expected to get his voice mail, but he picked up. She told him about the news story and the girl from the salon. He hadn't made the link between them.

"What can you tell me? For some reason, I feel a connection to her."

Kyle hesitated a moment. "The body was found off a trail in the regional park by an early morning dog walker. Her name was Brianna Bauer. She appears to be a victim of human trafficking—she had been branded with WE on her wrist—something we've seen before. But we'll know more once the coroner has finished their investigation." He paused again. "Jessica, there wasn't anything you could have done differently. Even if you had pulled the girl into the back with you, you had no way of knowing if the man was armed. He could have started shooting up the salon or taking hostages. Many times the victims willingly go back to their handlers because of the emotional dependency they create. You offered to help. It was probably the kindest thing anyone had done for her recently."

She dashed more tears away. Great, she'd go on a date with puffy eyes. "Thanks, Kyle. Will you let me know if you find out anything more?"

"Sure."

She changed her clothes and touched up her hair and makeup, examining herself in the mirror. While she was waiting to be picked up, she did a quick search on human trafficking and was shocked how prevalent it was. Not just in her town or in the states close to the border or big metropolitan areas, but in small towns and every place across the US.

A chill passed over her when she realized how lucky she was nothing bad had happened to her when she had been out drinking and not paying attention to her surroundings. She could've so easily stumbled into a dangerous situation. It was only by the grace of God she hadn't suffered much more than miserable hangovers, cringe-worthy memories of her own behavior, and broken relationships she was desperately trying to repair.

When Kim texted they were on their way, Jessica went to the family room and hugged both of her parents. She couldn't imagine the worry she had put them through. Pushing that thought away, she determined to have a good time tonight.

Austin's Honda pulled into the driveway. She was headed out the door as he walked up to meet her. "Hi. You look great." He leaned over and kissed her cheek.

That she hadn't expected. Her face heated. "Thanks." He smelled great. Freshly showered—his black hair still damp at the neck, spiky on top—and something spicy. This really was feeling like a date.

He opened the door for her, and she slid in, saying hi to Matthew and Kim in the back seat. Poor Matthew. His long legs were up to his chin in the small back seat. "Are you sure you don't want to sit up here?"

"Nah. It's a short ride."

Once they arrived at Outback and were seated in a booth, Jessica couldn't help but be aware of Austin's presence. And yet the tingles of being on a date with him competed with the heaviness she felt over the missing girl. Human trafficking. She hadn't suspected that. Maybe a possessive boyfriend or a bad date or something, but not modern slavery.

As they placed their orders, she scanned the restaurant. She couldn't help but see her town with new eyes. Where were the traffickers? Where were the girls—and sometimes boys—kept?

Kim nudged Jessica's leg under the table, and she looked up. All eyes were on her.

"Sorry, what did I miss?"

"We were just talking about the camping trip," Kim said.

Jessica didn't even remember the server taking the rest of the orders and leaving. She had to get it together. Austin deserved a good first date with her. Hopefully, there would be more.

"I'll make sure we have tents and sleeping bags." Matthew pushed his straw up and down in his drink.

Kim looked at Jessica. "What do you think the weather's going to be like? What kind of clothes do we need to bring? When we were there before, it was June and we weren't camping. It's August now, but Holcomb Springs is also at seven thousand feet."

"Layers are a good idea." Matthew had more camping experience than any of them. "It'll be cool at night and in the morning, but once we're hiking around, you'll want to shed some layers for sure."

Kim talked about the menu. Since she was on the planning committee, she was privy to the activity list Jerod had put together.

Jessica turned to Austin, wanting to include him in the discussion. "What do you think? What are you looking forward to about the trip?"

He shrugged. "I'm not convinced I should go. I've got a big thing going on at work, plus I'm not a fan of group activities."

Jessica's heart sank. He had to go. She was counting on them getting away from their responsibilities so they'd have some time together to hang out and get to know each other in a more relaxed environment.

"You survived the weekend away in June." Kim pointed at

him. "You were a big help to me with unloading the minivan and setting everything up."

"True, but I didn't really know anybody, and that was to my advantage. No one expected anything of me."

Matthew stared at him. "No one will expect anything of you on this trip either."

"It's a lot closer quarters with tents. I like my space and privacy."

Jessica turned toward him. "It doesn't sound like there's a lot of structured activity. It's supposed to be a time to get away, to recharge, relax, and be in nature. You'll be encouraged to spend time with the Lord, and you can always go for a walk in the woods by yourself." She took a sip of her drink. "I can run interference for you. Between Kim and me, we can talk to anybody about anything. No one will drag you into a conversation if you don't want them to."

He gave her a wide grin that made her stomach swirl. "Yeah, that doesn't surprise me at all. I appreciate it."

Their food came, and Matthew asked the blessing before they dug in. But he picked the conversation back up. "You need a break from work. You need to get away and give yourself some perspective. Nature will help with that. Also, Bernie's going. And as long as we don't have a forest fire chasing us, it'll be a win." Matthew grinned and cut into his steak.

Austin stopped, his fork in the air. "Wait. Bernie's going? I'd forgotten he was part of the group."

"Yep. And let's face it, you're going to need him in your corner. As part of the executive team, he's going to be able to convey to Edward that you are a human and not a robot, that you have the capacity to lead a team and have the soft skills a leader needs."

"Says the person who just figured out how to handle his direct reports' emotions." Kim nudged his shoulder.

"That's why I know what I'm talking about."

"If I can get through the stack of leadership books I ordered, then I'll go." Austin returned to his meal.

Jessica studied him while she ate, and the conversation turned to other things. Somehow she had to find a way to convince him to go. It wasn't like she had a business degree and could help him. But she knew people who did.

"Do you think Melissa would be available or willing to do some business coaching?" Jessica looked at Matthew.

"Isn't she busy planning her wedding? I wouldn't want to intrude." Austin sipped his drink.

"That's a great idea. We could both talk to her." Matthew set down his fork. "You heard her about the wedding. It's not going to be a big deal. I'm sure she'd like to talk to us. We can buy her dinner."

Kim sat forward. "I have an even better idea. Why don't we make her dinner? We can do it at my place, then she can talk business with you all—I wouldn't even mind listening in—and then Jessica and I could help with any wedding plans."

Matthew nodded. "Sounds good. I'll ask her tomorrow."

Austin shrugged. "If it's not too much bother."

Jessica pushed her finished meal away. Good. One thing had gone right today. Maybe Austin could learn to rely on them as friends who wanted to help, and he'd be more willing to include himself with their activities. And selfishly, she wanted to get to know him better. She sensed a deep strength about him. The way he considered his words before speaking. His steadiness was in contrast to her wildness, and she needed that balance.

If only he could find something as equally intriguing about her.

Austin enjoyed the food, but he wanted the focus off him. He knew they were trying to help, but it was an unusual —and uncomfortable—feeling. He was glad when they left the restaurant and headed to the movie theater. Once the movie came on—an action-adventure flick with a bit of romance—he wouldn't have to talk.

It'd been a long time since he'd taken a girl on a date, and there hadn't been many at that. He kept an eye on Matthew and followed his lead. Once they bought their movie tickets and headed inside, he and Jessica got in line at the concessions stand behind Matthew and Kim.

"I know we just ate, but it seems odd to watch a movie without something to snack on." Austin glanced at the menu board and back at Jessica. "What's your favorite movie snack?"

"Junior Mints. And popcorn. But the important question is, what do you put on your popcorn?"

"Butter, of course. Is there any other way?" He smiled. This, when it was just the two of them, was good.

"I'm glad we can still be friends, Austin. If you didn't like butter on your popcorn, I'd have my doubts." She leaned into him for a brief moment, and he wished it were longer.

What would it be like to take her in his arms? Too soon to find out tonight, that was for sure. But it was the one thing that made the camping trip attractive. For her, he'd be willing to go.

The silence between them grew, though there was plenty of noise in the movie theater lobby. This line was moving incredibly slow. He hated making small talk.

"So was your dinner good?" He shoved his hands into his pockets.

"Yes, it really was. I like Outback."

This was a lot easier when they'd been running from a forest fire. "How was work this week?" Had he asked her that already?

Jessica looked at him. "Work was fine, but I had a strange situation that's been bothering me." While they waited in line, she told him about a girl that had showed up at her salon and who'd subsequently turned up dead. And how Kyle had told her the girl had been a victim of human trafficking.

They moved up to the concessions counter just as she

finished telling her story. He placed their order then turned to her. “That’s got to be difficult. I can see why you were distracted earlier.”

“You noticed?”

“Of course.”

The worker brought over their order, and they took their snacks and headed to the theater, Kim and Matthew far ahead of them. They found their seats, and Austin settled the popcorn bucket between them. The pre-show with local advertisements and trivia played on the screen, so they had time even before the previews started.

“So Kyle will let you know if he finds anything out?” He nudged the popcorn toward her.

“Yeah, but who knows when that will be.” She met his gaze. “I know there’s nothing I could have done. It just seems so… unfair, I guess. She was so young, had her whole life ahead of her. I've never known anyone before who had been murdered. Not that I really knew her, but we had an encounter. I can’t help but be thankful nothing like that had happened to me.”

“It seems hard to grasp why God allows bad things to happen to some people and not others.” He paused. Should he tell her? Only Matthew knew, and he’d been sworn to secrecy. But if he wanted a chance at a relationship with her—and he did —he was going to have to stretch out of his comfort zone and let her in. “My dad was diagnosed with dementia last year.”

She laid her hand on his arm, heat shooting through him. “I’m so sorry. That must be tough.”

He nodded. He wanted to hold her hand, but was the time right? Matthew was not a good example since he had his arm around Kim. They’d been dating a lot longer. Austin didn’t move and hoped Jessica didn’t move her hand. “Yeah. I was angry for a while. My dad is the strongest person I know. To get such a senseless disease that will take his mind before his body seems so cruel. And since we don’t know what causes it, if it’s genetic or not, there’s no guarantee I won’t get it. I can’t imagine taking that as graciously as he has. My mind is everything to me. I can't imagine losing it. So, I get why you're struggling with understanding what God allows."

She met his gaze. "Thanks for sharing that with me. I don't take that lightly."

The lights dimmed as the screen flickered. Jessica slid her hand down to his and squeezed it. But as she started to pull away, he captured her fingers, intertwining them with his.

Chapter Seven

Jessica stood in front of her closet, deciding what to wear. It wasn't a date; not really. But she still wanted to look good since she was seeing Austin again. She was thankful for the shorter workday on Saturdays. Her mind was on last night's date a good portion of the day. She and Austin had held hands throughout the movie. He'd walked her to the door and kissed her cheek as he said good night. It was sweet and perfect. So unlike the bad boys that she used to date.

She had to force herself to keep her mind on work. She didn't want to screw up someone's cut or mix the wrong color for Madison. But once she'd gotten the text from Kim that Melissa was on for dinner tonight to dispense business advice and talk final wedding plans, it got harder to concentrate on work. She hurried through the cleanup so she was ready to walk out the door the minute Madison was done.

And now she had to figure out what to wear. She decided on a peasant blouse and skinny jeans. Casual but cute.

Once she was ready, she checked the terrarium that sat on her old desk under the window. She sprayed it a bit with water. It had turned out better than she expected. Maybe Monday she'd see about getting a few more things for it. Maybe some cute fairy garden items. Wait a minute. She went to her closet and sorted through the boxes on the shelf, finally pulling one down. Lifting the lid, she touched the various "treasures" she had collected over the years. Lots of memories there. Buttons, pins, rocks collected from family vacations, trinkets. She set the box next to the terrarium. She didn't have time to travel down memory lane now, but maybe Monday.

With a final glance at her reflection—would Austin find her appealing?—she hopped in her car and headed over to Kim's.

She thought about Austin holding her hand and kissing her on the cheek last night. He was such a sweet, stable guy. Just what she needed. But could he like a girl like her? He knew she was in recovery. They'd had that conversation at Heather and Kyle's wedding. It hadn't seemed to bother him. But it was one thing to know that about a friend, another to get serious with someone who had her background. Had he just gone along on the date because Matthew and Kim wanted them too? Maybe he wasn't picturing a future together with her. She wouldn't blame him, honestly.

Then again, Austin didn't seem the type to play with a girl's feelings. Still, they were pretty different. But didn't opposites attract? She let out a sigh as she pulled into a parking spot at the base of Kim's stairs. Looked like she was the first one here. Good. She'd hoped to get there early to help Kim with the food.

God, please help me to not make a fool of myself tonight. And if Austin isn't in to me, let me down gently.

Austin followed Matthew into Kim's condo, the smell of spicy meat and hot tortillas making his stomach growl. He'd been looking forward to this all day, as he'd skimmed through the various leadership books he'd bought, taking notes, writing down questions he wanted to ask Melissa.

But, if he was honest with himself, he also wanted to see

Jessica again. While there'd been a few awkward moments on their date last night, they'd found their footing. Holding her hand and kissing her good night, even if only on the cheek, had sent heat coursing through him that he wasn't sure how to handle. And he didn't like not knowing things. But there was something a little intoxicating about the feeling, living on the edge. The way she looked at him made him feel capable and admired.

But relationships took resources, and he was feeling spread pretty thin, with work and Dad's illness. Throw in camping, something he hadn't done before, and he wasn't sure he could handle yet another new thing in his life. Though work and camping would be over and done with soon. Jessica… Well, he hoped Jessica could be around for a long time.

While Matthew hugged Kim, Austin stepped around and saw Jessica in the kitchen. He set the bag he carried on the counter and pulled her into a brief hug. "Hey, Jessica. How was work?"

The sweet, floral-and-vanilla scent of her floated around him, intoxicating him so he barely heard her response.

"Good. Saturdays are short days, so that helped. Is that the ice cream?"

"Yep, and hot fudge sauce."

"Yum. I'll pop it in the freezer." She opened the bag and removed the containers, putting the ice cream in the freezer and the jar of sauce on a clear spot on the counter.

He couldn't stop watching her.

"What did you do today?"

He didn't get to answer before Kim interrupted.

"Dinner's almost ready." Kim had moved out of Matthew's arms and hovered over the various bowls on the kitchen counter. "We can eat as soon as—" A knock at the door interrupted her. "Melissa's here."

Matthew let her in. She greeted everyone, Kim gave directions about the food, which was a serve-yourself taco bar, and soon they were seated around Kim's living room eating.

Jessica sat next to him, cross-legged on the floor. They used the coffee table as a table.

The food was delicious, but he had a hard time concentrating with Jessica next to him, occasionally bumping his elbow.

Between bites, Melissa asked if they had any specific questions.

Austin pulled up his list from his phone, forcing himself to focus on it. Matthew had a few once Austin got the ball rolling, and before he knew it, they had eaten and Jessica and Kim were cleaning up.

"You guys ready for ice cream?" Kim asked, scoop in her hand.

"I'm always ready for ice cream," Melissa replied. "Unfortunately."

As they ate dessert, Matthew told Melissa that Bernie was going on the camping trip.

Melissa nodded. "Good. I've known Bernie for a few years now. We started that singles' Bible study together. Can't believe I won't be in it much longer. He'd be a good guy to get to know, Austin. He's easygoing, has a life-of-the-party vibe, but he's excellent with numbers. I know DataCorp jumped at the chance to grab him when they moved into town."

Austin disliked the idea of relying on anyone. "Shouldn't I get the job on my own merits, because I'm the best person for the job? I don't like playing politics."

"It's not like that. Bernie wouldn't say anything that wasn't true or try to manipulate anyone." Melissa ran her spoon around her bowl. "But every job requires you to work with other people. You have to show that you're a team player, not only in your department but with others. Having someone from outside your department vouch for you isn't a bad thing. Matthew will support you, but he's your roommate, so it won't count for as much."

Jessica carried her bowl to the sink. "Austin has accomplished a lot in a short period of time. Unless he had an agenda of schmoozing with folks from other departments, it makes sense that he hasn't had much time to meet other people. His team has been busy since the moment they got here. And he also made a big move from another state, away from his parents."

Matthew laughed. "Hey, just because you still live at home doesn't mean it's that traumatic to leave."

Kim threw a napkin at him.

Jessica put the ice cream containers in the freezer. "No, it's not that. I mean, with his dad's—"

Austin's head snapped up at her words.

She froze, a look of horror crossing her face as she met his gaze.

Kim glanced from Jessica to Austin to Matthew, and she frowned. "What about his dad?"

Matthew looked from Jessica to Austin then took Kim's hand. "Uh, just that his folks are getting older, like all of ours."

Austin shot Matthew a tight, grateful smile. But he'd lost his appetite for ice cream. He carried his bowl to the sink, ignoring Jessica who stood rooted to the kitchen floor.

She leaned toward him, lowering her voice. "I'm so sorry. I didn't mean—"

He clattered his bowl to the sink. "Matthew, are you ready to go? I've got a lot of reading to do."

"Uh, sure." He gave Kim a quick kiss on the cheek and stood.

Austin knew the women were looking at him oddly, but he didn't care. He needed to get out of there. Now.

Something had clicked shut in his heart. She'd done the unthinkable. She'd revealed something he'd told her in confidence. Even if she hadn't meant to do it, he couldn't trust her. She was right about her ability to talk about anything. But he couldn't be with someone who repeated what he told her.

They couldn't have a future together. And that bothered him far more than he would have thought.

JESSICA BLINKED AWAY TEARS AS SHE PUT AWAY THE FOOD and cleaned up the dishes. How could she have been so stupid? When would she learn to think before she opened her mouth? She'd seen the look on Austin's face. He'd shut her out, and it was her own fault.

Kim came over to the sink after she'd seen the guys out. "Thanks for doing all that. Are you okay? The vibe between you and Austin took on a definite chill."

"I'm fine." As much as she wanted to, talking about it with Kim would just make it worse. "So, Melissa, tell us what you've got planned and how we can help."

Melissa shot her a sympathetic look. Great. Everyone knew she'd screwed up. But she didn't say anything.

They moved into the living room and got comfortable.

"Good news on lots of fronts." Melissa sat on the floor, putting her phone on the coffee table where everyone could see. "First, the house is closing in three weeks, just after we get back from our honeymoon. Jessica, would you be able to keep any eye on it while we're gone? It would be just my luck that something would spring a leak while we're gone."

"Sure. Want me to house-sit?"

"That would be great."

"Maybe I can get all my friends to stagger their vacations so I can go from house to house." She grinned, though it felt strange.

"There has to be some advantage to living at home." Kim nudged her.

"There are a few." Jessica leaned forward from her spot on the couch. "What's the other good news?"

"I found the perfect wedding locale. Salt Creek Grille. They had a Sunday night opening. There's a garden patio with a separate entrance. We can have it set up with rectangular tables for ten around the perimeter." She showed them photos on her phone. That will leave room for a dance floor in the middle and an arch at the front for the ceremony. Best of all, they'll arrange for the food, flowers, cake. Music will be from a playlist. Which I'll need your help with."

The location was beautiful. A secluded gardened surrounded by trees and greenery, just up the hill from the ocean. And since it was August, twilight would linger. This seemed exactly like Melissa.

"So did you talk to Allie?"

Melissa ducked her head. "No. Once I heard about Salt Creek Grille, I knew it'd be perfect. And I'm afraid the more people know, the more of a chance someone will try to talk me out of it. Am I terrible for not telling my sister? I'm afraid she'll feel obligated to help. I just want her to enjoy the day with us and not feel like she has to always be helping. You know how she is."

"After all I went through helping with Heather and Kyle's wedding, I know what it's like." Kim touched Melissa's knee. "I think Allie will be relieved to not have that on her plate too."

"Good. Okay, I called Pastor Tom. He's in. He and Scott and I have been meeting weekly over Zoom for pre-marital counseling since shortly after we got engaged, since we knew we didn't want it to be a long one. It helps that he knows both of us already. Me better than Scott, but still."

She swiped to another screen that had a sample electronic invitation. "I'll start emailing invites and making calls tomorrow. Probably the biggest issue will be my family, but if anyone can't come, oh well. Someone can FaceTime them in."

"What are you going to say on the invitations and phone calls? What excuse are you giving them for the party?"

"I'm telling everyone that it's the last time Scott will be in town for a year and that my townhome sold, so I'm moving up to Washington. We want a going away party but don't want to interfere with Joe and Sarah's wedding. The garden only holds sixty people, which is perfect, until I started thinking about the guest list. I want to go over that with you two as well. I've got former work friends and colleagues, church people, their families. The sixty slots will go fast, so I'll have to prioritize and get verbal commitments from people when I talk to them." Melissa blew a piece of mahogany hair out of her eyes.

Jessica had always admired Melissa's beautiful, thick curls.

"Regretting the short time frame?" Kim asked.

Melissa shook her head. "No, I've pulled off more complex projects than this in less time. I just don't want to hurt anyone's feelings or have anyone feel left out."

"I'm sure that's bound to happen at every wedding. But this day is about you and Scott." Kim grinned. "Have you decided where you're going for your honeymoon?"

"Scott said he made reservations, but he hasn't told me where. It's a surprise."

"Ooh, fun. Okay, now let's talk about your dress." Kim pulled up her phone. "I have a couple of ideas for you. Tell me what you think. All of these are in Lynnae's store. We can try on your favorites, and I can alter anything. Is Scott wearing his uniform?"

Melissa swiped through the pictures. "Yes, his service dress whites." She looked up. "Will that give something away? Will people wonder why he's in uniform?"

"Are you doing the ceremony before or after dinner?" Jessica asked.

"After. That way we'll have the ceremony, cut the cake, and have the first dance and be done with the wedding part."

"Why doesn't he slip out at the end of dinner and change? That way the speculation will be short lived."

"Great idea, Jessica! That's perfect. And you know what else is perfect? This dress." Melissa tapped the screen.

Kim leaned over and smiled. "I thought of you when I saw

it. I would be surprised if it needed any alterations, but we can go try it on tomorrow after church."

Jessica studied the picture. A pale-pink lace bodice dress with a sweetheart neckline and lace cap sleeves. The fit-and-flare silhouette skimmed to a graduated hemline, just above the knees in front, calf length in back. The perfect combination of sweet and sexy, dressy without being overly so.

"It's you, Melissa." Jessica could picture Melissa in that dress, at the garden patio, marrying her handsome naval aviator. She blinked back tears. Would that ever be her someday?

They moved onto the guests and playlist, Kim making most of the suggestions and Jessica just listening. It had been an exhausting day emotionally, and she just wanted to go home. But this was her opportunity to be a good friend. She didn't want to blow it.

She reminded herself of what her Inspiration for Today app had said.

"I don't know what your destiny will be, but one thing I know: The only ones among you who will be truly happy are those who have sought and found how to serve." --Albert Schweitzer

She was trying. She'd spent so many years selfishly focusing on her own pain that she'd been blinded to everyone around her. And she desperately wanted to change that.

"Okay, girls, my head is spinning. Thanks a ton for your help. I need to get home and get those invites out." Melissa stood and gave each of them a hug. "See you tomorrow at church. And let's plan on doing that fitting afterward. We'll make some excuse on why we need to miss the traditional after-church lunch."

Yeah, Jessica had no desire to sit near Austin and feel the weight of his condemnation on her. She'd have to try to talk to him at some point. But what could she do to make up for it? Nothing.

As soon as Melissa had left and Kim had shut the door

behind her, she turned to Jessica. "Okay, spill. What was all that between you and Austin?"

Jessica shook her head. "I was stupid. I started to let slip something he'd told me in confidence. And that is something very important to him. He doesn't trust personal information easily with people. He's very private."

"I know. Matthew has said that too. And it must be a big deal since Matthew seemed to know what it was and he hasn't told me."

Jessica nodded. "Yeah. I blew it. I'll try to talk to him and apologize in private, but I don't know if he'll even take my calls. I've really screwed this up big time. And considering what I've done in the past, that's saying something. It's not so much about the specific information; it's about his ability to trust me. I'm sure he thinks he can't now."

"Oh, honey." Kim pulled her into a hug. "God is still in control, despite our best efforts to make a mess of our lives. Maybe you and Austin will have some time to during the camping trip to work through it."

"If he even goes." Jessica pulled out of the hug and picked up her purse, catching a glimpse of her reflection in the glass patio door, the pink streaks shooting through her blonde hair. Maybe it was time to make a change. Maybe the new Jessica would make fewer mistakes.

Chapter Eight

Sunlight streamed through Jessica's bedroom window, waking her. She needed to get out of bed. The light glinted off her terrarium, reminding her of her plans today.

Her phone buzzed with a text. Her heart jumped up as she rolled over, hoping it was Austin.

But it was from Sarah. **Hey, do you have time to meet me for lunch today? I have something I want to run by you.**

Other than the terrarium and laundry, she didn't have any other plans. Sarah probably wanted help with her wedding, which was great. Jessica was getting good at being a wedding assistant. If the hair stylist thing didn't work out, perhaps she could be a wedding coordinator. She laughed as she rolled out of bed.

Sure. Sounds great.

Awesome! Rubio's by the movie theater at 11:30?

See you then!

Jessica moved through her morning routine. Toast and coffee for breakfast, a shower, then getting dressed and doing her hair and makeup. Her thoughts drifted to church yesterday. Austin had kept his distance. Melissa and Kim had made an excuse afterwards about needing to do some shopping, and Jessica had claimed a headache. Which was true.

She had called Austin that afternoon but only got his voice mail. She tried a bit later and left a message this time. She needed to try again today, but he was at work, and she didn't want to bother him. So maybe tonight. Either he'd get tired of dodging her calls or maybe she'd give up. Either way, she had to keep trying to apologize to him. Even if there was no future for them, they were going on a camping trip together—at least she hoped he was still going. No matter what, they ran in the same circle of friends. They had to at least be friendly.

The only good news that had come out of that day was the picture Kim had texted her with the caption "Shh!" It was Melissa in the pink dress. It fit her perfectly. She absolutely glowed. Her brother was going to be blown away when he saw his bride.

She pulled open the trinket box she had gotten out of the closet Friday. Seemed like a lifetime ago that she'd heard the news of the girl's body. She didn't expect Kyle to have news for her any time soon.

She shook her head as she sorted through the box. Why had she kept this stuff? A rainbow pin from her rainbow phase, a plastic car that bore a faint resemblance to the VW Bug Kim drove, a few shells and rocks. At one point in time, these were important to her. She picked out the items and found spots for them in her terrarium. She remembered when she and Kim had gotten the car out of a machine. Kim had said she wanted one like it when she grew up. Jessica must have gone through a dollar's worth of change until she'd come up with the same car as Kim.

Funny how Kim now drove that car. Did she still have the plastic one?

Where had the dreams gone that Younger Jessica had had? She placed the rainbow pin, the rocks, and shells in the terrarium. Then she headed back to the closet. Maybe it was still here.

Yep, the art supplies she kept in a plastic fishing tackle box. She and Kim used to color and paint for hours, mixing colors, not worrying too much about the end product.

The paint trays were stained, and the palettes caked with cracked, dried paint. The brushes were stiff. Not much was usable. She put everything back inside and closed the lid. She'd toss this in the trash on her way out.

At one point, she thought she would be an artist. Her parents had signed her up for an after-school art class. The teacher really understood her and encouraged her boldness and creativity. Then the class was cancelled, and Jessica was devastated. Her parents bought her a DVD set of art lessons, but it wasn't the same.

Still, she hadn't thought about it in a long time. Maybe that's why she'd been drawn to cosmetology. Hair and makeup were a kind of artistry. And maybe she could pick up some paint supplies and start dabbling around again. It would give her something to do.

Putting everything back on the closet shelf, except for what she was tossing, she checked the time. Might as well head out for lunch.

She caught Mom in the kitchen.

"Smells good."

"Thanks. I haven't made homemade spaghetti sauce in a while. I thought I'd make a big batch and freeze some. I'll make lasagna for dinner."

"Yum. I'm off to meet Sarah for lunch. I might run some errands too."

"Have fun."

Jessica climbed in her car and headed toward the shopping center where Rubio's was. One benefit of living at home was that Mom still cooked most of Jessica's meals. And she was a good cook. After long days at the salon, it was nice not to have to worry about food.

She arrived at Rubio's to see Sarah already there. Jessica gave her a hug. "Did you order yet?"

"Nope, I just got here." She thrust a bouquet of flowers, clearly picked from her garden, into Jessica's hands. "These are for you."

"Thanks so much!" Jessica studied the beautiful arrangement of the flowers and how the colors complemented and contrasted. Purple statice, perfumed sweet peas, bright pink cosmos backed with a frothy greenery. Sarah sure had a way with flowers. "What's the occasion?" She gave a mock frown. "This isn't a bribe, is it?"

Sarah shrugged with a sheepish grin. "Um, maybe? Let's order, and I'll tell you more. I'm buying your lunch too."

Jessica raised her eyebrows. "This really must be a big deal."

They placed their orders and took their number to their tile-topped table and waited for their food.

They made a bit of small talk until their food arrived. Jessica loved the shrimp tacos, and the grilled meat with the chewy tortilla didn't disappoint.

"I told you about Joe's sister, Sophia, wanting to 'help' with the wedding. I thought since we'd nailed down all the big decisions that she wouldn't have anything left to do. However, she's obsessed with the favors and the place settings and the seating arrangements, and anything else she can think to micromanage. I get several texts a day from her. I can't deal with that on top of work. Plus, at some point I'm afraid I'm going to lose my temper with her and alienate her. I don't want to do that. I know she means well."

Jessica nodded. Her conversation Saturday with Kim and Melissa ran through her mind. She couldn't say a word of it to Sarah, but she could see why Melissa would opt out of all the drama with a surprise wedding. "So how can I help?"

"I thought maybe I could enlist you as a wedding coordinator of sorts. I could have Sophia text you her ideas and plans. You and I could go through what I already have, and then if

Sophia has something we've either forgotten about or I don't care about, then we can add that in. Plus, you'd be doing me a huge favor if you'd be the point person to make sure everything is coordinated the day of the event. I know it's a lot to ask."

Jessica sat back. "Wow. I didn't expect that." Sarah hadn't seen Jessica drunk, but surely Joe had informed her of the times he'd picked up Jessica when she couldn't drive home. The fact that Sarah was entrusting her with her wedding details was astounding. She wasn't quite sure she was worthy of the trust.

She reached across and squeezed Sarah's hand. "Yes, of course, I'll do it for you. I'm honored that you'd ask."

"It means so much to me, Jessica. I don't want to alienate Joe's family. I love them, but they can be overwhelming. And I overthink everything. It takes me forever to make a decision, so the amount of brain space it's taking dealing with Sophia is immense. I'm still trying to get our firm back on good footing without bothering my former boss, who retired to deal with his wife's illness. And I need to make sure all of my clients and projects are in good shape so I can leave for the wedding and honeymoon without worrying about work. You're taking a huge load off my plate."

"I'm happy to do it." Jessica played with the straw in her drink. Maybe her wedding coordinator dreams were coming true. She laughed. "I truly am. It's no secret I'm trying to keep myself busy. And if I can help you and Joe have a special day, all the better. Joe's been like a brother to me, pulling me out of bad situations since Scott was usually deployed somewhere else. And he didn't lecture me like Kyle did, so I would always call Joe first. He's a good guy. I'm glad he found you. And if taking the heat from his big sister means she's mad at me instead of you, it's a small price to pay."

Sarah laughed. "I don't think she'll be mad, but she is a strong personality. Probably comes from being the oldest of five kids. She was a teenager when their dad died." She pointed to the flowers. "Not only are those to say thank you, they're also to remind you that you are worthy of beauty. You have a talent for creating it, but you are also God's beautiful creation. And I just wanted to remind you of that."

Jessica fingered the bristly statice, blinking away tears. "Thank you. I can't remember the last time someone said something so nice to me."

"It's the truth." She held Jessica's gaze for a long moment. "Now, I can send you my wedding planning document so you can see everything, but let's go over it." She pulled out her tablet and swiped open an app.

In this space, Jessica felt like she belonged, like she was a dependable member of a team. So different than the competitive atmosphere at the salon. And this feeling was something she didn't want to go away.

WHERE WAS THE VAN REGISTRATION? ERIC FLIPPED through the documents on his desk. It had to be here. It wasn't kept in the vehicle, for good reasons. Yeah, if you got pulled over you were supposed to show it, but if Gordo got pulled over, they had worse issues than no registration. It was an innocent enough piece of paper, but if it fell into the wrong hands, it could link his legitimate business with his money-making but not-so-legitimate one.

His wife had become accustomed to the lifestyle he'd given her, the status in society, plus her own business that she dabbled in. There was no way he could risk losing all of this. He'd worked too hard his entire life for it to come crashing down on him. Brianna's escape was a huge problem. It set a bad precedent. The girls had to believe that this was their life now so they'd stay compliant. He couldn't have them trying to run away at every opportunity.

Gordo had seen to it that none of the other girls got any ideas from Brianna's escape. He'd caught up with her quickly.

And she'd been a good example to the other girls of what happened if they tried the same thing. There was a price to pay. He didn't think any of them would want to pay it after seeing what happened to Brianna.

The girl at the salon hadn't known anything other than Brianna wanted to use the phone. But to be on the safe side, they'd need to move the girls. He patted his shirt pockets, wishing he hadn't given up smoking. Instead, he reached for a butterscotch candy from the dish on his desk and popped it in his mouth.

He stepped out of his office to where his secretary sat. She only knew about his legit business. "Have you seen the recent vehicle registrations?" He had several vans and cars for his various businesses.

Michelle paused, hand lifted from her keyboard. "Yes, I paid them then put them in the correct vehicles when I put the new tags on them as they came to the office. You should be all set." She smiled like she'd done him a favor.

He kept his face neutral. Under ordinary circumstances, in an ordinary business, she would be being helpful. And there was likely nothing in the van to arouse her suspicions. The hooks in the floor were cargo tie downs. Nothing too unusual in that.

"Ah, thanks." He headed back to his office. He was going to have to be more careful. He couldn't have a leak from within.

AUSTIN PULLED A COLD COKE OUT OF THE FRIDGE AFTER work. He needed the caffeine and sugar. It had been a hot ride home, though no one had tried to run him off the road. He plopped into the recliner just as his phone buzzed. Jessica calling again. Guilt sliced through him. She'd sent a bunch of apology texts after leaving two voice mails. No funny GIFs among them. He should at least talk to her.

Matthew looked up from where he lounged on the couch. "Is that Jessica?"

Austin scowled.

"Aren't you going to get it?"

"I'll call her later." Work had been particularly draining. Randy had found out somehow that Austin was going for the director position, so he'd thrown his hat in the ring too. And had made sure Austin knew it. In the meantime, he'd decided to act like the position was already his, ordering everyone around and setting up regular meetings. It was annoying and ridiculous. And since Austin had blown off Randy's last meeting, Randy had gone over his head to Max.

Max's advice had been not to make an enemy of Randy, that even if Austin got the position, Randy would still be on his team, and it could come back to bite him. Austin thought that ship might have already sailed. When Austin tried to explain to Max about the research he'd done on presentations, Max had advised him to do what he did best and to not try to be someone else. Which had set his mind spinning, and he had some ideas.

"You're going to spend the whole weekend with her. You might as well straighten things out ahead of time."

"I'm not going." Sunday had been awkward enough. The only saving grace was that she hadn't come to lunch, pleading a headache. Kim didn't stay either, so he and Matthew had gone through In-N-Out and headed home.

"You have to. You agreed to. Remember, Bernie's going."

Oh, yeah. And after today with Randy, he was more determined than ever to get that director position. But his plan would take some time, something he had hoped to make progress on this weekend instead of going camping. Still, he did need to prove he could work with people, therefore, spending time with Bernie probably overrode working on his plan. Why did this have to be so complicated? Why couldn't everyone just do their jobs?

He shot the empty can across the room into the recycling

bin. Two points. He had done some research on camping and wilderness best practices. "Fine. But if I don't get this director position, Randy will be intolerable as a boss. I'll be forced to find another job, probably in Phoenix. You'll need a new roommate. So, yeah, let's have fun while we can."

Matthew climbed up from the couch and smacked Austin on the arm. "Good choice. Now call Jessica before your heart hardens any further. She actually didn't reveal any information, and if you recall the context, she was defending you. She clearly feels bad about it. Do you really think she'll reveal any of your secrets? You might consider that your expectations are a bit rigid." He turned and headed toward his room.

He had a point, as much as Austin didn't want to admit it. No one was perfect, and it was likely that people would step on each other's toes in a relationship. If he didn't let down his walls, he'd never have the opportunity to let anyone close, even if it did scare him.

But, hey, he was going camping. At this rate, he was going to become a daredevil with all the risk he was taking.

He picked up his phone and swiped Jessica's number.

Chapter Nine

Jessica examined her hair in the mirror at Madison's station. She and Lyric, at the next station, were cleaning up after clients. "What do you think about this pink streak? I'm considering getting rid of it. It was great when I was experimenting with color at school, but now I need something more serious. I was considering balayage." She turned to Lyric. "What do you think?"

Lyric came over and lifted pieces of Jessica's hair, looking at it in the light. "I think that's a great choice. Your blonde hair with darker undertones would look gorgeous and would cover the pink. Very beachy. And I'd love the practice. We can figure out a time this week after hours if Crystal says it's okay."

Jessica was a bit surprised that Lyric had offered. And was slightly concerned. Would Lyric do something crazy to her hair? No, it would reflect badly on her work. Jessica only wished she had a similar opportunity to show off her own work.

She cleared it with Crystal, whose only stipulation was that she got to see the results.

Two nights later, Jessica studied her new sun-bleached beachy waves with darker roots. No more pink. And Lyric had even given her a cut to play off the high- and lowlights. She looked more professional and stylish, instead of a rebel.

And she liked it.

Crystal was impressed too. More points for Lyric.

She couldn't help but wonder what Austin would think. They seemed to be back on better footing after he'd called and accepted her apology, admitting he'd overreacted. She'd asked him about work, and he'd been excited about a new program he was creating that he thought would show off his talents to the best light and give him an edge over Randy. He even seemed to be looking forward to the camping trip. The timing couldn't be better.

Gordo stepped into Eric's office, shutting the door behind him.

"Did anyone see you come in?" Eric stepped from behind his desk, checking to make sure the blinds were closed. His secretary had left hours ago.

"No. I'm not stupid." He crossed his tat-covered beefy arms over his chest.

"Didn't say you were. Do you have the registration?"

Gordo flipped the paper onto Eric's desk. "I'll cut to the chase. I want a bigger share. I'm taking all the risk driving from place to place. If I get stopped, it's my head on the line."

"Don't do anything to get stopped. You're not the one fronting the money, erasing the paper trails, and making sure certain people get paid to look the other way. You have no idea the pressure I live with."

Gordo gave a wicked smile. "I could always go to the cops with what I know."

Eric scoffed. "Yeah right. You're just as guilty. You think you'd get any kind of immunity? Think again." He stepped into

Gordo's space. "Don't push me. I've got a lot riding on this. Or I might drop the dime on you."

Gordo's smile morphed into a sneer. He hit a nerve. Gordo had served time before.

"Remember who you're dealing with." Eric took a step back. "I didn't get to be where I am by being stupid. I'm a businessman with a product, and I know what needs to be done with it. Those girls gotta be moved." He handed Gordo a piece of paper with where they should stay on their way to their final destination. Out-of-the-way places where the girls wouldn't be spotted and no one would ask questions. "Now get out of here and don't let anyone see you."

Gordo put his hand on the doorknob. "We're not finished with this discussion."

"Yes, we are."

Gordo narrowed his eyes.

Eric shot a glance to his desk drawer where he kept his Sig. It would be messy if he had to shoot Gordo, but it would be self-defense in a robbery gone wrong. But then he'd have to get someone else to move the girls, and he didn't have the time. Why were there always complications?

Gordo didn't miss Eric's glance. He narrowed his eyes and left.

Eric ran a hand over his face. He spent all of his time managing people, and it was getting to him. He needed a vacation. Instead, he grabbed a butterscotch.

Chapter Ten

Jessica pulled into the church parking lot Friday afternoon. Austin, Kim, and Matthew were already there with his truck, the back full of camping supplies and coolers. She wasn't sure who all was driving—or going, for that matter—but her twelve-year-old car wouldn't be a good bet to make it up the mountains. Kim had assured her there would be plenty of room for her in one of the vehicles.

A Ford Escape pulled up next to Matthew, and Gary got out. Jessica had met him a few times before. He had pale brown hair, a thin build, and a habit of pushing his glasses up his nose.

Austin glanced her way as she made her way toward the group. He paused a minute before lifting his hand, but that was it. She was hoping he'd at least comment on her new hair. Kim had loved it.

More cars arrived in the parking lot, and everyone loaded their gear into the back of Matthew's truck.

Jessica glanced around the gathered group. Ryan and Macy were still missing. She didn't see his signature Mustang anywhere.

A new Toyota RAV4 screamed into the parking lot, making a sharp turn and braking hard before the group. Ryan Bradley popped out of the driver's side, pushing his sunglasses up on his stylishly spiked hair. A woman climbed out of the passenger side, laughing, flinging back her long, wavy dark hair.

"Hey, everyone. This is Macy Villanueva." He slid his arm around her shoulders. "She came to see what a good time can be had camping with our singles' group."

She rolled her eyes at him. "Hi, everyone."

She looked like she was dressed for a photo shoot instead of camping, her clothing leaving very little of her generous curves to the imagination. Jessica forced herself to rein in her negative thoughts. Macy had aged well since high school, and Jessica found the insecure grade-school girl coming back up. For a moment, the past and present overlaid each other, and she struggled to find her footing.

Should she mention she was Scott's sister? No, that would likely bring back bad memories. Macy wouldn't remember her. Ryan had asked them to be welcoming to her. She stepped forward and extended her hand. "Hi, I'm Jessica. I'm one of the newest members. Me and Austin." She gestured to him and gave him a smile.

He stepped forward and shook Macy's hand. "Nice to meet you."

"Very nice to meet you." She held on to his hand longer than Jessica liked. Well, it was Austin's problem, not hers.

The rest introduced themselves.

Ryan raised his voice. "Okay, do we have everything?" He looked at Kim.

"Yep." She nodded. "We're all set."

"Good. Everyone know where they're riding?"

Jessica glanced around the group. Confused looks flew among everyone but Kim and Matthew. Um, no? At least she wasn't the only one.

Ryan patted the RAV4. "I'm driving this, so whoever wants to ride with me, hop in."

Macy leaned against the passenger door talking to Bernie. Austin made his way over and got in the back.

Really? Jessica didn't know what to think. He obviously couldn't ride with Matthew and Kim. The cab was too crunched for three people for that long of a trip. But she figured he'd ride with her since she was the only other person he knew well. And she thought they had something—well, special—between them. They had gone on a date. She sighed. Guess not.

Gary raised his keys. "I can drive and take the rest."

"Thanks." Jessica climbed in along with Laurie, a quiet girl she hadn't talked to much. Guess this would be a good chance to get to know both of them.

She cast a longing look toward Austin as the RAV4 sped out of the parking lot. But he wasn't looking her way.

AUSTIN WISHED MORE THAN ANYTHING HE COULD PUT HIS Air Pods in to block out Macy's chatter. Matthew had nudged him to make sure he rode in the same vehicle as Bernie, since that would be a good opportunity to get to know him and even talk about work. He just wished Bernie hadn't chosen the same car as Macy. Austin would have much rather been riding with Jessica.

And what had she done to her hair? The pink dye was gone, and she had different shades of blonde and brown streaked through in a style that made it look like she'd spent plenty of time in the sun. It looked pretty on her, in a sophisticated way, and he couldn't help but want to touch one of those curls to see what they'd feel like running through his fingers.

As usual, she'd figured out how to make something as casual as jeans and a shirt open over a tank top look good.

While he hated making small talk, Matthew had given him a few tips to get people talking about themselves, taking the pressure off Austin to maintain the conversation. So he asked Bernie how he came to be involved with this group.

Bernie told Austin how he and Kyle had gone on a men's retreat together several years ago and were roommates. Then they both ended up in the singles' Bible study Melissa was starting. They moved on to talking about work, what Bernie did before coming to DataCorp. It made the time pass, even though Ryan's driving might make him sick.

Ryan sped up the straightaways then braked hard to squeeze them around the mountainous curves. Either the side of the mountain or nothingness dropping away to the valley floor greeted Austin when he looked out the window. Ryan might have been testing the SUV's handling capabilities, but Austin wanted to remind him this wouldn't handle the same as his Mustang. But Ryan didn't strike him as the kind of guy who took direction well.

Instead Austin kept his gaze inside and concentrated on asking Bernie questions about his leadership experience, drawing on his conversation with Melissa and the books he'd read.

But he couldn't wait until they got to the campground and he could talk to Jessica.

On the way up, Jessica's heart beat faster the closer they got to Holcomb Springs and evidence of the fire of just two months ago became clear. She hadn't expected that. Though if she'd thought about it at all, she should have. Much of the area was scarred, black ground, and the remaining trees resembled charcoal toothpicks. Then for no reason at all, there'd be a patch of untouched trees. Some were burned on only one side.

As they came to the side of the lake near the marina, her heart was pounding nearly out of her chest. She concentrated on breathing, on feeling the seat under her, pressing her hands on her thighs. *There's no fire. I'm safe.*

Was Austin feeling the same things?

The Treasure Island park hadn't been rebuilt yet, but the melted playground structure had been removed. The marina was intact, however. Hopefully Captain John hadn't lost too much business.

They continued around the lake. Jessica wasn't entirely sure where they had been rescued. Everything looked different from this angle, and her thoughts had been on getting her kayak to the helicopter, not the scenery, which was all on fire anyway. She was amazed at how many of the homes had survived, even if the fire had clearly burned right up to them. The firefighters had done an amazing job on structure protection.

Had Jerod known how badly this area had suffered? The campground would have to be intact since they took the reservation, but would anything else have survived? She was beginning to rethink this whole weekend. Especially if Austin was going to spend it drooling over Macy.

But as they continued around to the other side of the lake, more stands of trees, sage, and chaparral survived, and the area around the campground was in good condition. Maybe they had set up a defensive perimeter here to protect the campground and nearby homes. She let out a breath and relaxed her shoulders.

At the campsite, Jessica and Laurie helped Kim set up the cooking area while the guys set up the tents. She needed to keep her hands busy and her mind occupied. She hoped she didn't have nightmares tonight. She hadn't had them in a while.

The campsite was nestled among the tall pines, giving them a sense of security. Holcomb Lake was down the bike path from their site.

Jessica had gotten to know Laurie a bit on the ride up. She was an elementary school teacher and had lived in Laguna Vista her whole life. She'd never gone camping before and was a little nervous about it. Jessica reassured her that it would be a fun trip. Luckily, Laurie had been sitting in the front seat and didn't see

Jessica nearly hyperventilating as they drove through the burn scar.

Once the camp stove was set up, Kim set Laurie to browning the ground beef. She and Jessica chopped the tomatoes, lettuce, and avocados and opened packages of shredded Mexican-blend cheese. They also got out a can of olives and in another pan heated up refried beans.

Jessica was impressed by how Kim had everything set up and organized.

"I got help from Melissa. I watched what she did on our Great American Road Trip. She had lists and plans. Everything went smoothly. So all I had to do was borrow her lists and menus. Piece of cake."

Once the ground beef was cooked and seasoned with taco spices and the beans heated, Kim told Ryan dinner was ready. It felt early, but it got dark sooner up here because the trees and mountain ridges hid the sun before it set. The lack of city lights made the darkness even more pervasive.

Ryan gathered everyone around and read off the meal assignments and cleanup crews. Then he asked the blessing on the food, and everyone made their way through the food line.

Kim explained how it worked. "We're having walking tacos. That means you grab a bag of Fritos, crunch it up a bit, then open it and add in some taco meat and whatever else you want. We have cheese, lettuce, tomatoes, avocados, and olives. There's beans for a side dish. And s'mores for dessert. Drinks are in the cooler at the end of the table."

When everyone had gone through the line, Jessica and Kim helped themselves. Matthew waved them to chairs next to him and Austin.

Jessica grabbed Laurie. "Come sit with us." Otherwise, the only other girl was Macy. And Laurie and Macy were about as opposite as you could get.

Jessica eased herself down into a chair by Austin. This wasn't going to be awkward at all.

"These are good. I've never had them before."

Jessica glanced over at Austin's comment. He was looking at her. "Oh, yeah. Kim's idea. It's easy to set up and easy to clean up. And everyone likes tacos. These are just less messy."

He nodded. "I'm going to get another one. Can I get you anything?"

She stared at him a minute. He was acting like everything was fine between them. She wasn't sure what to make of that. "Um, I'm still working on this one. But thanks." She turned to Laurie. "Do you need anything?"

Laurie smiled up at Austin. "I'm good. Thanks."

He nodded and moved to the food set out on the picnic table.

She and Laurie chatted about the food. The group was small enough sitting in camp chairs around the fire pit.

"Okay, icebreaker while we're finishing up." Ryan raised his voice. "The theme of this weekend is restoration. So we're going to go around the circle. Everyone say your name, what city you were born in, what you do, and what restoration means to you in one word. I'll go first. I'm Ryan Bradley, but you all know that. I was born in Palos Verdes, and I'm the worship pastor. Restoration means rejuvenation to me. Macy?"

They went around the circle. Jessica didn't care about Macy's answer, and she knew about Kim and Matthew, so she studied the trees soaring above them. A faint vanilla smell drifted above the piney one. The sun had disappeared behind the trees, making the shadows increasingly longer and making her wish they'd get a fire started soon. Most of her anxiety had dissipated under the beautiful surroundings. The mountains had always been a peaceful place for her when she'd come up here as a kid with her family. She was hoping to replace last trip's memory with good ones.

Her ears perked up at Austin's turn. He was born in Honolulu, though his family moved to Arizona when he was two. DataCorp had three employees present. And the various answers for what restoration meant centered on some form of the word rest. Except for Austin, who said, "Wholeness."

Jessica was thinking about his answer when it was her turn. Restoration was a big part of her recovery process. And her goal, while she wouldn't have picked that word, was wholeness. Could she make a step toward that this weekend?

"I'm Jessica Blake. I was born in Laguna Vista. I'm a hair stylist at Salon Moritz. And I like Austin's word *wholeness.* It fits." She glanced at him.

He smiled at her.

"I'm Laurie—"

"Wait," Macy interrupted. "Did you say your last name was Blake? I knew a Scott Blake."

"That's my brother." Let the awkwardness commence.

Macy studied her a minute. "Oh, I see the resemblance. You have the same color eyes, but I guess he got all the height in the family."

"Yep." She was short, nothing she could do about it.

"Huh. I was at his house a few times. I don't remember meeting you."

Jessica gave a tight smile. She sure remembered Macy.

Ryan glanced between the two of them. "Um, Laurie, why don't you continue?"

The conversation moved on to Laurie, but Jessica turned her gaze back to Austin. He ever-so-slightly tilted his head toward Macy and rolled his eyes. It was all Jessica could do to keep from bursting out laughing. For a moment, it was as if it were just the two of them.

Austin leaned over the arm of his camp chair. "Stealing my answers, huh? Wholeness."

"If they're good ones, why not?"

"I see how it is."

"You're the smart one here. Why wouldn't I take your ideas? You're always going to have the best answer."

"You think I'm smart?"

His words were soft, and Jessica didn't have time to respond before Ryan started talking again.

"Okay, great. Now that we all know each other, here's how the rest of the night is going to go. Everyone, make sure you put your trash in the bags hanging off the table. They have to go to the Dumpsters. No food in the tents; no food left outside. You will attract unwanted critters. Racoons are mean if you corner them, but bears will just take what they want. And people in sleeping bags are like soft tacos to them."

Laurie yelped.

Maybe not the best move by Ryan.

"Cleanup crew for one meal is the prep crew for the next. That way you can find the stuff you put away the time before. Tonight's crew is Matthew, Austin, and Gary. I'm sure Kim will help you if you need anything."

Kim nodded.

"Once that's done, we'll come back here for a devotional and a few songs. Then we'll make s'mores. Any questions?"

No one had any, so the guys stood and headed to clean up. Kim went with them to make sure they could find everything. She and Matthew had worked together on their Great American Road Trip under Melissa's direction, so Jessica was sure they'd work well as a team. She glanced after Austin, who was listening to Kim. Maybe someday she'd be a team with him. There was hope.

She turned to Laurie. "You know Ryan was kidding, right? Bears aren't going to come into our tent." She pointed to the bear box. "That's where all the food will stay, where the bears can't get it. And we'll keep all our toiletries and such in the cars."

Laurie nodded but didn't look convinced.

Jessica leaned her head back against the chair and studied the sky. "My brother taught me to study the sky and look for when the first star appears."

Laurie tilted her head up too. "Seems like it would need to be darker."

"You'd be surprised. But just don't get confused by a plane." She laughed. She was glad Scott was marrying Melissa and they'd get to be together. But she was going to miss both of them. Maybe she'd be able to visit. What were the stars like in Washington?

She glanced toward Austin. He caught her eye and smiled. If she didn't feel like she'd be abandoning Laurie, she'd go over to the food area on the pretense of helping Kim. But Laurie was the kind of person who probably got left alone at all sorts of social events. Jessica didn't want to be that kind of person. She thought about her Inspiration for Today quote: "The time is always right to do what is right," by Martin Luther King, Jr.

So she focused on Laurie. She'd find time with Austin at some point. The weekend was just beginning.

Chapter Eleven

Austin listened to Kim's instructions and helped put the food away while keeping one eye on Jessica. Her words played through his head. She thought he was smart. Huh. Of course, he knew that he was intelligent; it was something he prided himself on, one of his assets. But it never occurred to him that Jessica had noticed and appreciated it about him.

Ryan plopped in the chair Austin had vacated. He leaned over the arm and talked to Jessica and Laurie. It sounded like they were talking about camping. But why was Ryan leaning into Jessica's space? Because, face it, Ryan was more Jessica's type, even if he was older than her by about eight or ten years. He was the good-looking, outgoing kind of guy that drew women to him effortlessly. A faint pink over Laurie's cheeks showed that she wasn't immune to his charm.

Jessica's gaze wandered past Ryan to Austin. Her smile was hesitant, but then she frowned and turned back to Ryan.

Matthew nudged his arm. "What are you frowning about?" His voice was low.

"I'm not."

Matthew raised an eyebrow.

Was he?

"Don't worry about him." Matthew zipped the plastic bag closed as he tilted his head toward Ryan. "Just find some time to spend with Jessica."

"That's the plan."

Ryan kept up his conversation with Jessica and Laurie. But if Macy was his guest, why wasn't he including her?

She sat on the other side of the fire ring scrolling through her phone, frowning. There probably wasn't good service here. He remembered that from their time on the lake, though he hadn't bothered to even get his phone out since they'd arrived.

Macy stood and wandered over to where they were cleaning up. "Hey, guys. Anyone know where I can get cell service?"

"Probably not very good service anywhere around here." Matthew spoke up. "At least that's how it was last time." He smiled. "Besides, we're supposed to be communing with God and nature. Don't need phones for that."

"I've got a big PR push for a nonprofit at work, and I don't want to miss any emails. I didn't know I wouldn't have service."

"I'm sure it'll be fine for the weekend." Kim smiled at her.

The smile Macy returned lacked warmth. She turned back to Matthew. "I'm sure I can find some distractions this weekend."

Austin knew he wasn't the best at reading people, but even to him that seemed a bit flirty. But the cleanup was nearly done.

Out of the corner of his eye, he spotted Jessica rising from her chair and heading toward them. He also noticed that Ryan had turned to follow her with his gaze.

Jessica shot him a quick smile then walked up to Kim, who pulled her close and spoke into her ear. They giggled.

He and Matthew loaded the rest of the coolers and food bags into the bear locker. Kim pulled out the s'mores supplies. "We can lock these in one of the cars, since it's just a small bag." She brandished one of the skewers and lowered her voice. "Unless I 'accidentally' poke someone with this."

Jessica laughed.

Austin hefted the bulging trash bag and met Jessica's gaze. "Know where the dumpster is?"

She stepped closer. "I think I remember seeing it on the map. I'll go with you."

Yes. He tried not to appear over eager. "Okay."

The sound of the campsite receded as they walked down the roadway. "I think it's next to the bathrooms. I wanted to see where those were anyway before it got dark." The silence hung heavy and awkward between them. The easiness of earlier had disappeared.

"What did you think of dinner?" She looked at him. "Have you had walking tacos before?"

"No, but they were good. I like how Kim fried up the taco shells at her house, but that seems like a lot of work. It's not as hard to open a bag of Fritos."

"Exactly."

More silence. The bathroom building came into view. The smell of campfires and the chatter of children floated to them. A few kids zoomed by on their bikes.

The dumpster was on the other side of the building. "Hey, I want to check out the bathroom real quick." Jessica pulled open the heavy door and peeked inside.

What was it with women and bathrooms? He grinned when she came out. "Find anything surprising?"

"No, thank goodness. Surprises are not what you want to find in a bathroom. Especially camping. I just didn't want to see any spider webs or bugs. Those are bad enough in the daylight, but at night?" She shuddered.

"Good point. Hey, think Ryan will be too upset if we walk down the bike path? I want to take a look at the lake." And he didn't want to return to the campsite right away.

"I don't care if he is." She grinned. "He's not the boss of me."

Austin laughed. This was the Jessica he knew and was fascinated by.

They stepped off the road onto the bike path. The mossy

smell of the lake grew stronger. The sagebrush and goldenrod rose up around them on both sides of the path, enclosing them in their own little world. He wanted to take her hand like on their date, but this wasn't a date. It was one thing being around Kim and Matthew, but he wasn't sure he wanted anyone else knowing how he felt about Jessica. He wasn't even sure of his own feelings.

"When we were driving up here, I was surprised by how much it freaked me out going through the burn area. I didn't expect that."

He nodded. "I had thought about it, but since it was in the past and we survived, I didn't expect it to bother me. It was weird driving through the burn scar. And seeing the marina from the road. I'm glad it survived. Hopefully, they'll replace the playground too."

The path turned, and the lake opened out before them. Their steps slowed as the path paralleled the lake.

"Wow," Jessica breathed.

Her hand found his. He was surprised but didn't pull away. It felt…right.

The burned hills stood across the lake from them, where the marina was. And off in the distance to the east was the beach area where they had been rescued.

"I can't believe we paddled across that whole lake." His voice was low, and he threaded his fingers through hers, tugging her a bit closer, surprised by the emotions the memories evoked. And how they made him feel even more protective of her.

"Yeah. Well, it took us all day, and the wind helped too. But with all the smoke, most of the time we couldn't see the shore. I had no idea where we were."

He glanced at her. "Were you ever worried we weren't going to make it?"

"Most of the time. But you helped. You never let me get too far away from you. You stayed next to me, shouting encouragement the whole time. With my short arms, I just couldn't get the same kind of leverage as the rest of you. There was a point where the shore never seemed to get any closer, no matter how hard I paddled. I really thought the helo was going to leave without me."

"I wouldn't have let that happen. But I did wish we'd had a double kayak like the rest of them." Because more than once he'd been worried he wouldn't be strong enough or fast enough to help her.

"No one anticipated the fire."

"No, but I like to prepare for trouble. I missed that one."

She cocked her head. "So how did you prepare for this trip?"

"I ordered an emergency kit off Amazon. I figured we should have one at the apartment anyway for when there's an earthquake. So we've got medical supplies, emergency repair kits, even some food and water."

"You and Melissa would get along well. Though, the surprise wedding was unexpected. But once she explained her reasoning, it made total sense."

It would be dark soon. They should head back.

She nudged his arm with hers. "One thing you forgot."

"What's that?" The playful tone in her voice did strange things to his heart.

"We came out here without a flashlight, and it's getting dark."

He grinned. "Hey, I was just going to take out the trash." He *had* thought about the flashlight, but it would have been obvious if he'd taken the time to retrieve it.

"It's a good thing I came along then, so you could see the lake." She grinned back. "Actually, if we keep walking along the path, it loops back to the campground road down a bit farther, if I'm remembering correctly.

"You are."

She looked at him. "Oh, of course you studied the map. You didn't need my help at all."

"Nope. If you recall, I didn't ask for it. I just asked if *you* knew where the dumpster was."

She laughed. "Testing my knowledge?"

"Something like that." Or nothing like that.

The path came out at the far end of the campground, where it was more isolated. A lone paneled van was parked in one of the slots. Austin's steps halted. He flashed back to the moment when he thought a van just like that one was going to take him out.

"What?"

He shrugged and started walking again. "Nothing. That van reminds me of one that almost ran me off the road when I was biking home a couple of weeks ago. Though, I'm sure it's not the same one. But it made me wonder how many people still drive those big vans. Doesn't make a lot of sense if you don't provide some sort of a service. The gas must be crazy expensive."

"You almost got run off the road?" She shivered.

"It was no big deal. Are you cold?"

"Not really. Just a little freaked out by the idea of you nearly getting hit."

Warmth shot through him at her words. She worried about him?

Their campsite was in view, and their private moment would come to an end. Walking into camp holding her hand was like making an announcement of some sort. While he wouldn't mind if Ryan thought she was taken, he wasn't ready to have everyone else commenting on his love life.

A campfire was burning in the pit, and it looked like they had already started on the s'mores. Everyone glanced their way.

He dropped her hand. And immediately regretted it. He moved his hand to her low back, out of sight, but maintaining a connection. "Do you want to get a hoodie or something? I can grab your bag."

"Yeah, sure." But her voice was subdued.

He pulled her bag from the back of Gary's car.

She rummaged through it, grabbed a fleece, and shrugged into it.

But as they made their way to the fire and found their chairs, he couldn't help but wish he could wrap his arms around her and keep her warm.

The rest of Jessica's evening remained covered by the warm glow generated by her walk with Austin. Even if she did wish he was still holding her hand. But they'd listened to Ryan's devotional, sung some songs by the fire, and played the Ungame while eating s'mores. They were Kim's special s'mores—though she gave credit to Melissa—made with one's choice of candy bars instead of just chocolate. Austin's wry commentary on the others' answers, meant for her ears alone, had her suppressing a smile most of the night. Who knew he had such a dry and delightful sense of humor? She was enjoying getting to know this side of him.

She stifled a yawn. The fire had burned down to coals, and it was getting chilly. "I'm ready to head to bed. Anyone want to make a bathroom trip with me? I know where they are."

Kim and Laurie agreed. Macy said she'd be along later.

When Jessica stood, Austin rose with her and handed her something. "Here." It was his flashlight.

She laughed. "What? You didn't think I had one?"

"This one is right here. And I have an extra. You can keep that one in case you need it in the middle of the night."

His concern touched her. "Thank you."

She flicked the light on and headed to the car to pull out her bag. Once Kim and Laurie were ready, they headed to the bathrooms, which were surprisingly clean. Typical bathroom. Stalls, sinks, a couple of showers at the far end. Tile everywhere. No bugs.

Jessica had hoped for a moment alone with Kim to tell her

about the walk with Austin. But she didn't want to ditch Laurie or make her feel left out.

The three of them each had a sink to wash their faces and brush their teeth. Kim glanced in the mirror from Jessica to Laurie. "I saw Ryan come over and talk to you two while we were cleaning up. What was that all about?"

Jessica shrugged. "He asked about work and about Scott. I noticed he didn't ask about Joe and Sarah, though I doubt he knows that I know the story." She sent an apologetic look toward Laurie. It wasn't something she could explain, since it was now gossip, given that none of the involved parties were here and it reflected badly on Ryan. She regretted bringing it up and once again wished she'd thought before speaking.

But Laurie didn't seem concerned. When she went into one of the stalls, Jessica leaned over and whispered to Kim. "What do you think is up with Ryan and Macy? She seemed awfully flirty with Matthew and Austin."

Kim nodded. "Those were my thoughts about Ryan with you. I have no idea. It was not the dynamic I would have expected."

Once they were all ready, they headed back to the campsite and stowed their toiletries in the vehicles.

Austin and Matthew stood silhouetted by the nearly dead fire. They both turned when the women came back into camp. "You guys in for the night?"

Kim slid her arm around Matthew's waist and pulled him into a hug with a quick kiss. "Aw, you guys waited for us."

"We did."

Jessica took a step to the side to give them privacy, and Austin did too. "Goodnight, Jessica. If you need anything in the middle of the night, just let us know." He reached out and squeezed her hand.

"Thanks." She looked around the campsite. "Where are Ryan and Macy?" Gary and Bernie were already in their tent given the silhouettes from the light on inside.

He shrugged. "They walked off while you were gone."

Interesting. "Well, see you in the morning." She turned and headed to their tent.

Laurie had gone ahead and turned on the lantern. She was rolling out her sleeping bag.

Jessica did the same, and Kim came in a minute later. Soon they were all snug in their bags.

"Ready for me to turn out the light? Or should we leave it on for Macy?" Laurie asked.

Jessica exchanged a glance with Kim. "Hopefully, she has a flashlight with her and won't step on any of us."

Laurie switched off the lantern.

Exhaustion settled over Jessica. It had been a long day, and the altitude was tiring. Plus, her heart had bounced around with competing emotions and a whole bunch of adrenaline from the memories of the fire and Austin's presence. She thought about their walk and her hand in his. And then how he'd dropped her hand when they'd gotten back to camp. Was he being sweet by making sure she had something warm to wear? Or was he trying to cover the fact that he didn't want to hold her hand in front of everyone? She wasn't sure what to make of it.

Still, he was a private person. Perhaps that extended to public displays of affection. He probably wouldn't want people he barely knew to speculate about his relationship with her. She wasn't sure what it was beyond them getting to know each other.

The tent zipper slid open, and Macy stumbled in. "Sorry, guys. Are you already asleep?"

"Not yet," Kim responded. "We just turned out the light."

Laurie switched the lantern back on.

"Thanks." Macy found her bag and rustled for a while until she was settled. "Hopefully, I can sleep tonight. I've never slept in a sleeping bag before. The things we do to catch a guy's attention."

Jessica didn't dare look at Kim, or she'd burst out laughing.

"I think we're supposed to be getting away from it all." Kim's voice came out of the dark.

Macy laughed. "There's no point in getting away from it all if you can't do it with a cute guy. I'm just glad there's an outlet in the bathroom so I can use my flatiron tomorrow. We might be roughing it, but I definitely don't want to let my looks go."

"Why does it matter?" Kim's voice was more curious now. "At some point, don't you want someone to love and appreciate you for who you are as a person, regardless of your looks?"

"You're in fashion, right? And Jessica, you're a stylist. You two should know. You're in the image business. Women pay a lot of money to look good for men. We wouldn't do that if it didn't matter. And neither of you would have jobs if they didn't."

She was right that women did spend a lot of money on their looks. But Kim was right too. Shouldn't there be something more? While she wanted Austin to find her attractive, she wanted him to see her as a whole person and to love the inside as much as the outside, if they ever got that far. And even though she'd recently changed up her hairstyle, she was working a lot harder on her inside lately than her outside.

Makeup and beauty was fun, but it wasn't all there was. Jessica let out a sigh. "I get what you're saying, but I'd like to think that the image we present to the world is at least in part a reflection of who we are inside. Ultimately, I want someone to love me for me."

Kim laughed. "Matthew has definitely seen me at my worst. I think camping is good for that."

"You girls believe what you want. But if a guy wants to buy me dinner because of how I look in jeans, who am I to pass that up? You have to use the assets you've got to make your way in this world. Wait until you've lived a few more years like I have. You'll see." She motioned to Laurie. "You can turn that off now."

The lantern switched off.

If that's really what she believed, then Macy might be the loneliest person Jessica had ever met.

Chapter Twelve

The light coming through the tent had Austin up and awake earlier than he normally would have been for a Saturday. Of course, his bedroom at home had light-blocking curtains. After a quick trip to the bathroom to freshen up, he came back to find Matthew, Gary, and Bernie in various stages of readiness.

He lowered his voice and stepped near to Matthew so as not to wake Ryan and the women, who were apparently still sleeping. "What time were we supposed to have breakfast ready by?"

Matthew shrugged. "No one said. I guess we can go ahead and get started so it'll be ready once everyone is up."

They pulled the supplies out of the bear box and the vehicles. Matthew had just lit the camp stove when the women's tent unzipped, and Jessica and Kim stepped out.

"Morning." Kim stepped over to Matthew and kissed his cheek. "How long before coffee's ready?"

"As soon as I can get the water to boil."

Austin turned to Jessica, who was finger-combing her hair. "How did you sleep?" He'd seen her in a lot of different situations, sooty and tired their last trip here, dressed perfectly after he'd picked her up from work and for their date. But he'd never seen this fresh-faced, newly awake look on her. And the vulnerability of it took his breath away. He was definitely looking forward to spending the whole day with her.

She shrugged. "Not too bad. I think the elevation helps to knock you out, even though the ground could be softer. What about you?"

He could barely process her words. "Um, fine."

Laurie climbed out of the tent, and the women headed off to the bathroom. Gary started making pour-over coffees, and Matthew manned the stove, frying up pancakes and bacon.

Austin managed the paper goods and condiments. When Ryan had returned to the tent last night, he hadn't seemed to be in a very good mood. Perhaps he and Macy had had a falling out. He'd looked at Matthew and then Austin. "Tell you what, guys, always maintain the control in a relationship. Once women think they have the upper hand, they'll break your heart and take your money. It's better to focus on your career and finding success. God gave you gifts to use, and women can be a distraction from that."

Bernie had chuckled. "There's a better solution, Ryan. Stay broke, then you'll only attract women who aren't interested in money."

Austin wasn't sure what to think about that. He didn't know Ryan well, but that didn't seem to be the kind of advice he'd expect from a worship pastor. Maybe more about surrendering to God's will and keeping your focus on him? Yes, use your gifts, but success—at least by the world's standards—wasn't necessarily in the cards. Still, thinking about his own situation at work, he had to admit he liked having a goal to strive for, having something to accomplish, having others acknowledge his contribution.

Matthew spoke up. "That sounds awfully cynical. Maybe you just haven't met the right woman, Ryan."

"And you have vast experience?" Ryan shot back. "People in

the music world appreciate me and my gifts. I'll focus my energies on where I'm wanted."

After that, the tent had quieted down, and the guys had apparently gone to sleep.

The women returned from the bathrooms, breaking his thoughts. He might not know a lot about women, but he didn't think Ryan had it right.

Macy emerged from the tent, grabbed a cup of coffee and her bag, and headed toward the bathroom—Austin assumed—not speaking to anyone.

Eventually, everyone filtered past the picnic table grabbing food and drinks and making their way to their chairs around the cold campfire. It would have been nice to have its warmth, but they would have had to put it out again before they left.

When they were done eating, Ryan gave a short devotional from the Psalms about God's creation. Then he talked about the day's events.

"We've got a lot of options for the day and three cars, so we should be able to split up and do something everyone will like. I'm renting a boat and going out on the lake. Maybe do some fishing. Who wants to do that?"

Austin shot a look at Jessica, who shook her head. Neither Kim or Matthew seemed on board with that either. Not with their last experience on the lake. But Gary, Bernie, and Macy raised their hands.

"I'm not fishing," Macy said with a shudder. "But laying out in the sun on the water sounds good."

Laurie looked torn. She leaned over to Jessica. "I don't know how to swim. What are you guys doing?"

Jessica shrugged and looked around. "We'll probably hike around the woods a bit. Maybe go into town. We won't be on the water."

"Is it okay if I go with you, then?"

"Sure."

"Has anyone checked today's weather?" Austin asked. "I

looked before we came up, and afternoon thunderstorms were forecasted. I wonder if that has been updated."

Ryan shrugged. "Not much cell service here. I'm sure they'll let us know at the marina. As soon as we clean up from breakfast, we'll get things out so everyone can make their sack lunches. Me, Macy, and Bernie are on the cleanup and lunch crew. The sooner we get done, the sooner we can leave."

Jessica stood and collected Austin's plate and Laurie's, carrying them over to the trash bag hanging from the picnic table.

Ryan stepped over to her. "Sure you don't want to come on the boat with us?"

Bernie looked up. "Yeah, it'll be fun." He glanced over toward Austin and the rest of them still by the fire pit. "We should all go. We can get a big pontoon boat."

Austin didn't want to go back on the lake. But if Bernie was going, maybe he should consider it. Getting to know Bernie was part of the reason for this trip.

Jessica shook her head. "No, our last experience on that lake was enough to last us for a while." She tossed the trash and walked back toward the fire pit. "So, where do you guys want to go?" She slid her hands in the back pockets of her jeans, her gaze on Austin, and smiled. "You picked out something already, didn't you? Where's the map?"

Matthew glanced over. "The one he's been studying for days?" He laughed.

Austin shrugged. He had picked out several hiking routes he thought would be interesting. And it was just for the afternoon. He could talk to Bernie tonight over dinner. "I like to know the environment." All eyes were on him, but they were eager to hear what he said, not making fun of him. "Uh, there's a trail that runs along Holcomb Creek that looks pretty good. Nice views, not too difficult. Crosses the Pacific Crest Trail if we want to take part of that. But we should go by the ranger station first and check out the weather forecast."

"Good idea." Matthew stood and looked around the group. "One problem. It'll be a tight fit for all five of us in my truck. That back seat isn't made for adults."

Gary raised his head. "You can take my Escape, and we can take Ryan's RAV."

"Thanks, man."

They made up their sack lunches with sandwiches, chips, fruit, and water bottles. He noticed Macy stood to the side, not actually participating in the cleanup. There wasn't much to do, but after Macy had looked at Ryan and said, "I don't cook," he put together her sandwich and sack lunch.

They spent some time rearranging the contents of the vehicles, stuffing most of the bags in Matthew's truck. Once the site was cleaned up and put away, the groups split up. Gary tossed Matthew his keys before he climbed into the back of the RAV with Bernie. They pulled out of the campground and left.

Austin tossed the emergency bag in the back, along with their lunches and backpacks, and climbed in the back of the Escape, letting Kim have the front seat with Matthew. It wasn't going to be a long drive anyway. Jessica slid in the other door, taking the middle seat, just like he'd hoped. It put her close to him, their shoulders and thighs bumping as they made their way out of the campground and toward the ranger station.

Let the adventure begin.

JESSICA WAS ACUTELY AWARE OF THE HEAT COMING FROM Austin's body next to hers. The trip was short but intense, and soon Matthew turned into the parking lot of the ranger station. They all hopped out and headed inside to the small building with map-covered walls and a counter dividing the lobby from the work area.

Matthew told the ranger where they were thinking of

heading and asked about the conditions and the weather forecast.

"You'll need to buy an Adventure Pass. And here's a map." She produced something larger than Jessica would have expected. Looking more like a small newspaper, it had information on the history and local spots of interest as well as trails and their difficulty. The ranger opened it to where they were thinking of going. "That's a good hike. Not too difficult and pretty scenery. Are you going now?"

"Yeah, that's the plan."

"Thunderstorms are forecast for this afternoon. They pop up quickly. That creek has the potential to flash flood and this road here—" she pointed to a spot on the map— "often does, so you won't want to get stuck on the other side of it. Especially since that area is downstream of the burn scar, there could be a significant debris flow. Watch the clouds, and if you hear thunder or it starts to rain, get out of there."

"Thanks." Matthew paid for the Adventure Pass, which the ranger dated and handed over.

"Oh, and there's no cell service there at all. So make sure someone knows where you're going and when you're expected back."

Matthew nodded, and they all said thanks as they left. Once they were back in the car, he handed the map to Kim.

"Just like old times, huh?" She turned and smiled at him. They'd shared his truck on the Great American Road Trip last March, and while Melissa had mapped out most of the journey, Kim and Matthew had found their own points of interest to explore.

Austin held up his phone. "We have a signal here. Someone should text Ryan where we're going and when we expect to get back."

"I'll do it," Kim said. "How long do you think we'll be gone?"

"I imagine we'd be back by three," Austin said. "I checked

the weather, and that's when the thunderstorms are forecasted to start. If it rains, they'll need to come in from the lake too."

Matthew backed out and headed down the road the way they'd come. "What are we going to do for dinner if it rains?"

"Go into town," Kim said. "I'm serious. It's too difficult to cook outside in the rain. We could go to that Italian place we went before, Belle Sorgenti. That was good. I bet they have good pizza."

That was the first time Jessica had met Austin. They'd sat together at dinner, but she'd gotten the impression that he didn't quite know what to make of her, that the whole group overwhelmed him. It was amazing, really, that he'd stuck around and befriended them. She was grateful he had.

Matthew turned off the pavement onto the forest service access road. They bumped their way down the gravelly dirt, knocking Jessica into both Austin and Laurie. She put her hand on the seat to brace herself a bit.

A moment later, Austin's warm hand covered hers, and he leaned his shoulder into hers so she no longer bounced against him.

She glanced over at him, and he smiled at her. The bumpy ride didn't seem so bad.

Kim turned around. "Hey, guys, there's a short hike to the top of Little Bear Peak, just under two miles. Should have some great views of the lake. Want to try it?"

Agreement went around the SUV.

Kim pointed to a sign along the road near a turnout. "Pull up over there."

They hopped out and grabbed their backpacks from the back of the SUV. The trail was marked by an opening cut in a fallen log. The dirt trail was wide enough for two across. Matthew and Kim led out with Laurie behind them. Austin and Jessica trailed, something they both seemed to agree on. She liked that they were thinking along the same lines. The trail meandered up and down through the pines and chaparral. The fire had come through parts of this, leaving huge swaths of charcoaled ground in the distance and even running black up to the trail in some spots.

Before too long they reached the summit. Holcomb Lake spread out before them, dotted with boats and other watercraft.

"They're down there somewhere." Jessica pointed.

"If we had binoculars, we could probably spot them." Austin pulled a map out of his backpack.

"Did you bring any?" Jessica grinned.

"Nope, but I'll add it to my list for next time." He looked at the map and pointed to the mountains in the distance. "Those are the San Gabriels. That's San Gorgonio."

Some bird of prey made a lazy circle above them. Thunderheads piled up over the south ridge of the mountains, near San Gorgonio.

"It's incredibly peaceful here." Jessica leaned close to Austin. The others had wandered off to different viewing spots.

"It is." He met her gaze. He brushed her hair back over her shoulder, letting a lock run through his fingers. "I like what you did with this."

"Thanks." Was her voice really that breathy?

His fingers lightly skimmed over her shoulder, and he took a step closer, his gaze on hers.

Was he going to kiss her?

A scuff of a shoe on dirt behind them. Jessica turned. Laurie was holding up a rock. "This one sparkles. Think we'll find any gold up here?"

Austin took a step back. "This is gold country. There are mines scattered all through these hills. See these X's on the map?" He pointed. "But that's probably quartz. It sparkles, and it's often found near gold."

Laurie tucked it in her pocket. "I'm going to keep it as a souvenir."

Matthew and Kim joined them, and they headed back down the trail faster than they came up.

Back in the SUV, they continued down the dirt road. It was impossible to judge how far they had gone because of the twists and turns and low speed. But Austin had covered her hand with his once again, so she didn't care.

They found the creek, pulled over, and got out. A dirt path ran alongside it. This late in the summer, it was down to a trickle, but the debris of trees and rocks scattered across a much wider area testified to how raging it could become.

They wandered down the path, marveling at nature. Jessica hung back a bit, hoping she and Austin might have another chance at that kiss. But he walked along the rocks in the creek bed, bending over, looking for something.

The wind came up, cool, and the sky darkened. Jessica scanned the sky. It wasn't just the shade of the trees blocking the sun. The clouds were dark and heavy.

Austin bounded over to her. "Here." He held out something.

She reached out, and he dropped a beautiful pink quartz stone, long and slender, into her hand. It was damp from where he'd washed it in the creek. "It's beautiful. Thank you."

"It kind of reminds me of the pink you used to have in your hair."

She laughed. "Should I put the pink back in it?"

"Only if you want to. I think it's pretty either way." He stepped closer. "Actually—"

A fat drop of water landed on her head. She looked up and got another in the eye.

A second later, the sky opened up and poured.

"We'd better go." Austin grabbed her hand just as lightning flashed above them followed too quickly by the crash of thunder. "I should have been paying better attention. I thought we had more time." He pulled her back toward the car as Kim, Matthew, and Laurie came running in their direction.

They ran toward the SUV but had come a lot farther in their wanderings than she had remembered. The decomposed granite on the path was slick under their feet, making the path more treacherous as the rain continued to fall. Without Austin's hand holding her up, she would have slipped more than once. A stitch developed in her side. She couldn't even remember the last time she'd run. PE class, maybe? She wanted to catch her breath, but the closer flash of lightning, followed far too quickly by thunder, made her eager for shelter, and not from a tree, which could easily be struck. The saving grace was that the creek bed was lower than the surrounding terrain, since lightning tended to strike the tallest objects.

When they reached the SUV, they were completely soaked through, and the creek was already more than a trickle. It had turned a muddy brown with branches and twigs bobbing in its current.

Matthew popped the locks, and they all climbed in, catching their breath as the rain pounded on the car roof, drowning out other sounds.

Jessica looked around the inside of the car, wiping wet hair out of her eyes with equally wet hands. They didn't even have anything to dry off with. "Ugh, we're going to owe Gary a car wash and detailing. We've got water and mud everywhere."

"I don't think he'll be too upset." Matthew glanced around. "We'd better get out of here. Kim, guide me back."

"Will do."

Matthew maneuvered the SUV through the now-muddy road back the way they came. As the rain fell harder and the thunder cracked over them, those were the only sounds, other than Kim's directions to Matthew at forks in the road. The windows fogged up with their wet clothes and warm bodies. Kim flipped on the AC and defroster as Matthew hunched over the steering wheel peering out the window in the small clear spot.

"Watch out!" Kim yelled as a fallen tree lay partly across the road.

Matthew swerved at the last moment.

They came around a curve, one Jessica remembered as close

to the main road, when a larger rumbling noise seemed to be growing. Too long for it to be thunder. "What's that—?"

"Mudslide!" Austin shouted. "Get us out of here."

The SUV lurched forward as Matthew tried to go faster in the treacherous conditions.

Jessica bent down to see half the hillside above them—trees, rocks, and mud—flowing down like icing off a hot cake. She closed her eyes and squeezed Austin's hand. They weren't going to make it.

Chapter Thirteen

Austin wished more than anything he was the one driving. Not that he could do a better job, but he'd feel more in control. He hated feeling out of control, and ever since he'd almost kissed Jessica at the top of Little Bear Peak, he'd felt as if he was standing on the edge of a cliff, waiting for a stiff breeze to push him over.

She was a distraction. If he hadn't been so intent on finding her the perfect stone she could keep as a memory of today, he would have been paying better attention to the sky, looking up instead of down. If they didn't get out of this mess, it would be his fault. And this wouldn't be a day she'd want to remember.

The Escape's automatic traction control must have kicked in because they pulled away from the slide with only the back end getting tagged by the debris flow, pushing it slightly sideways before they evaded the mudflow.

Kim called out the final turn in a quiet voice, and soon they were back on the paved road.

Matthew pulled to the side and let out a long breath before turning around. "Everyone okay?"

Laurie opened her eyes. She had been whispering what Austin assumed were prayers.

Jessica still held his hand.

He should have never let things get this far. That's what happened when he let his heart rule instead of his head. And she was going to get hurt when he pulled back. Why couldn't he have just been content to be friends with her? Romance was an area so far out of his comfort zone. He wasn't Matthew, and he shouldn't have tried to be.

No one said anything as they made their way back to the campground. Once at their site, it was still pouring rain. No one wanted to get out in it.

"Anyone have an umbrella?" Matthew grinned, catching Austin's eye in the rearview mirror.

He removed his hand from Jessica's under the pretense of leaning forward. "I'm not sure I own an umbrella," he replied. "But we could grab our bags out of your truck and drive over to the bathrooms and at least get changed into dry clothes. No point in going in the tents. We'll just get them muddy. We could throw some towels down on the seats in here and wait it out, eat our lunches." Now that they were out of danger, he realized it was well past lunch, and he was hungry.

"Good plan." Matthew pulled the Escape close to his truck. "You ladies stay here. We'll grab the bags."

With what could have been practiced movements, Austin and Matthew grabbed bags from one vehicle and transferred them to the next. He didn't think he could get any wetter. Luckily, it wasn't cold out, but the wind didn't help. And wet jeans were just miserable. Dry clothes would feel great.

Matthew drove them up next to the bathrooms. They weren't the only one with that idea. The van from earlier was pulled up close. And the women's bathroom door was propped open with a rock. A big guy with a scruffy beard sat behind the wheel of the van. Austin got a weird vibe from the whole thing, though maybe it was the residual feelings of irritation and resentment from the van that ran him off the road. The guy was probably just waiting for his wife or girlfriend. Plus, it wasn't like he could go inspect the women's bathroom to see if it was safe. And Jessica would think he was nuts for suggesting it.

She was a capable woman, and he and Matthew wouldn't be far. It was probably nothing. He grabbed his bag and headed into the men's room without giving Jessica another glance.

Jessica noticed immediately when Austin had disappeared inside himself. It was like he went into a fortress and pulled up the drawbridge, shutting her out. She didn't know why or what she had done. How could they go from almost kissing to this? Maybe she'd just misread everything. She'd only known bad boys who wanted one thing for so long that she didn't know how to read the signals a good guy was—or wasn't—giving. Once again, she'd made the wrong choice and humiliated herself.

She glanced at Laurie and Kim. "Ready to make a run for it?"

The three of them dashed inside the restroom, a bit easier feat since someone had propped the door open with a rock.

Once inside, she plopped her bag on the sink and got a good look at herself in the mirror. She looked like a drowned rat, her hair dripping around her face, dirt smudges on her cheeks. She grabbed her towel and comb from her bag and got to work on her hair. Until it stopped dripping, it would get her dry clothes wet too.

In the mirror, Jessica saw a girl emerge from the stall. And she stopped. It could have been her in high school. She even had pink streaks in her blonde hair. The resemblance clicked something into place. Could it be the girl they had gotten the Amber Alert about several weeks ago? Jessica had remarked on the similarity then, especially since it had come just before the missing girl whose body had later been found. Her rabbit hole of research had led her to know more about those girls and their lives than any other news story before or since.

She put down her comb and watched the girl. "Do you need the sink?"

The girl bit her lip. "Uh, sure."

Jessica grabbed her bag and moved out of the way, studying the girl. "Are you here camping?" Her mind scrambled to remember what she'd heard about trafficking and how to help.

The girl nodded, washing her hands. But her provocative clothing didn't look like it would be comfortable or practical for camping.

"With your family or friends?"

"Friends." She choked on the words, and her eyes darted away.

Jessica noted some abrasions on the girl's wrists. And something that made her blood run cold. A WE was tattooed on her wrist. Just like Brianna. "Are you okay?"

"I'm fine." The answer came back too quickly.

Jessica pointed to her wrists. "Those look like they hurt. If you're not safe, we can help you."

Kim moved next to her. "Please. Let us help you. We can get you some place safe."

The girl's eyes darted toward the open door. "I have to go. He's waiting."

"The guy in the van?" Jessica asked.

The girl didn't answer, just headed toward the door. But Jessica jumped in front of her. "You don't have to go." She met the girl's gaze. One girl looking for help had gotten away from her and ended up dead. She wasn't going to let that happen to another one. "Are you Mia?"

The girl's face crumpled, and tears welled in her eyes. "How do you know my name?"

"There's an Amber Alert out for you. Your parents reported you missing."

Sobs wracked Mia's body as she fought for control, wiping

her eyes. "I have to go. He'll hurt one of the other girls if I don't come back."

Kim stood next to Jessica, blocking the door. "You can't go back. We'll help you. And the other girls."

Mia shook her head.

Jessica gently took the girl by the shoulders. "It's going to be okay. You can trust us. Kim's brother here is a detective on a local police force."

Mia's eyes went wide. "I don't know about any cops. I—"

"Don't worry. You won't be in trouble, no matter what you did or didn't do. It's not your fault." Jessica met Kim's eyes. "What's our plan? How do we get her out of here without him noticing?" She glanced around the bathroom. The windows were glass block. No help there.

Laurie stood frozen in front of the sink, eyes wide. No doubt this was more than she'd bargained for on this trip.

"The guys can help. I'll go out and hug Matthew and whisper in his ear. It'll just look like we're being affectionate." Kim studied Mia then Jessica. "You guys look like you could be sisters. Jessica, give her some of your clothes to change into. Then if the three of us stand on the outside of her and get in the Escape, he won't notice. He'll be looking for Mia in her old clothes by herself."

Jessica was pulling clothes out of her bag before Kim stopped talking. "Good plan." She pushed them in Mia's arms. "Hurry."

Mia froze. "If I don't come back…"

"We'll get help for the other girls too. I promise." She turned Mia and gently led her to the stall. "Kim, when you are outside, get the license plate or have the guys do it. We'll head straight to the ranger station. It's closest."

Laurie slung her bag over her shoulder. "Maybe I'll just head back to our campsite. The others should be back soon."

"No!" Jessica practically shouted. "Sorry. But you can't go back there by yourself. It's not safe. We'll get ahold of Ryan from the ranger station. Just stick with us, okay?"

Laurie nodded, but she didn't look convinced.

Mia came out of the stall in Jessica's clothes, and the resemblance was eerie. Jessica shoved a hat on Mia's head.

"Kim, you ready?"

She nodded and disappeared out the door.

Jessica wished she had Austin's planning ability. But this ploy would have to do. It had to work.

It just had to.

AUSTIN STOOD WITH MATTHEW UNDER THE SHELTERED porch area outside the bathrooms. He could hear the women's voices. What was taking them so long?

Kim came out. Still wearing her soaked clothes. Why hadn't she changed? She plastered herself to Matthew in a hug, whispering something in his ear.

His eyes darted around, and he nodded then gave her a quick kiss on the cheek.

She headed back inside the bathroom.

"What was that about? Why aren't they ready yet?"

Matthew dug the keys out of his pocket. "Hop in the Escape. I'll explain."

They dashed through the rain and into the car. "There's a girl in the bathroom with them that they think is being trafficked. The guy in the van is the trafficker, watching her. They're going to hustle her out of there dressed in Jessica's clothes into the car, and we'll take off and head to the ranger station."

Austin saw so many potential problems with this plan. But there was no time to come up with a better one. Still, he had an idea. "Be right back." He hopped out and jogged over to the van, his dry clothes getting spotted with rain again, but at least he had a shell jacket on now.

The driver glanced back and seemed to be talking to someone.

Austin motioned for the guy to roll down his window. With any luck, the guy would be distracted by him and not the women getting into the SUV.

The guy scowled at him. "Yeah?"

"I was just curious, what kind of gas mileage do you get on this thing? You don't see too many of them around. Is it worth it?"

The guy shrugged. "It sucks, but it does the job."

"Must be helpful on a day like today with all the rain. Lots of room to stay dry."

The guy just stared at him.

"Okay, thanks. Just curious." Austin jogged back to the car and squeezed himself in, barely getting the door closed before Matthew took off.

The back seat now held Jessica, a girl he didn't know, and Laurie. Not legal, but desperate times… He shifted his hips and laid his arm across the back of the seat, allowing Jessica a smidge more room.

"This is Mia," Jessica said. "Matthew's the one driving, and this is Austin."

Mia nodded.

Austin glanced out the rearview mirror. The guy had climbed out of the van and headed toward the bathroom. "Step on it. He's going to find out in two seconds that Mia's not in the bathroom."

Mia whimpered.

"It'll be okay." Jessica squeezed Mia's hand. "Matthew, did you get the license plate?"

"Yep."

"It won't matter," Mia said. "He steals them off other cars all the time."

Austin swayed into Jessica as Matthew sped around a corner. She was still in her wet clothes too. She couldn't be comfortable, but he'd seen the tenacity in her eyes. She was going to protect Mia, and nothing would get in her way. It was one of the things he most admired about her. She couldn't have seen this coming, but she jumped into action anyway to do the right thing.

Matthew turned into the ranger station parking lot. It was eerily empty. Austin checked his phone. It wasn't that late. Shouldn't it still be open? "There's a sign on the door. I'll go see." He hopped out and ran up the steps. CLOSED DUE TO AN EMERGENCY. This was an emergency, but he supposed given the mudslide they encountered earlier, there might be other problems in the area.

Back in the car, he told them about the sign. "We can't sit here. The guy will be after us soon."

Matthew pulled out of the parking lot and headed toward town. "Pull up where the sheriff's station is. I think it's housed in a common building."

"His name is Gordo," Mia said in a flat voice. "The guy driving the van."

Kim gave Matthew directions while Austin dialed 911. "What's your emergency?"

"We have a girl here who was the subject of an Amber Alert." He moved the phone from his mouth. "Mia, what's your last name?"

"Latham."

He relayed the information to the operator, but the phone crackled, and he didn't hear what she said. "Could you repeat that?"

She asked for their location, and he told her.

"Are you in a safe place?"

"Not really. We're driving away from the man who had her and suspect he's following us." He gave her a description of the van and the license plate, adding that it was likely stolen.

"Can you get to the nearest sheriff's station?"

"We're heading there now."

"No, we're not." Matthew braked.

Austin leaned over Jessica to see out the front. A massive debris-slide blocked the road.

Mia stared stoically out the front window. Jessica put her arm around her, the wetness from her clothes soaking Mia's, but she figured the girl could use a comforting touch more than worrying about wet clothes. "It's going to be okay. We'll figure something out."

"Kim, find us another way." Matthew turned the SUV around.

Austin reached over the back seat while still on the phone with the 911 operator. "The main road is blocked by a debris-slide. We're going to try and find another way, but the cell service isn't good." He grabbed a map out of his backpack. He opened it across his lap and Jessica's. "Sorry, there's not much room," he whispered.

"That's fine. What are we looking for?"

His finger skimmed over the paper. "This is where we are." Then, "This is where we want to be. There are a few back roads that can get us there. And I'm guessing not everything is on this map. Show this to Kim."

Jessica took the map and leaned between the front seats, pointing it out to Kim while Austin relayed their plan to the 911 operator.

Kim nodded. "Got it."

As they came around the corner, the white van appeared in the distance coming toward them.

"Change of plans." Matthew whipped into the next road. "Kim, find me another route."

"This road's not on the map. It might be a smaller one that goes back to someone's cabin."

Austin studied the map then looked behind them. "He followed us."

"Great." Matthew swore under his breath.

Austin continued to update the 911 operator.

Mia shivered under Jessica's arm. "You nice people are going to have a bunch of trouble because of me."

Jessica gave a small laugh. "We find plenty of trouble on our own. And we've survived every time. This will be no different." But she kicked her prayers for wisdom and safety into high gear.

Austin studied the map over the jostling road. "I think this one should loop around and join up with a bigger road. If we can gain some distance and whip onto the next road and get out of sight, we might be able to get him to drive past us. Then there are a couple of different options we can take. I think the main goal right now is to lose him. There are plenty of back roads up here. He won't know where to find us."

Matthew sped up, dangerously, it felt like, but the van disappeared behind them. The SUV slid around a muddy turn and onto an even smaller, more rutted road. At the first bit of widening, Matthew pulled behind some trees.

Austin turned around and stared out the back window. It felt like everyone was holding their breaths. Finally, "He just went past. Didn't even slow down." He turned back around. "Okay, we've got a minute. Let's plan this out." He studied the map intently. "If we loop back here, we can eventually get to our original road and get to town."

Jessica took the map and showed it to Kim.

As they got on their way, Mia spoke quietly. "There was one girl who tried to get away. Unlike the rest of us, she never gave up, never stopped fighting. Even when they beat her. Her name was Brianna. They kept us in this building…I think it was still in Laguna Vista. We didn't go far. She was able to shimmy up a pipe to a window and escape. Gordo went after her when he found out, but I never saw her again. He showed us a picture of her, said that—" Her voice broke. "But I didn't want to believe him." She turned watery blue eyes to Jessica. "Did she make it? Do you know?"

Jessica knew the minute her face gave her away, because Mia's crumpled. "What happened?"

Jessica swallowed. Would Mia hate her for not doing more to help Brianna? Would she understand? "Brianna managed to find her way into the salon where I work. I didn't know it was her or that she needed help. She asked to use the phone. I went to get my cell phone, and when I came back, she was gone. I went outside, and I think I saw a man hustling her into a van." She took a shuddering breath. "Her body was found in the regional park a few days later by someone walking their dog. I'm so sorry."

Mia's sobs filled the car. The rain pounding on the roof made Jessica think creation was crying too.

When Mia wiped her eyes, she shook her head. "Just take me back. Maybe if I go back on my own, he won't hurt me—too much. I'm not brave like Brianna was. But if he catches me—" Her voice broke.

"We're not taking you back. We'll get you and the other girls safe, and Gordo will go to prison." Jessica's voice was much more confident than she felt.

"I'd never heard of him killing anyone. Not good for business, you know, to kill the source of income." Mia's voice dripped resentment. "Maybe it was because of what Brianna found out."

"What was that?"

"One time when we were all locked in the van being moved from one place to another, we stopped for a few hours. She managed to get to the glovebox and found that the van was registered to EM Import Export."

Jessica tucked that bit of information away to tell Kyle and whoever else they talked to. Maybe they had a real chance to bring this ring down.

"Where are we, anyway?" Mia asked.

"The San Bernardino Mountains. Holcomb Springs," Jessica said. "You didn't know?"

She shook her head. "No, we never knew where we were. I tried to guess by how long we drove anywhere, but mostly they seemed to be short trips within town. But this had been a much longer trip. I think when Brianna got out, she must have done something that scared them, because it wasn't too long after that they started moving us all over the place, a lot of back roads where there weren't a lot of people."

"Where are you from? Where's home?"

"Laguna Vista."

"Same with us. Our friend Kyle, the detective, said they were investigating the trafficking ring there. Maybe they got close." Jessica squeezed Mia's shoulder. "There's hope. Hold on to that."

Mia shook her head. "Cops can't be trusted. Whoever owns us has money, and he pays people off."

"Not Kyle. He's one of the good guys."

Mia just shrugged but clearly didn't agree.

They bumped along in silence, even the rain appeared to have let up to just sprinkles. They came over a rise and began to descend when Matthew stopped. A muddy lake was where the road had been.

Chapter Fourteen

Eric's burner phone rang. He and his wife were at home having cocktails by their pool. Their expensive pool that she insisted on designing to resemble a tropical island hideaway. He excused himself to go inside. "What?"

"We have a problem. Some do-gooders helped Mia escape."

His blood pressure shot through the roof. "Get her back. At any cost." This was far worse than Brianna escaping. Other people were involved now too.

"Working on it. I've got the license plate of the SUV that took her. There've been mudslides, so we're all trapped up here. I had to hike a bit to find a spot with cell service."

"Give me the license plate number."

"It's a Ford Escape." He read off the number.

Eric found a piece of paper in the kitchen drawer and jotted the number down. "What about the other girls?"

"Duct taped and secured." He gave an evil chuckle. "Believe me, I told them exactly what would happen to Mia when I got her back. They won't get any ideas."

"I'll send someone to help." Eric ran a hand through his hair.

"Can't. Roads are washed out. And we have another problem. They've seen the van. They probably know about the girls.

We're going to have to ditch it soon. I'm guessing they called the cops. The mudslides are keeping everyone busy, which buys us a little time."

"What are you going to do?"

He chuckled. "I have a plan. They're going to have to return to the campground at some point. There's nowhere else for them to go. And when they do, I'll be waiting."

Eric let out a breath. "Take care of it. Otherwise, you're no longer useful to me. And you know what happens when people have outlived their usefulness." He hung up the phone and paced the kitchen. He hated not being able to do anything. Why was it so hard to get good help? And why was even nature working against them?

Well, he could do one thing. He punched a number into his phone. "Hey, I have a license plate number I need you to run." After he'd given the information, he tore the paper into tiny shreds and threw it in the kitchen trashcan.

Matthew and Austin got out of the SUV to examine the water. "How deep do you think it is?"

Austin shrugged and scanned the area. Finding a large rock, he heaved it into the water. It disappeared completely. "Too deep for the Escape. Time for Plan B."

"I think we're on at least Plan D by now." Matthew smacked his shoulder. "At least Gordo isn't on our tail. Maybe we should go back to the campsite and get my truck. He didn't know which site was ours, and he wouldn't know my truck. I doubt he would go back there. He has no idea who we've told what. If he couldn't stop us, then he probably hightailed it out of here."

"Which is bad news for the girls with him."

"I'm sure the sheriff's put a BOLO on him. But he's going to have a hard time leaving the area with all the mudslides."

Yeah, law enforcement would be on the lookout for a white

van. At least until he ditched it and found something else. The enormity of the situation fell heavy on him. He didn't know how Kyle and others dealt with this kind of thing daily. Evil seemed to be winning everywhere he looked.

Except when he looked at Jessica. She had to be uncomfortable in her wet clothes, but she continued to encourage and strengthen Mia. She wasn't going to back down in the face of evil.

Austin considered Matthew's suggestion. "If we go back to the site, the women can change into dry clothes, and we can eat. If we can't get to town, Ryan and the others can't get back to camp. And without cell service, we have no way to contact them. Except at the ranger station."

"We can go by there first."

"We need a contingency plan. We are sitting ducks at the campsite. I don't think we should spend the night there. Gordo is going to be a desperate man, and desperate men are unpredictable. He probably won't go back there, but what if he does? We need to get Mia to the authorities. I was studying the map, and there are two forest service roads that go over the mountain down to the desert on the back side. One might even connect to the main highway. I'd have to look again. I don't know if the Escape can handle it, but your truck has four-wheel drive, so worse comes to worst, you can go on and get Mia to safety."

Matthew crossed his arms and considered Austin's words. Austin himself wasn't even sold one hundred percent on this plan. They weren't law enforcement. They had no business rescuing anyone.

Except they were all Mia had. And there was no way he'd be able to live with himself if he didn't do all he could to help someone God had put in their path. *God, I hope you have a plan for all of this. Show us what to do.*

Matthew nodded and slapped him on the back as he walked back to the Escape. "Let's do it."

Austin opened the door to the back seat, and Jessica slid

back over tight against Mia. At least once they had Matthew's truck, they'd be able to spread out a bit. And Mia and Jessica would ride with Matthew and Kim. Leaving him with Laurie. She was quiet, so she wouldn't mind if he was too. And it would get him away from the sweet torture of being so close to Jessica.

They consulted the map and charted another path. The rain had stopped, and the sun was peeking out from behind the clouds, sending brilliant rays through the trees, lighting up the raindrops like diamonds. It would be a beautiful day in God's creation if it weren't for the mission they were on.

Perhaps the mission made it more beautiful. After all, what was God's crowning glory of creation? Woman. Saving one of his beloved creatures had to be one of the highest callings. *I feel so inadequate to the task, Lord. We don't have the resources.*

Austin explained the plan while Matthew drove and Kim navigated. Mia paled when he mentioned returning to the campsite but reluctantly agreed. He hoped she didn't try to run off in some misguided attempt to protect them. He'd have to speak to Jessica about that.

They came around a bend and down an incline when Matthew slowed. "Whoa. That's not good."

Austin leaned over Jessica to see out the front windshield, her scent—even over her wet clothes—enveloping him. In front of them, not only was the road washed out, apparently a truck had tried to cross it and had flipped over on its side, water rushing all around it. A log had lodged against the back tires, causing the water to shoot up around it.

"We'd better go see if anyone is trapped inside." He hopped out just as Matthew did. But he heard Mia say, "We can't stop. What if Gordo catches us?"

Jessica said something to her in return, but he didn't hear the rest of it. He reached the truck at the same time as Matthew. They stayed on the edge of the raging water. "Hello? Anyone in there?"

Over the water, a cry for help. Sounded like two different voices, a man's and a woman's.

"We're on our way. We'll help you." Matthew turned to Austin. "We can't just wade into the water. It's too fast. One of us could easily get swept away, especially if any of that debris knocks into us. We need to see if we can make a rope of some kind."

"Got one in the emergency kit." Austin ran back and popped open the back of the Escape. He grabbed rope, gloves, and a multitool and came back.

A woman's head poked out of the passenger side window, the highest point. "I can get out with help, but Tony's stuck. He's wedged in there."

Austin slipped the gloves on. "I'm going to toss you the rope. Tie it around your waist, and we'll pull you out." When she nodded, Austin tossed the rope to her. Most of it landed in the open window, and she was able to grab it and get it around herself.

"We have to hurry. The water is getting up to his chin."

Austin held the rope taut, and Matthew grabbed onto it as well as he waded into the water a bit.

The woman climbed out. Austin could feel the tug of the current trying to pull her away from them. A giant branch floated toward her. They hauled her out of its path just in time. As she reached the shore, Jessica and Kim came alongside her, helping her untie the rope and then escorting her back to the Escape.

"The first aid kit's in the back," Austin called, and Jessica nodded. He coiled the rope back up and stepped closer to Matthew. "What's the plan for getting the guy?"

Matthew wound the rope around his waist. "If I go under, haul me back up. I'll see if I can get the guy loose. Otherwise, we might need a knife or a pry bar."

Austin handed him the multitool. "The Escape probably has a tire iron that would work."

Matthew nodded, slipped the tool in his pocket, and waded out. Austin braced himself then felt a tug behind him. Jessica had taken up the rope too.

Matthew waded to the truck and hauled himself into the window then lowered himself down.

Austin couldn't see or hear anything. "Is Mia okay?" he said over his shoulder, keeping his eyes on the truck as the rope moved through his hands at Matthew's movements.

"Yeah. I told her and Laurie to stay in the car. Kim's with the woman. She just had a cut on her head."

Matthew's head reappeared and the man's a moment later. Matthew tied the rope around the guy's waist and helped lower him into the river. The man lost his footing a couple of times, and Austin was glad for the extra strength Jessica provided on the rope.

When the man reached shore, he untied the rope, and Austin flung it back to Matthew.

"Are you okay?" Jessica asked.

"Just messed up my shoulder. We high-centered on something as we tried to cross. Probably a rock I couldn't see. Then a big tree slammed into us, lifting us up and over. My shoulder took all my weight, and I slid under the steering wheel. Couldn't get any leverage to get myself up. Grateful you guys came along when you did. I'm Tony."

Austin glanced back at the man then felt the rope go tight. His gaze shot back to the river. Matthew had gone down. More debris rushed down the river. Austin dug in his heels and pulled, hand over hand, rope cutting into the gloves as Matthew fought to regain his footing. A branch cut between the shore and Matthew, yanking the rope loose. Austin retrieved it, but his foot slipped just as Matthew regained his feet, throwing him off balance. His side step landed him on a rock, his foot rolled off, and his leg went out from under him, twisting his knee at an unnatural angle.

"Austin!" Jessica's voice reached his ears, but she didn't drop the rope until Matthew was on shore, soaking head to foot.

He collapsed on the muddy soil, closing his eyes against the pain in his knee. He just twisted it. Once he took a few deep breaths and straightened it, it would be fine. He leaned his weight on his hands and scooted back, straightening his leg. The pain did not get better. It got worse. And then it settled into a squeezing throbbing.

Jessica was down in the dirt next to him. "What's wrong?"

"My knee." His voice sounded strained. "There's an ace wrap in the first aid kit. I'm sure that's all it needs." He wasn't, but the options weren't good right now.

Jessica didn't leave. She began gently tugging his jeans up over his knee. It had to be done, but it didn't feel great. Matthew handed her the ace wrap then lifted Austin's foot slowly so she could get the wrap around his knee.

"You're pretty good at that," he joked, trying to lighten the mood.

"Scott showed me. Lots of football injuries." She smiled at him. "Yours is more heroic." She pulled the jeans back down over it. With the bulk, he wasn't going to be able to fold his legs in the back seat. She leaned forward and kissed his forehead. "Matthew, can you help him stand? There's a boulder over there he can sit on."

They each got under one of his arms and lifted him to his feet. He hated feeling helpless, having Jessica see him this way. But there wasn't another option. He could put weight on his leg, but it was painful. Once he was on the boulder, he waved Matthew off. "Go see to our guests. Figure out something."

Tony came over. "I feel terrible you got hurt rescuing us. I can't even help, since I think I dislocated my shoulder."

"I'll be fine. Just a sprain. It's no big deal."

Tony shook his hand. "I'm still grateful." He looked at the Escape. "Looks like you've got a full load already." He turned to Matthew. "If you can get me and Maria to a spot where I can get cell service, I can call someone to get us. We've got friends nearby."

"We haven't been able to get service anywhere but close to the ranger station off the main highway. We can take you there. Some of us can hang out here since it's not raining." Matthew looked at Jessica. "You mind staying here with Austin?"

"Not at all. But take Mia and Laurie with you. If you're heading to the ranger station, maybe you can get help for Mia. And Laurie will feel safer." She counted heads. "I guess that means Kim needs to stay with us too. Can you figure out how to get back to the ranger station without her help?" Jessica grinned.

Matthew nodded. "I think I can manage if she leaves me the map. Anything you need before we go? I'll be back as soon as I can."

Austin knew that could be awhile given the condition of the roads. "Leave us our lunches and the emergency kit and our backpacks."

"Will do." Matthew returned shortly with the items.

Jessica arranged them behind him on the rock.

Austin watched as Matthew hugged Kim and kissed her before leaving. He thought of how close he'd come to kissing Jessica, how much he still wanted to. Getting caught in the thunderstorm earlier—was that still today?—paled in comparison to everything that had happened since. None of which was anyone's fault. So perhaps that didn't mean Jessica had pulled his focus away from what was important. Perhaps she was what was important. And it looked like they'd have some time here to find out.

Chapter Fifteen

Jessica spread out their lunches on the rock behind them. It was kinda perfect, slanted on the face to make it easy to lean against or sit on, then flat toward the top to hold their food and backpacks. Maybe getting some food in Austin would help his pain. She handed him his sandwich.

"I'll look for some pain medicine in the emergency kit. There's got to be some ibuprofen or something." She dug around in the pack and its little compartments, finding a packet of Advil. She tore it open and handed it to him with a bottle of water.

"Thanks." He took them from her and swallowed the pills.

Kim climbed up on the rock and started in on her lunch. "I'm glad the sun came out. I'm over these wet clothes. Maybe we can dry out a bit."

"I hope so too." Jessica dug into her lunch. She was starving, and she hadn't realized it, being so consumed with taking care of Mia and now Austin. Only the sounds of nature surrounded them, the rush of the wind through the trees and the cascading creek.

Austin broke the silence. "What did you tell Mia in the car?"

Jessica frowned. "What do you mean?"

"When Matthew and I jumped out to rescue those folks out of the truck, Mia protested. She was afraid Gordo would catch up with us."

"Oh. I told her everyone was worthy of rescue. And that whether she knew it or not, Jesus had come to rescue her."

Austin nodded. "You've been good for her."

Jessica shook her head. "I don't know. I just wish we could get her safe. And then find those other girls. After what happened to Brianna, I can't let this go."

Kim slid off the rock and dusted her hands. "I'm going to see if I can get any kind of signal anywhere. Or even a better patch of sun. The tree limbs keep showering me with raindrops. I won't go far." She gave Jessica a wink as she wandered off.

Jessica knew what Kim was doing, and she wished she could have told her there was no point in leaving them alone. Austin wasn't interested. She glanced at him. "How's the pain now?"

"Bearable."

"It's too bad we can't elevate it to keep the swelling down."

"I'll be fine."

O-kay. She drummed her fingers on the granite, noticing the multicolored specks that comprised it. "I wonder how long it'll take them to get to the ranger station and if they'll be able to get help. I should have given Mia my phone number. If they are able to get her safe, I want to be able to stay in touch with her."

Austin's hand covered her drumming fingers, stilling them, surprising her. "It's going to be okay. Someone will make sure we stay in touch. With everything going on today, I imagine first responders will have their hands full. Just look at what we came across. I'm sure that was just a small part. A big thunderstorm over a burn scar will create a lot of problems. Mia will likely come back with Matthew and Laurie."

"Does it sound bad to say I hope so? I want her to get help, but I don't want her to feel like we've just dumped her off to be someone else's problem."

His thumb moved over her hand. "I don't think she'll think that at all."

Jessica wasn't sure what to make of his actions. He'd been so closed off before, trying not to touch her at all in the SUV, an impossible feat. And now… Was he just trying to comfort her? While she had some time alone with him, maybe she just needed to be direct. One thing she'd learned about him: Austin didn't understand subtle.

She drew her knees up and wrapped one hand around them, leaving the other under Austin's touch. "This might be one of my weirder Saturdays. And I've had some weird ones."

"The fire chasing us across the lake was pretty unusual." He leaned his shoulder into her.

She laughed. "Yeah, true." She paused a moment. "I told you I was a recovering alcoholic. I spent quite a few Saturdays drunk, recovering from being drunk, or planning on getting drunk. Such a waste." She stared out into the trees. "Mia reminds me of how badly things could have gone for me. And it raises questions. If God was watching out for me in my stupidity, then why did he allow Mia to get into her situation? It's one of those things about him that is hard for me to understand."

Austin nodded. "I don't know. And I don't like saying I don't know. But there are things about God that are unfathomable. I think it comes down to trust, trusting that his plan is best, that it does all somehow work out for our good and his glory. Doesn't make it easy, though." He fingered the shark's tooth necklace that had moved to the outside of his T-shirt.

She'd seen it before and wondered about it. "You always wear that, don't you?"

"Yeah." He was quiet, and for a moment she didn't think he was going to expand on that. But then, "My dad got it for me when we were visiting our relatives in Hawaii when I was in high school. He said that it represented strength and commitment. It was like he was bestowing a blessing and a responsibility on me. When he was diagnosed with dementia, I started wearing it again to remind me of his strength and to keep him in my prayers."

"That's a great memory. My memories of high school—and my family—aren't that great. I've wondered if we all could have done something differently, if our paths—my path—would have changed."

He met her gaze. "Did you start drinking in high school?"

She nodded. "I can actually remember the first time I got drunk. Over and over I've thought if I'd made another choice that night, what would have happened? I came home with a bad report card. I was struggling with algebra. I probably should have asked for help, but I thought school was hard and stupid."

She nudged him with her shoulder. "If I'd known you, I could have asked you to tutor me." Her smile faded. "Dad saw my report card and was disappointed in me. He didn't actually say it, but I felt it. I constantly felt that they were thinking, 'Why can't you be like your brothers?' Scott was off flying the not-so-friendly skies for the US Navy. And Christopher was dead. But he'd been a star before he'd died. I was replacement child, born after he had been killed by a drunk driver. And a poor replacement at that. They should have stopped at two kids."

"Jessica." Austin laced his fingers through hers.

"I know a lot of it was they weren't sure what to do with me. I was unexpected; I was a girl. I didn't like sports. I gave up T-ball after one season because I was bored. I was only an average student, except in art and music. But I didn't want to take piano lessons. I did take guitar lessons but stopped after a while because I never remembered to practice. Yeah. I was nothing like my brothers. I wanted to color or doodle or daydream. Anything other than boring schoolwork."

"So what did catch your interest as a kid?" Austin's gaze on her was steady, curious, not condemning at all. She was surprised…and not.

"I loved the after-school art program. My art teacher was the first person who I felt saw me as me, with my own ideas and potential. She didn't know my brothers or compare me to them. I was devastated when it was cancelled." The memory still brought tears to her eyes.

"So anyhow, it was no shock that I was failing algebra, and I didn't really care. I hid in my room to avoid the displeasure and disappointment in my parents' eyes, listening to music, talking with my friends. One of them texted me about a party that night. I wasn't grounded, but I knew my dad wasn't going to let me go to a party after a bad report card. So I wandered out to the kitchen and said, 'I'm going to Tyra's house. She's pretty good at algebra. Maybe she can help me bring my grade up for next semester. Then we'll watch a movie, and I'll spend the night.' Dad was quiet a minute then nodded."

"Were your parents particular about your friends or where you spent the night?"

"Not really. I'd grown up with the same group of kids since elementary school, but my parents were older, and frankly, I think they were just tired. But they knew Tyra, and the idea of my making an effort to bring up a grade appealed to them. So Tyra and I went to the party. This guy I liked, Landon, was there. He brought me a drink. I don't know what it was, but it had alcohol in it. But I wanted him to like me, so I drank it. He danced with me and kept bringing me drinks."

She paused for a moment. "The thing that I liked the most, though, even more than Landon's attention, was how all my problems just fell away. I didn't have to think or feel anything. I didn't have to see my dad's disappointment in me yet again. That's what brought me back to alcohol again and again." She shook her head. "Next thing I knew, it was morning. I was waking up on a couch in someone's house. Not mine. Not Tyra's. Cute guy Landon was snoring on the other end. I didn't know where Tyra was. Panic washed over me. I found my purse and dug out my phone and slipped outside. I called Joe to come get me. And he did."

Her eyes sought the trees as the memory washed over her. "I got a lecture but also a promise that he or Kyle would always come get me when I needed them. And they did." She gave a short chuckle. "I think the only person happier about my sobriety than me is them. They prayed for it for a long time."

He met her gaze. "Thanks for sharing that with me."

She nodded and took a breath. Now came the hard part. "Austin, we've become friends over the past several months, maybe more than friends, I don't know. But what I do know is that my heart is still tender when it comes to disappointment from other people, people I care about. So I'm going to be straightforward and honest with you, like I hope you will be with me. I can't ping-pong back and forth with you over what our relationship might or might not be. I know what that will do to me, and my sobriety is too important to risk it."

He didn't look away, didn't look horrified, so she kept going. "If we are just supposed to be friends, that's great. I'd be happy to have you in my life as a friend. But if we're going down the road exploring if we have something more than friendship, I need to know that too. I can't go back and forth wondering where we are today because you've shut me out." She glanced at their intertwined fingers. "Or getting my hopes up because you're now holding my hand. I was hoping this trip would give us time to spend together and get to know each other better, get a sense of where we might be going. So now, the ball's in your court. You don't have to respond right away. Just think about it and let me know."

She gave his hand a squeeze then removed her fingers and hopped down off the rock. "I'm going to go find Kim."

Her heart was pounding as she walked away, but she didn't look back. She had to do it, had to be honest with him. If there was a chance of them having a future together, he had to be honest with her too. And if there wasn't a future for them, better to know that now.

This had been a day of surprises, but one thing Jessica knew: She had made the right decision.

As Jessica walked away from him, Austin wondered if it was literally or figuratively. He didn't have too much time to process what she said because Kim met her coming up the road, and shortly after that, the sound of a vehicle grew louder over the sound of the water and wind. The mud-covered Escape appeared with Matthew, Laurie, and Mia.

So Mia had come back with them.

Matthew pulled up close so the passenger-side door was close to the rock Austin perched on. He hopped out. "You're still here. I thought maybe you guys would try to hike out."

"Funny guy." Austin slid off the rock, and Matthew got under his arm and helped him hop the two steps to the front seat.

Kim and Jessica pulled their bags off the rock, stowed them in the back of the Escape, and climbed in the back seat.

Matthew turned the SUV around and headed back down the road. He plopped the map in Austin's lap. "I'm getting good at navigating these roads, but I still need your help."

"How did it go dropping our guests off?"

"Ranger station was still closed, but they called friends who picked them up. Left a message for Ryan. Talked to the sheriff's department. They're overwhelmed right now with rescues and mudslides. They said if Mia wasn't in any immediate danger, she should stay with us until we could get her to help."

The trip back to the campground was quiet and uneventful, a relief after the day's activities.

Kim spoke up. "I think Jessica and I would like to change into dry clothes. Then we'll help pack up the site. It shouldn't take too long. Everything is going to be wet and muddy no matter what."

Austin hated that he couldn't help, that he was deadweight. And Jessica's words bit deep. She was right; it wasn't fair to start a relationship with her and then close up on her. If they were going to have a future, he was going to have to be vulnerable. But the risk felt like looking over a cliff. Was it worth it? Or would he end up broken in pieces beyond repair? It didn't seem like there was any good way to know.

They pulled into the campground and wound around to their campsite, no van anywhere. So far, so good.

The women grabbed their bags and took off to the bathrooms, Jessica's arm around Mia and Kim on her other side.

"If you can help me to the tent and grab my bag, I'd like to change into some sweatpants and get out of these jeans. With the ace wrap and the swelling, I can't bend my knee. I need something with more give."

Matthew threw an arm under his shoulder as they hobbled toward the tent. He half fell inside, leaving his feet outside the door until Matthew helped him pull his muddy shoes off. Feeling a bit like a contortionist trying to change without bending his knee too much, he managed to get into the sweatpants he slept in. Much better. Matthew helped him get his shoes back on just as the women came back to camp. Good timing, so they didn't have to witness his feeling like a toddler.

"Back to the Escape?"

"Yeah, I think that's the best plan. Jessica can drive it. You and Kim can go in your truck."

Matthew nodded. The rest of them began stowing the gear when a loud, jacked-up four-by-four truck roared up to their campsite.

Ryan climbed down, followed by Bernie and Gary.

Matthew walked over, and Ryan jerked his thumb at the truck behind him. "He's willing to take us down the hill, but he can only fit four of us."

Austin knew what Matthew was thinking. There was so much Ryan didn't know about how their day had gone. There were four women here: Jessica, Kim, Laurie, Mia. Where was Macy? Maybe this guy should take them down the mountain. And then what? They'd still be stranded. They could rent a car, maybe. It was still an hour and a half home from the base of the mountains. And what about Mia? Jessica wouldn't want to just abandon her.

Matthew met Austin's gaze and lowered his voice. "We don't know this guy. I'm not comfortable sending the women off with someone we don't know."

"I'm thinking the same thing. Maybe the guys want to go? It's going to be a tight fit in the two cars we have left." Austin swung his gaze to Ryan. "Where's the RAV?"

"I'll tell you later. Anyone want to go with this guy? Otherwise, we need to let him go."

Matthew shook his head. "We're just packing everything up. We have some options for getting down the mountain the long way. But you guys should go with him."

Austin looked at Bernie. So much for getting to know him better this weekend. A few other things had gotten in the way.

Gary wandered over. "How did the Escape do for you today?"

"Surprisingly well," Matthew said. "I owe you a wash and a detail though. It's pretty muddy."

Gary waved him off. "No worries. I'm just glad you had it. Austin, you want to head down the hill with this guy?"

No, he didn't. But the Escape was Gary's car, and it made sense that he'd want to drive it. But if they both stayed, it was going to make a tight fit in one of the vehicles. "I'm not sure I can get in that truck." He laughed, not feeling it at all. "But, no, I'm fine. We've kind of gotten a system down for navigating through the roads. If you don't mind us keeping your car, we can get it back to you tonight or tomorrow."

"I don't mind. I wouldn't even know how to drive it off road. If you don't feel like I'm bailing on you, I'm happy to get out of your hair."

Ryan, Bernie, and Gary conferred then Bernie and Gary grabbed their bags. They said their goodbyes and climbed in the truck.

Ryan shouted his thanks to the driver, and the truck took off.

Austin leaned out the window. "Where's the RAV? And Macy? Why didn't you just take the RAV down the hill?" They'd had a plan worked out and didn't need Ryan.

Ryan shook his head and put his hands on his hips. "I didn't feel right about leaving you guys up here stranded. Macy got into a snit about getting rained on and having to leave the lake. Then when we discovered we couldn't get back here due to the mudslide, we headed into town to a coffeeshop to get out of the rain and figure out a plan. She asked me for the keys. I thought she was getting something out of the car, but she took off. She had been saying we should just leave, that you all would handle the campsite, and there was nothing we could do by being stranded in town."

Austin raised his eyebrows. He'd noticed Macy didn't seem like a good fit for camping, but he wouldn't have expected that. Then again, he didn't know her at all.

"There were these two old guys in the back of the coffeeshop. They heard us talking about our situation. One of them called someone who had a big truck with four-wheel drive and knew how to get around the back roads. Some I don't even think were roads. So here we are. What have you guys been up to?" He spotted Mia. "Who's that?"

Matthew slapped Ryan on the shoulder. "I'll let Austin catch you up. I'm going to help get the truck loaded."

Ryan shifted his gaze to Austin, clearly wondering why he was sitting in the car. Austin gave him the rundown of what had happened from getting rained out to finding Mia to rescuing the folks from the overturned truck. He couldn't help but notice Ryan's gaze strayed to Jessica far too often.

"Wow. You've had a busy day. Why didn't you just leave this

Mia with the camp host or wait at the ranger station until someone came to get her? Seems like she's put you all in a lot of danger."

"She wouldn't have been safe with the camp host. And there was no one available to get her from the ranger station."

Ryan shrugged. "How come you're sitting in here?"

"I twisted my knee pulling Matthew out of the river after he went under."

"Ouch. Okay, I'll go help get everything packed up." Ryan tapped the roof of the SUV and headed over to the tent Jessica was taking down.

Unfortunately, that left Austin with a front-row seat watching Ryan charm Jessica, complementing her on her bravery in rescuing Mia. He explained to her about Macy when she asked, blowing it off like it was no big deal. "It wasn't like she helped out at all. Camping is definitely not her style. I thought maybe she'd loosen up and roll with things, but she doesn't have a sense of adventure. Not like you do." He gave her that winning, movie-star grin that Austin was sure had female hearts everywhere melting.

And here he was stuck with his bum knee, sitting in the car helpless. Yeah, the differences between him and Ryan were obvious. His gut twisted. Ryan and Jessica were a lot more alike: outgoing, friendly, easy conversationalists. Would his reluctance to let her in cost him a chance with her?

Chapter Sixteen

Jessica scanned the campsite for anything they'd left. They were racing the sun now. It would be dark in the woods a lot sooner than they'd think. It had been a long day, and she was physically and emotionally wrung out. It was good to get into dry clothes, however. She never knew how good they could feel.

She needed a call with her sponsor, Chelle, when she got home to process everything. But that was a long way off. They had to figure out how to get home first.

Laurie was already huddled in the back seat of Matthew's truck. That poor girl had gotten more than she'd bargained on this trip. Jessica figured she'd never agree to go on a camping trip again. But that meant she and Mia would be in the back of the Escape. With Ryan and Austin. That wouldn't be awkward at all.

Ryan and Austin were about as opposite as you could be. Ryan had light brown hair and blue eyes. Austin had black hair and dark brown eyes. Ryan was outgoing and friendly, but you were never quite sure if he was genuinely interested in you or putting on a show. Austin was quiet but as loyal as the day was long. If he said something, you knew he meant it.

Matthew conferred with Austin over the maps, and they marked out the route Austin had spotted earlier.

Ryan joined them, skepticism written all over his body language. "Isn't there another way? Why don't we just wait here until the road reopens?"

"Because we don't know when that will be, and we don't want to risk Gordo coming back." Matthew met Ryan's gaze. "The sheriff's department has their hands full right now. If we can get Mia to them, it will make everything easier."

Ryan shook his head, but he climbed into the driver's seat. Jessica and Mia got in as well, and once everyone was settled, they pulled out behind Matthew. They first stopped by the camp host's site to inform him they were leaving and to see if he had any information. But he still wasn't there. Or he'd come and gone.

Leaving the campground, they headed back into the woods. Some of the turns and natural features were beginning to look familiar to her, since they'd been this way a few times now. She glanced over at Mia, who leaned against the headrest and closed her eyes. The girl probably hadn't had a true moment of rest since she went missing.

Ryan muttered under his breath as they navigated the ruts and bumps of the forest service roads. From the rigid set of Austin's shoulders, he was either in pain from the jostling or wishing he could drive instead of Ryan. Or both.

As the road climbed around a particularly steep switchback, Ryan growled. "I don't think this is a good idea. What if we get stuck out here?"

"We're committed to it now." Austin's voice was steady. "Keep going. Just follow in Matthew's tracks."

Ryan muttered something else.

Jessica, seated behind Ryan, had a great view of Austin's profile. Occasionally, he would glance back at her, but mostly he kept his gaze alternating between the road and the map.

As they continued to climb, the trees grew farther apart,

letting in more sunshine. Then the vegetation stunted and became brush and chaparral. At least they would have a little more time before the light left them, now that they were higher and the trees weren't blocking the sun.

As the road turned sandy and became a series of switchbacks, Ryan slowed. She could almost feel Austin urging him to go faster, especially since they'd lost sight of Matthew. At a fork in the road, Ryan headed to the right.

"No, not that way. Left." Austin pointed.

"What? That can't be. This road is bigger."

"But it dead ends. It's not the one we want."

With a sigh, Ryan reversed and turned onto the correct fork.

They were nearly to the peak when they came to a spot where runoff had badly rutted the road and liberally sprinkled boulders across it. Matthew's truck sat on the other side, but the Escape didn't have the clearance to make it.

Ryan threw the car into park and hopped out. "Okay, so what's the plan now?"

Matthew was out of his truck looking around.

Jessica got out too. It would be good to stretch her legs. Kim had the same idea.

Matthew studied the underside of the Escape and the terrain. "I had to crawl over this rock here, but the this one won't clear it. I don't see a way forward."

Kim held up her phone. "Good news though. We have cell service."

Jessica looked around. One of the peaks in the distance had antennas poking up out of it. The whole wrinkled mountain range laid out before them. They could even see the blue smudge of the lake in the distance. It was beautiful. A sense of relief overcame her. They had made it. Freedom was in sight for Mia.

Austin met her gaze through the windshield. She couldn't read his expression, but he didn't look away. Something shifted in her heart, and she knew she could trust in whatever would come next. With or without Austin.

He rolled down his window. He must be feeling left out of the discussion. She inclined her head in his direction and moved over by him. The others followed.

"What do you think, Matthew?" Austin asked.

Matthew shook his head. "No way the Escape can get through. Between the rutted road and the washed-down rocks, there's just not enough space to make it. It was tough for me, and I was in four-wheel drive."

Austin looked at the map. "Not much farther then it's downhill to the high desert. It turns pretty quickly into a mining road and then goes to the highway. You can take Mia and meet up with the sheriff. We can turn around and head back and figure out what to do."

Jessica's heart sank at his words. She knew he was right.

Kim said, "Let me call Kyle and talk to him. See what he thinks." She wandered off with her phone to her ear.

Mia climbed out of the Escape and came to stand next to Jessica. "I'm sorry I'm such a pain."

"You're not." Jessica put her arm around the girl's shoulders. She didn't want to let Mia go; she wanted to be with her when she talked to the sheriff. She wanted to make sure they stayed in touch. She glanced at Matthew's truck. Laurie sat inside. There was no way she'd want to get in the Escape with Ryan and Austin. And if Jessica went in the truck, it would make for a cramped fit for the long trip home. For no good reason other than her wants.

Plus, should she leave Austin with Ryan? He was a big boy, but she didn't think Ryan would consider asking if Austin needed more pain meds or wanted something to eat. And Austin wouldn't ask. They would both survive, but it would be a better trip if she was along to moderate the testosterone.

Ryan walked over to her. "You need to let Mia go. It's going to take us awhile to retrace our route, and it's going to be dark soon."

He was right, though she didn't want to admit it, especially to him.

Ryan and Matthew began rearranging things, moving bags and equipment from the truck to the Escape.

In the back of the Escape, she found her backpack. Rooting around inside, she found a pen. Returning to Mia, she said, "Hold out your hand."

Mia gave her a questioning gaze, but she did it.

Jessica saw the WE tattoo on her wrist again. What did it mean? Initials for something? She gently took Mia's other hand. "This is my phone number." She jotted it on the girl's other wrist where it wouldn't get rubbed off. "Call or text as soon as you can. And this is something I want you to remember." She wrote LUKE 12:6-7. "It's a Bible verse that means a lot to me. It says, 'Are not five sparrows sold for two pennies? Yet not one of them is forgotten by God. Indeed, the very hairs of your head are all numbered. Don't be afraid; you are worth more than many sparrows.' Don't be afraid, Mia. You are worth more than many sparrows to God." She pulled the girl into a hug, only breaking it when Kim returned.

"I talked to Sheriff MacIntyre. Collins worked with her when he was up here, and Kyle put us in touch. She wants to meet us at a spot off Highway 18. We're about an hour away. She also said that the mudslide across Holcomb Springs Road would be cleared late tonight. A bulldozer is supposed to get to it in a few hours. So if you guys head back that way, you might have to wait a bit, but you should be able to get down the mountain tonight, though it'll be late."

Ryan climbed back in the Escape and, with Matthew's help guiding him, was able to turn it around to point downhill. He waved out the window. "Have a safe trip."

Jessica gave Mia one last hug and helped her climb in the back of Matthew's truck. She gave Kim a hug. "Keep an eye on her."

"I will. I'll text when I know something."

"Thanks."

"Come on, Jessica. We've got to go." Ryan waved at her impatiently.

With one last wave, Jessica climbed into the back of the Escape. She barely had her door closed when Ryan headed the Escape back down the hill. She fastened her seatbelt.

Ryan shook his head. "We made this whole trip for nothing. Mia could have gone with them from the beginning."

"Not really." Austin spoke up. "If we were able to make it over that one spot, we could have met up with the sheriff and headed home. Even when we get back to the main road, we'll likely have to wait for it to be cleared. We'll be getting home much later than Matthew, Kim, and Laurie. Assuming the road is even cleared tonight. We might want to think about going back to the campground to sleep and trying again in the morning."

Jessica's heart warmed that Austin had defended her. She prayed for Mia. And she prayed that the road would be opened so they could get home. Because she knew one thing. She did not want to camp with Ryan and Austin tonight.

THEY HADN'T MADE IT OUT OF THE WOODS BY THE TIME darkness fell. Austin flicked on his phone's light to read the map until they got back to Holcomb Springs Road. His leg ached, and he was hungry and stiff from being in this seat for hours.

Jessica had been uncharacteristically quiet the whole way. Mia had really affected her. He thought about what Jessica had shared with him on the rock about her past and her honesty with him about what she needed from him.

What if he couldn't give her what she needed? And then he looked at Ryan. He could do better than Ryan would. Ryan would never appreciate all the facets that made up a woman like Jessica.

Another thought entered his mind. What if he could give her what she needed? What would that look like? He was so used to seeing the limits to his resources like time, energy, and finances that it was a struggle to open his mind to the possibilities that he was enough, he could be enough. With God's grace.

Heading down the main road, they passed the campground, the ranger station, and finally came to several ROAD CLOSED barricades across the street. But construction lights shone in the distance, and the sound of heavy equipment carried through the night air.

Ryan pulled to the side of the road. "What do you want to do? I think our options are to wait here or head back to the campground, put up a tent, and get some rest. I'm tired. It's been a long day. Who knows when the road will be open. I say we go back to the campground."

Austin glanced back at Jessica. "What do you want to do?"

"I want to get home. But Ryan has a point. However, I'll sleep in the Escape. I don't want to share a tent with two guys."

"I don't like the idea of you sleeping in the Escape where someone could walk up on you in the middle of the night." But she had a point about the tent. He and Ryan could sleep in the car and give her the tent. But then, they might just as well hang out by the side of the road waiting for it to open if they were going to do that.

"One of the tents has those partitions," Ryan said. "Maybe that's the one Matthew tossed in. It's not like anything is going to happen. We'll all be in our clothes, tired and dirty. I don't think anyone wants to sleep out under the stars." Ryan turned the SUV around and headed back to the campground.

It would be good to stretch and straighten his leg out. Get some more ibuprofen and something to eat. He wasn't sure how he felt about sleeping in the same tent as Jessica. It seemed too private, somehow. But desperate times and all that. He had to admit that Ryan had a point.

They pulled into the campground and wound their way to

their site. A car was parked in it, but no one was around. There were no tents or camp chairs around the fire pit.

"Huh." Ryan idled in front of the site. "Did they give our site away? We should have it through tomorrow morning."

"Maybe they thought we left." Austin shifted in his seat. "I mean, we did leave."

"I guess we can go find the camp host and ask him." After another look around, Ryan pulled away.

"Stop at the bathrooms, will you?" Austin asked.

"Sure. I can walk to the host's site from there. Are you going to need a hand?"

Austin shook his head. "I can manage." He heard the growl in his voice, but he didn't care. He could limp a few steps into the bathroom. He just didn't want to have to walk all the way from the camp site. If they still had one.

Ryan pulled in front of the bathrooms. Austin couldn't believe how much had happened since they'd left this spot earlier today. He pushed his door open.

Jessica jumped out too. "You can lean on me, if you need to."

Nope. He didn't care how much it hurt. "I'm fine, thanks."

She watched him a minute then went into the women's bathroom.

While it hurt to put weight on it, it also felt good to stretch out the rest of his body. It was just a sprain. He'd had them before, and he'd put a brace on it and be fine in a few days. The ace wrap helped. He washed his hands and face, cleaning up as best he could. They all looked like they'd been rolling in the mud to some extent.

At the Escape, Jessica had the back open. "I thought I'd see what we had for food." She handed him a bottle of water and another ibuprofen pack.

"Thanks."

"Want a granola bar? We've got that, some trail mix, marshmallows, graham crackers, and an assortment of candy bars that we didn't use up on Kim's special s'mores."

"Ah, the healthy stuff. I'll take a granola bar."

Ryan came striding across the road. "The host said he didn't know who was parked in our site. He said he wouldn't have given it away since we had it until Sunday, but that folks who were trapped by the mudslide had been looking for places to stay for the night. Unfortunately, since no one is around, we can't ask them to leave. I suppose we could park next to them and set up our site again."

Austin raised an eyebrow. "We don't know what kind of people they are. What if they get angry? Is there another site we could go to?"

Ryan shook his head. "No, he's given them all out."

Jessica held out a granola bar to Ryan, who took it. "I guess we're sleeping in the Escape then. The question is, do we do that here or over by the road closure so we can leave as soon as it opens up?"

Ryan sighed. "I guess by the closure. Maybe we'll get home before dawn."

Austin eased himself back into the front seat. This was beginning to feel like the day that would never end.

They returned to the road closure. They weren't the only ones with the idea. A dozen different vehicles had pulled along the shoulder. In the dark, it was hard to tell how much progress they'd made on the road.

Jessica pulled out snacks from the back and handed them around.

"I have the Ungame in my backpack," Ryan said. "We could play that."

Austin couldn't think of anything he'd rather not do.

"Or we could sing."

Except that.

"Ungame," Austin said quickly.

Jessica handed Ryan his backpack, and he came up with the small box of cards, handing the pile to Austin. "You can go first."

Great. He wouldn't mind talking to Jessica, but Ryan? No thanks. But here they were. He repressed a sigh. "'Talk about a joyful time in your life.'" He thought for a moment. He'd had a good time with Jessica at Kyle and Heather's wedding. But he didn't want to talk about that with Ryan listening.

He went back further. "When I was in high school, I had gotten pretty good at coding and found I really enjoyed it. I would write programs for everything. If a teacher mentioned a problem or that they wished something could be a certain way, I'd write a program to solve the problem, even if it ended up being a bit Rube Goldberg-ish in its utility. I did some attendance and grading programs that generated reports and letters. But there was one I wrote for my English teacher that helped her figure out if students were using previous students' papers or plagiarizing and so on. Last Christmas, she sent a card to my parents' house and included a note saying she was still using it. So I guess I get joy out of being useful and solving problems."

He glanced back at Jessica.

A smile crossed her face in the dim glow leaking over them from the construction lights. "That's really cool."

"Nice." Ryan handed the stack to Jessica. "Your turn."

She took a card. "'What do you think is your purpose in life?'" She gave a short laugh. "I wish I knew. It's been the question of the year." She blew out a breath. "I do believe God has a purpose and plan for us, but unlike you, Austin, I don't have any fantastic skills that can help people. I like art and beauty and music. So I'm just trying to follow where he leads and help the people he puts in my path."

"People like Mia," Austin said softly.

She met his gaze, but he didn't think she could see his face in the shadows. "Yeah, people like Mia."

The silence pulled a bit then Ryan grabbed a card. "Okay, my turn. 'Talk about the importance of faith in your life.'" He laughed. "Well, I'm a worship pastor, so I guess it had better be important." He sobered. "I do really love seeing people respond to worship. There is something, a spirit, that moves over a group that is all praising God together. Being able to be part of that is really a privilege."

A buzzing filled the car. "My phone." Jessica pulled it out. "I forgot we had cell service here. It's Kim. Hello?"

Jessica chatted with Kim for a moment. From the side of the conversation he could hear, it sounded like Kim, Matthew, Laurie, and Mia were heading down the hill.

"I'll let you know when we're home, no matter how late. Bye." Jessica turned to the rest of them. "The sheriff took a report and had Kyle and Collins on speaker phone, so they are all up to speed. She let Kim and Matthew take Mia home to her parents, and Kyle and Collins will follow up with them tomorrow."

She let out a long sigh. "So she's safe. She's already talked to her parents, and they are thrilled to have her home. Kyle knows someone who does trauma counseling for trafficking victims, so he'll put her in touch with that resource as well."

Austin reached his hand back and found hers and squeezed it. "Good job, Jessica. She's safe because of you."

She shrugged. "Anyone would have done it."

"Probably not. But the fact is, you did."

Ryan rattled the Ungame box. "Another round?"

Austin shook his head. "Nah, I think I'm going to try to close my eyes. The ibuprofen is kicking in."

"Good idea." Ryan laid his seat back, crowding into the back seat where Jessica was.

She scooted to the middle. "Austin, if you want to lay your seat back, go ahead. I'll just put my feet over the center console."

That didn't look comfortable, especially for the whole night. "I'm fine. If you lean against the door behind me, you can stretch your legs out under Ryan's seat."

She rummaged in the back. "Anyone want a jacket or sweatshirt to use as a pillow?"

"I'm good." This from Ryan.

Of course he was. He had a headrest, not a hard window to lean against. Austin wished he could trade places with her. But if he was in the back, she wouldn't be able to lay the front seat back either.

Jessica rustled around and then settled down, and quiet fell over the car. Austin let his mind spin out over the day's events. He wished he and Jessica were alone so he could talk to her. Instead, he stretched out as best he could and closed his eyes.

Gordo kept to the woods. He'd seen them come into the campground and then leave again when they couldn't find a spot. That just narrowed down their options and made things easier for him. He stashed the van off the road, but with all the cars parked along the highway waiting for the road to reopen, he had to be careful not to be spotted or heard. He hated nature. His shoes and jeans were soaked. Sticks and bushes had scraped up his arms and legs. And someone was going to pay for his bad mood.

These people were all alike. Self-righteous, thinking they were above folks like Gordo and his clients. But they used people too. They bought and sold each other all the time; they just didn't call it that. At least Gordo and his colleagues were honest about what they were doing.

He spotted the Escape. He watched for a long moment. They were close enough to the road closure that the construction lights spilled over the area, leaving little shadow for him to hide in. The good news was the racket from the bulldozers would drown out the noise he would make.

Nobody stirred, either inside the Escape or the surrounding cars. But was it the right Escape? It was too dark to see the license plate without being right up on the car. Hoping that if anyone saw him they'd think he was checking on the progress of the road clearing, he wandered along, edging toward the Escape. Light shone on blonde hair against the back passenger window. Mia!

He forced himself to slow down. Yeah, the guy sleeping in the front seat was the same guy who'd talked to him when Mia escaped. Mia must be leaning against the back door. He could pull it open and yank her out, but the doors were likely locked. All he needed to do was to get them to open up. Should be easy with a couple of do-gooders like them.

And to keep them from getting away… He pulled the knife out of his pocket and bent down next to the tire like he was tying his shoes and plunged it into the sidewall. He repeated it three more times, making sure no one noticed or the occupants didn't wake up.

As he finished off the last tire, he rose and looked inside. Wait. The girl wasn't Mia, but she looked a lot like an older version of her. Was she related to Mia? What did they do with her?

It was the first question he was going to ask. He lifted his fist to pound on the driver's window, but a light caught his eye. He dodged back behind the car.

Someone was walking this way with a high-powered flashlight, stopping to knock on windows. From the shadow profile cast by the construction lights, he could tell it was a sheriff's deputy.

He swore under his breath then duckwalked back to the woods.

Chapter Seventeen

A pounding startled Jessica out of sleep, and she jumped. Where was the sound coming from? Had Gordo found them? Her eyes searched the darkness as she remembered she was in the back seat of the Escape.

Austin and Ryan stirred, and someone pounded on the window again, shining a flashlight inside.

Ryan raised his seat upright and rolled his window down.

"Road's open. A pace car is going to lead a group of you down. Be ready to go in five minutes. Just follow the car in front of you." The sheriff's deputy started to move on, then he stopped. "Hey, you've got a flat tire." He swung his flashlight to the other tire. "Two flats." Frowning, he moved around the other side then came back to Ryan. "All of your tires are flat. Looks like someone slashed them. Did you see or hear anything?" He spoke into the mic on his shoulder.

Ryan look around. "No. Did you guys?"

Austin shook his head. "I was asleep."

"Me too." Jessica straightened up and stretched a bit. Now what were they going to do? And who would have slashed their tires? Did it have anything to do with Mia? She wasn't awake enough to ponder what all it could mean.

The deputy bent down. "I've got a tow truck coming. I'll get the rest of these folks going then I'll come back." He walked away, and Ryan rolled up the window.

"Now what?" Ryan looked from Austin to Jessica.

Austin stretched his arms in front of him. "When he comes back, tell him we were part of the group that found Mia Latham. The guy in the van knows this car. He might have come back and slashed the tires out of meanness."

"But why stop at that? Why not come after us in some way?" Jessica rolled her head, trying to loosen the kink in her neck.

"Maybe he got interrupted," Austin said.

"Gary is never going to let us take his car again." Ryan rubbed his eyes. "Four tires aren't going to be cheap."

"His insurance should cover part of it. We can all pitch in to cover the deductible."

Jessica couldn't help but stare into the woods, wondering if Gordo was out there, if he had something else planned for them. He probably didn't know Mia was safe now, or soon should be.

She texted Kim the latest. And then they waited for the deputy to come back.

Even though she was expecting him, his knock at the window made her jump.

Ryan rolled the window down again.

"A tow truck is on its way. I'll need to file a report."

"We're part of the group that helped the trafficked girl, Mia Latham," Ryan said. "Our friends met with the sheriff earlier tonight. This might be related to that. The guy who had her is probably still stuck up here."

"Then the sheriff is going to want to talk to you." He spoke into his mic again. "She's on her way. In the meantime, I'll start the report. I need your names and the registration for the vehicle."

By the time they'd given him the information he needed, a sheriff's SUV pulled up behind them. A woman got out and made her way over. "Hey all. I'm Sheriff Shannon McIntyre. I hear you guys are heroes."

Ryan grinned. "We just happened to be in the right place at the right time."

Jessica wanted to roll her eyes at him and his *aw shucks* demeanor. He hadn't been the biggest fan of Mia's rescue, but now he was lapping up the praise.

Sheriff McIntyre looked at the deputy. "Did you get what you needed, Brett?"

"Yes, ma'am. And the tow truck is on its way."

She nodded. "Why don't you folks let me give you a ride back to the station? Bring your bags. We've got hot showers, some okay vending machine food, and I can get your statements. I'll have to wait until morning to ask Art to open up his shop to fix your tires. He doesn't usually work on Sundays, but he'll do it for me." She winked. "We've got a few cots where you can catch up on your sleep too."

"That sounds great. Thank you." Ryan waited for them to step out of the way, then he opened his door. Austin and Jessica also got out. Her legs ached, and she stretched a bit. She could only imagine how Austin felt. He was definitely limping as he moved to the back of the Escape.

Ryan popped the back, and they grabbed their bags and backpacks.

"Need to have someone look at that leg?" the sheriff asked. "You're limping pretty bad."

"It's just a sprain. No big deal."

She nodded. "Sit up front. There's more leg room."

They climbed into her Explorer and headed past the barricades and down a bit before turning onto the main road that went through downtown Holcomb Springs. A short while later they were pulling up in front of a town complex that looked like it housed the sheriff's department, fire department, and town offices, with a community center thrown in for good measure.

The sheriff showed them the men's locker room, and Austin

and Ryan disappeared behind the door. She took Jessica to the women's and went inside with her. "Let me show you where we keep the good stuff." She opened a cabinet that contained Bath and Body Works shampoo, conditioner, and body wash. "The guys can use the stuff they put in the dispensers in the shower, but I prefer it if my hair doesn't end up like straw."

Jessica smiled. "Thank you. A hot shower sounds wonderful. I feel like I've been rolling in the mud."

"When you're done, exit to the right. You'll see my office a short way down the hall behind the glass windows."

"Got it."

The sheriff left, and Jessica used all of her energy to get undressed and step into the steaming shower. It felt amazing, like the best shower she'd ever had. She wished she could just fall asleep under the spray. But she couldn't. Reluctantly, she dried off and changed into her last set of clean clothes, glad she'd brought extra just in case.

She combed through her wet hair and pulled it up into a messy bun then put the toiletries back in their hiding places. Grabbing her bag, she headed out to the sheriff's office.

Ryan and Austin were already there, fortified with soda and bags of chips.

She took an empty seat. "Thanks so much. I feel human now."

The sheriff smiled from behind her desk. It had to have been a long day for her, but her golden blonde hair was pulled into a neat bun at the nape of her neck. She looked to be in her late thirties or early forties, though she did have a stressful job, so maybe she was younger. Then again, she'd probably had to put in a lot of years to get this position. Her soft brown eyes were kind. "A hot shower does wonders." She glanced over to the doorway.

A man in a firefighter's uniform came through. "Hear there's someone who has a sprained knee?"

Austin shot a glance at the sheriff.

"This is Marco. He's one of our firefighter paramedics. They were just playing cards." She winked. "Need to keep him busy so he earns his keep. You can use the conference room for the exam."

Marco shook his head but took Austin's arm as they headed to the windowless room and shut the door.

"They've actually been out all day on rescues. I had food sent over there, so I knew someone was still up. Might as well make sure there's nothing serious going on with that leg." Sheriff McIntyre looked between Ryan and Jessica. "Who wants to go first?"

Ryan gestured to Jessica. "How about I go get you something to eat and drink while you tell your story? You were more instrumental than I was. I just drove around."

She nodded, and he left the room. She told the sheriff everything that happened from the time they found Mia in the bathroom to when they left her with Matthew, Kim, and Laurie.

The sheriff took notes on her computer, asking a question now and again.

Ryan had brought her a Diet Coke and a bag of Doritos.

Austin had come out with Marco. He sat in a chair with his leg up on another one and an ice pack on his knee.

"I think that's everything. I have your contact information, and I know Detectives Taylor and Collins will also be in touch. I understand you all are friends as well. I told him I'd make sure we took good care of you. Jessica, if you head back into the women's locker room, there's a door on the other side that leads to the rack room. There are cots where you can crash for a bit."

"Sounds good. I can barely keep my eyes open, even after this." She shook the Diet Coke can and got to her feet. "Thank you for everything."

"Thank you for doing something for Mia. You've changed her life."

Jessica nodded and left the room, following Sheriff McIntyre's instructions and finding the rack room. She plopped on the cot nearest the door and slid her bag and backpack underneath. She texted Kim another update then laid down and pulled the blanket over her. Her mind spun with the events of the day, with all the what ifs. She didn't know if she'd be able to sleep, even as exhausted as she was.

She was just drifting off when Ryan and Austin came in and found cots nearby. But her mind was filled of images of a van chasing them down, a faceless man grabbing Mia and coming after them with a knife.

What had she gotten them all into?

Chapter Eighteen

It only seemed like she'd had about fifteen minutes of sleep when Austin was shaking her shoulder.

She blinked at him. "What?"

"Time to go. One of the deputies is taking us to the coffeeshop to wait while the Escape gets new tires."

"It's the middle of the night."

He laughed. "Nope, it's nearly eight a.m."

She pushed upright. Almost five hours since she'd laid down. She felt the top of her head. Her bun had slipped, and she could only imagine what she looked like. "I'll meet you outside the locker room." She grabbed her bags and scuttled into the women's.

Ugh. Her hair stuck up funny. She pulled the bun out and finger combed it, then washed her face and brushed her teeth. Good enough. It would have to be.

Outside the locker room, Ryan and Austin leaned against the wall. They looked up when she came out.

"Hey, Austin. I have an idea." Ryan darted into the closest office and pulled out an office chair. "Sit. I'll push you to the door."

"I'm fine."

"Come on." Ryan patted the chair back.

Jessica took Austin's bag from his hand. "Go ahead. Take advantage of Ryan's labor." She grinned. Man, she was punchy when she was tired.

Austin reluctantly sat, and Ryan wheeled him to the back door where a deputy's SUV sat. It was probably a longer walk than Austin could have comfortably made. He stood. "Thanks, Ryan."

Ryan gave him a salute and wheeled the chair back while she and Austin climbed in.

A different deputy sat at the wheel. "I'm Roberto. I hear you guys have had quite an adventure."

Austin nodded.

Ryan hopped in and the deputy took off. "I'm taking you to the Jitter Bug Too. Cassie, the owner, is the sheriff's sister. She has great coffee and makes the best scones. Art's auto repair is just down the street. He'll call Cassie when your car is ready."

Roberto pulled up in front of the store, parked, and got out. But the sign on the door said CLOSED. That didn't stop him. He opened the door, and a heavenly aroma of coffee and baked goods floated out. Maybe someone had forgotten to flip the sign.

A woman with an athletic build and curly, dark hair smiled at them. She pushed a to-go coffee cup and a bag across the counter. "Morning, Roberto. These are for you."

"Cassie, you're the best. Thanks for taking care of our guests."

"Happy to."

Roberto swept up his goodies. "Best of luck to you all." And he headed out the door.

The woman came around the counter. "Hi, I'm Cassie."

"I'm Ryan, and this is Jessica and Austin."

"Nice to meet you, though I'm sure you wish the circumstances were different." She moved past them and locked the door. "What can I get you? Blueberry scones are hot from the oven. I can make any kind of coffee drink. And it's on the house." When Ryan started to protest, she raised her hands. "My sister insists. And she's the sheriff, so I do what she says. That, and she's my *big* sister." She laughed.

They placed their orders, and Cassie showed them to a booth, bringing a big plate of scones over to them. They were the best things Jessica had ever tasted.

As Cassie was bringing their coffees over, someone knocked on the front door. She waved them away. "We're closed. It's Sunday."

There was a muffled response, but Cassie just laughed and deposited the coffees. "You need anything else?"

"Wait. You're closed? Then why are we here?"

Cassie pulled over a chair. "Small towns. We like to help people out when we can. You guys did a good thing, and my sister feels the least we can do is get some good food and coffee in you. I agree."

Ryan sipped his coffee and looked around. "Is this connected to the Jitter Bug in Laguna Vista?"

"In a way. Same original owner for both. He came up here to semi-retire and opened this shop. I bought him out last spring."

They ate scones, drank good coffee, and heard about life in Holcomb Springs. "This is the second time I've been up here, but I've never seen the charming side of it." Jessica swallowed the last of her coffee. That was an understatement.

Cassie brought over another pot to refill their mugs. "You'll have to make another trip, then."

"Agreed, but no camping and no being on the lake."

Austin laughed. "I'm with you on that."

The coffeeshop phone rang. It was Art saying their car was ready.

Ryan hopped up. "I'll grab it and swing by here so you don't have to walk far, Austin."

Within a few minutes, they were saying goodbye to Cassie and heading down the mountain. Dirt, mud, and rocks piled up on the side of the road where the mudslide had been. But after a while, Jessica's eyes drifted closed as they wound their way down the mountain.

At the base of the mountain in the town of Highland, Ryan said, "One of you want to find a place where we can grab something to eat that serves breakfast? Those scones weren't very filling and it was like three hours ago."

"Sure." Austin slid out his phone. "There's a Jack in the Box." He directed Ryan there. They placed their orders, grabbed their food, and headed back on the freeway.

The food helped wake Jessica up a bit and tasted far better than it would have at any other time. Their speed on the freeway seemed almost unreal, and she leaned forward to check the speedometer. Yes, Ryan was speeding, but just by the typical California amount. After the rutted, muddy roads and the twists and turns, a freeway seemed like flying.

Jessica must have dozed again because she awoke to the feeling they were slowing and exiting the toll road.

Ryan glanced back. "Your car is at the church, right?"

The last church service was already out, so the lot would be mostly empty. "Yeah. Austin came with Matthew though. But I can take him home."

"That'd be great. I'm meeting up with Gary, and he's taking me to get my car from Macy. She texted me that she'd returned the RAV and picked up my car." He shook his head.

Ryan pulled up to Jessica's lonely Nissan in the church parking lot. Her muscles ached as she got out and popped her trunk. She and Ryan transferred everything to her car. She could sort it out with Kim and Matthew later.

Austin hobbled around the Escape and into her passenger seat. A few minutes later, everything had been moved.

Ryan pulled Jessica into a hug. "Thanks for everything you did. I know I'm not always that flexible when it comes to changing plans. I felt responsible for the whole group. But you did the right thing."

She stiffened, not expecting the hug or his words. "Thanks." She pulled out of his embrace, not sure what to think of any of it. She just wanted to get home.

Ryan gave Austin a wave and drove off. Jessica followed him.

"How's the leg? Really."

"It's just a sprain. Marco rewrapped it. The ice helped. It'll be fine in a few days. I'll probably see my doctor tomorrow just to make sure. It's more inconvenient than anything."

They rode in silence a bit, Jessica more awake now that she was at the wheel.

"Do you still have that quartz I gave you?" Austin's voice came out of the quiet. When she glanced over, his gaze was steady on her.

"Yeah. It's in my backpack. I thought I'd put it in my terrarium."

"You have a terrarium?"

She laughed. "It sounds silly, but I liked the idea of something growing in my room. A miniature garden of sorts. I put some trinkets in there from when I was a kid. It's like a living memory box."

He nodded. "I like that. It's a good place for your quartz. I know a lot of people believe stones have different meanings, kind of like flowers do. But it reminded me of my shark's tooth." He touched it where it rested on the leather strip.

She pulled up in front of his and Matthew's apartment. "It means a lot to me. Thank you."

Their apartment door opened. "I texted Matthew from the church," Austin said.

"Good thinking." She popped the trunk.

Matthew came out, followed by Kim.

"Did you get any sleep?" Kim hugged Jessica.

"Eh. What about you?"

"Same. I figured keeping busy today would help me sleep tonight. Plus, since I'm my own boss, I can sleep in if I need to."

"Must be nice."

Austin reluctantly took the shoulder Matthew offered and made his way to the door.

Jessica grabbed Austin's backpack and followed them.

At the door, Matthew ducked back out. "I'll unload your trunk."

Austin reached for her hand. "Come here." He pulled her into a hug, a long one, not saying anything. When he pulled back, he trailed a finger down her cheek. "Look up the meaning of rose quartz. I'll talk to you later." He stepped back and into the apartment.

Jessica waved and then headed for her car.

Matthew hefted an ice chest out of the trunk.

Kim opened the lid. "I wonder if any of this food is good. Want some of the candy bars?"

Jessica shook her head. "Nope, I had enough to last me until our next camping trip."

"I'm sure Matthew and Austin can make good use of them." Kim closed the lid. "Have you heard from Mia yet?"

Jessica shook her head. "No. Text me her contact info, and I'll reach out to her if I don't hear from her soon."

Kim did. "What about Melissa? The wedding is a week from today."

Jessica shook her head. "I'm sure she thinks we're just getting back from the camping trip. It's hard to believe everyone doesn't know what happened to us."

Kim grinned. "We didn't make the news this time."

"So much for creating good memories though."

Matthew put a hand on Kim's shoulder. "We'll just have to keep trying."

"I'll pass." Jessica let out a sigh. "I'll talk to you later this week." She climbed into her car and headed for home.

This weekend had been mind bending, for sure. She'd have to call Chelle tomorrow.

But right now, all she could feel was Austin's arms around her as he hugged her.

The girls were loaded up in the back of the U-Haul truck Gordo had rented with a fake ID. He checked the van for any identifying traces before wiping everything down and climbing in the truck. The longer it took for someone to find the van, the better. He hit the road, going in the opposite direction the Escape had taken. They were Eric's problem now. He was back on schedule to get the girls delivered, and it was going to be a long, hot day through the desert once they got off the mountain.

The original plan had been to travel at night, but he'd have to find some place to hole up first. A U-Haul would be an eye-catching site at a campground, unlike a van. And if he took the girls through the desert during the day, he could kill the inventory. And that wasn't good for business. Once again he cursed Mia and those do-gooders for making his life more complicated.

His burner phone rang. Eric. "Yeah?"

"Where are you?"

"Back on track, heading down the mountain. But I had to ditch the van."

Eric's sigh came through the phone. "I'll report it stolen. What happened with the people who took Mia?"

"Don't know. Found the car. It had two guys and a girl that looked like she could be Mia's older sister. Fooled me for a minute. But a cop came up, and I had to bail before I could question them. But you've got the license plate. You track them down. I got problems of my own." Like driving this stupid truck around mountain curves without going over the edge.

"You bet you do. Call me when the girls are safe at the next stop."

Jessica had pulled her bags out of her car once she got home. Everything was going straight into the laundry. She had texted her parents that she'd be home a little early from the trip so they wouldn't be surprised.

Her mom pulled her into a hug as she came in the door. "Your dad and I want to take you to lunch so we can hear about your trip. Sounds like a lot happened from the little you told us. Is everyone okay?"

"Yeah. Austin sprained his knee, but other than that, everyone made it home safely." She hoped Mia would text her soon. If not, she'd reach out. "Lunch sounds good. I'm starving. We didn't get much to eat yesterday." It'd been a long time since she'd gone out to eat with her parents.

After Jessica started a load of wash, they climbed into Dad's Lexus sedan and headed to Islands for burgers and shakes. As they ate, Jessica told them the whole story.

Mom reached over and grabbed her hand. "You were so brave. It means a lot that you had the courage to do the right thing. We're very proud of you."

Jessica swallowed and blinked back tears. She couldn't remember the last time her parents thought she'd done the right thing or were proud of her. It was always her brothers. She wasn't sure what to make of it or of the strange things it did to her heart.

When they got back home, Jessica finished unpacking her backpack. The quartz from Austin fell out, and she fingered its smooth sides. She placed it in the terrarium where she could easily see it, next to the flowers Sarah had given her, which were drying nicely. Then she did a quick Google search on the meaning of rose quartz. Her heart pounded when the results came up: love, trust, and harmony. Did Austin know that when he gave it to her? He must have. He was the kind of guy who had all his facts straight before he acted. He wouldn't have given her something without knowing how it could be interpreted. In fact, he was the one who'd encouraged her to look up the definition. Was he letting Google say something he couldn't?

She thought about texting him, seeing how his knee was doing. But…no. She was going to give him space. She'd told him what she wanted. The ball was in his court, and he was going to have to deal with it.

She didn't want to obsess over Austin. She remembered the acronym HALT—hurt, angry, lonely, tired—which meant that if she was feeling any of those things, she needed to be careful not to make any rash decisions. And she was tired, a soul weariness that would take more than sleep to resolve. She'd reach out to Chelle. Maybe they could meet for lunch tomorrow. She needed to process this weekend with someone.

A tired restlessness invaded her. She didn't know what she wanted to do. She could finish her laundry and text Chelle. And Melissa. And Mia, if she hadn't heard from her.

Huh. She had a lot more people depending on her than nine months ago.

She kinda liked it.

Her phone buzzed. Before she could pull it out of her shorts pocket, it buzzed again. And again. It was a string of several long texts from Sophia. She laughed. She had expected this before now, but Sophia had only sent her a couple of ideas. But this list was extensive. From welcome baskets for out-of-town guests to party favors, Sophia had been spending way too much time on Pinterest.

Her phone buzzed again. This time it was Sarah. **Sorry! Sophia is on a tear. Heather said you guys are back from camping. Joe's working. Want to come over?**

That sounded exactly like what she needed to do.

Be there in a few.

She told her parents where she was going then hopped into her car, pulling up in front of Sarah's condo a few minutes later. It was too hot to sit out on her pretty patio, at least for a few hours until the sun went behind the other building. But Sarah had a pitcher of passion-fruit iced tea ready for them.

She poured them glasses, and they sat in her cute living room. Sarah leaned forward. "Tell me about the trip. Heather gave me some of the highlights."

So Jessica did, for the second time that day. Telling Sarah was different than telling her parents. There was an eagerness and a willingness to believe Jessica's decisions were the right ones. Plus, she could tell her about Austin, a part of the story she hadn't told her parents.

"Have you heard from Austin today?" Sarah asked.

Jessica let out a breath. "No."

Sarah reached out and touched Jessica's hand. "Just because he needs space doesn't mean he's going to abandon you. He needs time to process. Guys don't deal with their emotions as well as we women do." She smiled. "Let him choose to come back. I bet he will."

Peace flowed over Jessica at her words. "Even if he doesn't, I'll be okay. It'll hurt, but I'll be okay."

"Yes, you will."

The subject turned to Sophia's list and Jessica made note of how to respond. For the sake of family harmony, Sarah had agreed to let Sophia organize the bridal luncheon the Friday before the wedding, even though that honor should have gone to Heather as matron of honor. Heather said she didn't mind.

All the planning made her think about Melissa's wedding. Most of the items on Sophia's list weren't things they had planned for Melissa. She'd reach out to Melissa tomorrow.

At least she didn't have to work Mondays. One more day to recover from all of this.

When she left Sarah's, she was determined to head home and get a nap. But Sarah's soft words of encouragement were like a balm to her soul. It was one thing to believe she was strong enough herself; it was another to hear someone else speak it into her life. The words flowed like a sweet oil over her soul, soothing the sore and scarred places.

AUSTIN SPENT THE DAY ON THE COUCH WITH HIS LEG UP and an ice pack on his knee. With Air Pods in his ears, he created his own environment and didn't have to talk to anyone. Of course the only person around was Matthew, and he was good at giving Austin space. He needed to recover from being around people for so much of the time, and not just physically.

Except for Jessica. He didn't just want to be her friend. He knew that. But he wasn't sure how to handle her. His mind kept returning to her, despite his attempts to put off thinking about her. He didn't want her to think he was shutting her out. She had been honest about what she needed from him. How did he balance his needs with hers? Relationships involved sacrifice. How did he maintain the connection he wanted with her and get the recovery and space he needed?

He did what he always did when he needed answers: research. But after several hours on blog posts and YouTube videos on relationships, he wasn't sure he was in a better spot than when he started.

The front door opened, and Matthew came in. He dropped a bag of In-N-Out on the table in front of Austin. "I thought you might be hungry."

"Thanks, man." He sat up and grabbed the burger and fries. "How did it go with all the camping equipment?"

"Fine. We hauled everything over to Kyle's house so we could set up the tents, clean them off, and let them dry out on his back patio. The camp chairs got hosed off and are drying. Tomorrow after work, I'll go over and pack everything up and people can come claim their stuff." He stole a fry before landing in the recliner. "How's the knee?"

"Not too bad with the brace and ibuprofen. I'll call the doc tomorrow, but I doubt he'll say anything different. Guess I won't be riding my bike to work."

"Not for a while."

Austin set his burger down. "Can I ask you a question?"

"Shoot."

"How did you figure out what to do about Kim?" He ran a hand over his face. "I'm not even saying it right, but how do you balance what you need with giving her what she needs?"

"I didn't get it right at first. Still don't sometimes. I think it's something you spend a lifetime working out. Just when you think you've got it, something changes. But if she's the right person, it's worth the effort."

Austin nodded.

Matthew got up from the couch, and Austin finished his burger, thinking about what Matthew said. He was going to have to dig deep and be what she needed him to be, even if it felt beyond what he could do. Even if it was risky and uncomfortable. He needed to fight for her. She was worth letting his walls down for. If she'd protect a girl like Mia that she didn't even know, she'd protect and defend him too, if he'd let her. She pushed him into being a better man this weekend, and he needed that.

Now he'd have to figure out how to prove to her that she could trust him and also to convey when he needed space to recharge.

He'd noticed she hadn't texted him today. He half expected her to. But she'd kept her word. It was his decision to make.

Melissa and Scott's surprise wedding was Sunday. He didn't want to wait that long to see her. And if he did, she'd definitely think he wasn't interested. Joe's bachelor party was Saturday. Maybe they could go out Friday night. If his leg was up to it. He didn't really want to wait that long, but she often worked pretty late during the week.

Why was this so complicated? Just pick up the phone already. He hesitated, unsure of what to say.

Hey, did you get some sleep finally? Have you heard from Mia?

There was a long pause where he wasn't sure if she was going to answer. The text said DELIVERED but not READ. So she hadn't read it yet. Maybe she was too busy to get to her phone. Feeling too much like a middle school girl, he was just about to put his phone away when she responded.

Just now. A crying and laughing emoji sat between the words of her text. **I was taking a nap. No word from Mia yet. How's your knee?**

They texted back and forth like old times. Except it wasn't like old times anymore.

Let me call you, okay? He wanted to hear her voice.

Sure.

He tapped her number, and she answered on the first ring.

They talked a bit more about the trip—it was faster than texting—but he could hear the question in her voice as to why he called. The only time he'd called her before was to ask her on their double date.

"I wanted to know if you wanted to go out to dinner this week. Just the two of us."

Her response came back fast. "I'd love that. Let me look at my schedule."

They settled on Wednesday night. By the time he hung up the phone, he felt like he'd jumped off that cliff, but his parachute had opened, and he had a spectacular view of the future.

Chapter Nineteen

Jessica felt much better Monday morning. Likely from a full night's sleep, as well as her conversation with Austin. And it was going to be a busy week.

Mia had texted Jessica yesterday. Her folks wanted to meet Jessica and thank her. They asked her to come to dinner tonight. And she was having lunch with Chelle today. With her schedule this week, she was looking like a social butterfly. She laughed. It was only temporary. After the weddings were over in two weeks, life would go back to normal, whatever that was.

She opened her Inspiration for Today app while she ate breakfast. Today's quote was: "Develop an attitude of gratitude. Say thank you to everyone you meet for everything they do for you."—Brian Tracy. She certainly had been more thankful lately. The trip up the mountain had made her grateful for the protection God had given them, for her friends, for her family. The list got longer each day. It was a good reminder.

And she was thankful that God had brought Mia into her life.

She texted her. **How's it going now that you're home?**

They hover. Mia added a rolling eyes emoji.

I can imagine. They're worried.

She couldn't blame them. They'd lost their daughter for three weeks with no idea if she were dead or alive. And Jessica didn't know how much Mia was going to tell them about what she'd been through or if they suspected. Mia had a lot of hard work in front of her.

I talked to Detectives Taylor and Collins today. They've put out a sketch of Gordo. There are some leads they're following. I see the trauma counselor today.

Jessica's heart squeezed. It would be hard, but Mia was moving in the right direction. After confirming she was still coming for dinner, Jessica got ready for her lunch with Chelle. As many times as she had told her story of this weekend, she could only imagine what Mia felt like telling hers.

She thought about what Mia said, about how Brianna escaped. She couldn't have gotten far, not on foot. Especially since the guy in the van, probably Gordo, had caught up with her fairly quickly. It was an assumption, but one she was going on. Which meant that the building the girls had been held at had to be within walking distance of the salon.

She reviewed her mental map of the area. What buildings around the salon could be holding girls? She headed to her car to meet Chelle. Why was she worrying about this anyway? Kyle and Collins were good at their jobs. They'd for sure thought of it already. Besides, they probably had more information than she did.

Then again, she might be able to poke around unobserved. Kyle and Collins both screamed *cop* by their appearance and the way they carried themselves. Jessica wouldn't stand out in that way. Maybe she could drive around the area after lunch.

She headed off to meet Chelle at California Fish Grill. They ordered and got their food. Chelle mostly listened as Jessica talked in between bites, asking questions occasionally. Because Jessica was doing most of the talking, Chelle was finished with her meal way before her but didn't seem to be in a rush.

"I'm proud of you, Jessica. You did good. Just…be careful. It can be easy to get involved in someone else's problems, even with good intentions. Mia and her parents will have to do their own work. The best thing you can do is encourage that. Remember, you're still in recovery yourself."

Jessica nodded. "You're right. I just see so much of myself in her. We even look alike."

Chelle nodded, but caution lit her eyes.

They left the restaurant and hugged goodbye in the parking lot, with Jessica promising to keep Chelle updated and to reach out when she needed to.

As Jessica slid into her car, she realized how close she was to the salon. It wouldn't hurt to drive around a bit, see if she could narrow down some buildings so she could point Kyle in the right direction. Nobody would take a second look at her in her basic Nissan.

Using the car's Bluetooth, she called Melissa. "Hey, just checking in with you about the wedding." She told her about all the ideas Sophia had come up with for Sarah.

She almost could hear Melissa's eyes rolling. "This is exactly why we're doing a secret wedding. Almost like eloping, but with all our friends there and none of the hassle. Poor Sarah."

She chatted with Melissa until she reached the salon. Melissa didn't need anything else for the wedding, but Jessica and Kim were going to be there early, just to make sure any last-minute details were taken care of. Melissa was always so organized and on top of things. It was nice to see her relaxed and looking forward to her wedding.

Before Heather and Kyle's wedding in June, Jessica couldn't remember the last time she was invited to a wedding, and now she was involved with two in a two-week time span. It still amazed her how different her life was now. She'd even have her "own" place for a while house-sitting Melissa's townhouse.

After hanging up with Melissa, she pulled into the salon parking lot and studied the area. Too bad she hadn't seen the direction Brianna had come from. Had she come across the parking lot from one of the office buildings? Or had she come up the street?

The salon shared a wall with the building next door, some sort of office space, like most of the structures in the area. Across the parking lot was a professional building. She'd start there. She got out of her car and headed over. A list of company names and suite numbers was attached to the wall. Doctors, dentists, an architect. Nothing suspicious there. Unless one of them was a fake name.

She walked along the portico covering the building front. Each office door had a floor-to-ceiling window next to it. She slowed down as she passed, casually peering in each one. Each appeared to be exactly what they said they were, with waiting rooms and receptionists. Plus, she didn't think any place hiding girls would want a window by the door. So, not this building.

She checked out the closest buildings in either direction but found basically the same thing. There was one building that had a metal mesh security door to access the second floor, like a security screen door. It required a code. Hmm, something to mention to Kyle. And she could ask Mia tonight if she remembered going through a door like that to the second floor.

The afternoon nearly gone, she headed home. She had a bit of time, so she pulled up Google maps, printed out the area, and circled a few buildings that looked promising. She could walk around tomorrow on her break.

Her phone rang. Kyle. What update did he have?

"Gary's condo got broken into while he was at work today. I don't think it was a coincidence."

Poor Gary. Between his car and his house, he was never going to volunteer to do anything with the singles' group again.

"That Gordo probably got the license plate and figured out where he lived, not realizing Gary had nothing to do with rescuing Mia. Still, he's hanging out with Bernie until this gets resolved. As long as they think he is responsible for Mia's disappearance, he's in danger. Did any of you post on social media where Gordo could connect the rest of you?"

Jessica's heart pounded for a moment. They'd taken pictures. "No, the cell service was bad. I'd figured we'd do it when we got home but haven't thought about it. Been too wiped out."

"Good. I'll tell everyone not to. Be careful."

"I will. I'm meeting Mia and her parents for dinner tonight."

"I'm glad you're there to support her. She's going to have a rough time of it. But please make sure no one follows you. And don't go near Gary."

"I won't."

Austin left the conference room frustrated. His knee brace kept him from a long stride that would burn off some of his irritation. He'd seen the doctor yesterday, who'd agreed it was a sprain and said to keep wearing the brace, keep ice on it, elevate when possible, and to take it easy. He'd be better in a week.

He thought he'd nailed this presentation, but by the looks on their faces, he'd still missed the mark. He'd gotten with Matthew to understand the client and marketing side and was able to factor that into his presentation. He'd kept it short and to the high points, but it still hadn't been enough.

"Hey, Austin."

He turned.

Bernie took a quick step to catch up with him. "Got a minute?"

"Sure." It was kind of a dumb question. He would listen to whatever Bernie said. He'd need that information if he was going to pull his chances for the director position out of the nosedive that they'd taken.

Bernie stepped into a nearby conference room and closed the door behind them. "I know that was frustrating in there. It may not seem like it, but I see the progress you're making. The problem is you might run out of time before you can prove to Edward that you can handle the director position. He doesn't have a lot of patience. So, here's what you need to do. You're great on the facts and figures. You have those nailed down, and it's clear you know them backward and forward. Most of it goes over our heads, but we trust you with the numbers."

He stuck his hands in his pockets and paused before continuing. "What's missing is the warmth, the friendliness, the soft skills. Everyone in that room is evaluating you based on how they will work with you in the future. It's human nature to want to work with people similar to you, people you can relate to. So you have to prove to them you can do that. I know you can do it. I've seen that side of you. Now you need to let them see it."

Austin nodded, but he had no idea how to do what Bernie was asking.

He met Austin's gaze. "Let me ask you a question. Are you sure you want the director position? You're a great team leader. It's clearly your sweet spot. Why the director position?"

Austin's brain clicked through possible responses. What should he say? He didn't want to give away too much. What if it came back to haunt him? "I think I can best help the team from the director position. I'd be in a better place to prioritize projects, assign workloads, figure out how to best utilize each person's strengths—which I know because I've worked closely with them. I can make our department more efficient and the team members happier."

Bernie nodded. "I believe you. But you're forgetting that you'd not just be working with your team; you'd be working with the other directors as well. Convince Edward that you can do it." He clapped Austin on the shoulder and left the conference room.

Austin stood there for a moment, taking in Bernie's words. How exactly was he supposed to be friendlier? Should he go around and shake everyone's hands, asking them how their weekend was? How did he convince them that he wanted to be part of their team, that he could be a great asset?

Shaking his head, he left the conference room and headed back to his desk.

At the end of the day, he hobbled down to Matthew's car. Out of ideas, he told him about the presentation and Bernie's advice.

Matthew was quiet for a moment. Then he snapped his fingers. "Let Jessica help you."

"What? She doesn't even know anything about my job."

"Exactly. But she's good with people. She can come at this from a fresh perspective. You and I are too close."

Austin shook his head. "I don't want to burden her. She's got a lot going on herself. She doesn't need my problems too."

"I think she'd jump at the chance to help you. And I don't think she'd consider it a burden; she'd consider it a fun challenge."

"I don't know."

"That's right, you don't. And you'll never know unless you ask her."

Austin clenched his jaw. Fine. He was just going to put it out there. "What if I depend on her to help me, and then I keep needing her to help me do my job? And then she decides she doesn't want to be with me. Then what? That's exactly why I don't want to start down this path."

Matthew shook his head as he turned into their complex parking lot. "That's a lot of *what ifs*. Here are a few more. What if it turns out great? What if she wants to be with you forever?" He parked and turned off the car. "Stop expecting the worst."

Austin sat in the car thinking about Matthew's words long after Matthew had gotten out and gone inside.

Jessica got ready to meet Mia's parents, a little surprised at how nervous she felt. She hadn't heard all the details that led to Mia being taken by a trafficker. She figured Mia would tell her when she was ready. But she had a feeling that all was not well at home, and she hoped maybe this would be the crisis that would be the catalyst to heal their wounds.

She knew what it was like to be in a dysfunctional family. Hers was slowly finding their way to wholeness, but it would take a lot of time. Probably true for Mia's family too.

Jessica's phone rang as she was driving. Kyle. She answered it over Bluetooth.

"I have good news. I just talked to Mia and her family and told them. We found the girls she was being held with. The San Bernardino Sheriff's Department took Gordo's sketch to motels in the High Desert area. One of them got a hit at a motel in Victorville off Interstate 15. Someone had seen a U-Haul truck unloading girls from the back. They thought they were coyotes smuggling people across the border. The traffickers got away, but the girls are safe."

"Oh, thank God! That's fantastic news. I'm so glad the other girls are safe." Not being able to help the other girls had been something that had nagged at her, even though she knew there wasn't anything she could have done differently.

"Be careful. These guys are going to be desperate since they know we're closing in. Desperate people are dangerous."

"I will." With a much lighter heart, she pulled up in front of the place Mia and her family were staying.

Mia's parents had found an Airbnb to move to temporarily at since Mia's traffickers had taken her purse, had her ID, and knew where she lived. Her dad was already in the process of putting their house up for sale and buying a new one under his company name to provide some privacy.

Dinner went well. Mia's parents welcomed her. The food was

delicious, and the conversation flowed politely. There was a sense of hope that this nightmare was drawing to a close. Mia was an only child, and it was clear the gratitude her parents had at her return overflowed their hearts. Neither her mom or dad could keep their gaze off their daughter for long, as if they were afraid she would disappear.

They were effusive with their praise for Jessica, and after dinner, Mia's dad, Bruce, handed her a check. For a ridiculous sum. She handed it back. "This is very generous, but I can't take it. I didn't really do anything."

Bruce lifted his hands, palms out. "I'm not taking it back. I'd pay a lot more than that if it meant I'd get my daughter back. It's the least I can do."

The man was clearly used to getting his way. Probably was a great asset in whatever business he was in.

She took the check and put it in her purse. She'd figure out what to do with it later.

Across the table, Mia fidgeted. When she reached for her water glass, her hand shook. She pushed back her chair. "I'm going to show Jessica my room." As she met Jessica's gaze, she tilted her head in the direction of the stairs.

Jessica stood. "Dinner was wonderful. Thank you."

Mia practically dragged Jessica upstairs and into her room, closing the door behind them. "Sorry, I couldn't take another minute of it."

Jessica nodded. "Did your trauma counselor have any suggestions?"

Mia shrugged. "We didn't get into it too much. We had a lot of ground to cover. She gave me some techniques to deal with the nightmares and panic attacks. I'm supposed to start hippotherapy this week. Did you know that means horses, not hippos?" She laughed. "They're all acting like once the traffickers get caught, everything will go back to normal. Life will never be normal for me again."

Jessica squeezed her hand. Mia was right, and yet… Jessica

knew there was hope. You couldn't change the past, but you could make a new future. But Jessica didn't have the words to say that without sounding like she was minimizing what Mia had been through. Maybe there weren't any.

Mia turned to Jessica. "What I really need is a drink. My parents got rid of all the alcohol in the house. Can you take me somewhere to get some?"

Jessica studied her for a moment. She wanted to say, *But you're seventeen.* But then again, she'd been addicted to alcohol at seventeen too. "I can take you somewhere. Do you think your folks will be upset if we go for a ride?"

"If I tried to leave on my own, yes. But they think you walk on water. Let's go."

Jessica touched her arm. "Wait. I'm not going to buy you alcohol. I'm a recovering alcoholic. But I will take you to an AA meeting with me. There's one that starts in a few minutes. But it's your decision."

Mia looked at her then turned in the seat and crossed her arms. "I'm not an alcoholic. I just started drinking to make it all go away. Everyone uses something. I stayed away from the hard drugs."

Jessica nodded. "But you're craving a drink now. It becomes a crutch, and not a good one." She paused a minute. "I thought about just driving to the meeting and surprising you with it when we got there. But you've had too many decisions taken out of your hands. I want you to have agency over your own healing and recovery. You're the only one who can do the work. If you're not ready or don't want to, I won't make you. But if you do want to, I'll go with you every time."

Mia glanced around her room, and Jessica thought she was going to decline. But she turned to Jessica. "Let's go. It beats staying here."

Downstairs, Jessica saw the worry lighting Mia's parents' eyes when she explained where they were going. They'd probably live with that fear for a long time.

"It was nice meeting you. I'll have her home in a couple hours, I promise. Thank you again for the delicious dinner."

Mia dragged her out the door as she was saying goodbye.

Once inside the car, Jessica started it and headed toward the familiar meeting place.

"How did you become an alcoholic?" Mia's voice floated to her from the passenger seat.

Jessica let out a breath. "The short version is, I used alcohol to make my pain go away, to not feel anything. Probably the same way you did. But over time, it created more problems for me. I've discovered it's much better to face the pain head on and deal with it than to try to bury it."

At the stoplight, Jessica glanced over at Mia. A tear rolled down her cheek.

Eric's pocket buzzed. One of his phones. He excused himself from the dinner table he occupied with his wife.

She rolled her eyes and lifted her wine glass. "It's always business with you."

He kissed her cheek. "It's my business that keeps you living the lifestyle you deserve." He ducked into his office and closed the door. It was his burner.

"Mia's not at her house. No one is. The guy I left there hasn't seen anyone come or go. But they've got a monitored alarm system."

Eric swore. Her parents had probably taken her somewhere to keep her safe. "Mia doesn't know anything anyway. Except your face."

"That's only a problem if I get caught. And I'm not going to get caught. I got that load of girls transferred just fine at the next stop and made it back here with no problems."

"Except that guy's house you tossed who owned the Escape."

"Yeah, he wasn't either of the two guys in the car. But neither was Mia. Maybe he helped her get away."

"*Maybes* don't cut it. Keep your head down until this blows over."

Chapter Twenty

Jessica was glad Crystal assigned her the front desk during Kendra's lunch. She hadn't had a break all morning to walk around the buildings she had picked out from Google Maps. But from the front desk she could stare out the glassed-in front. Not that it told her much, but for some reason it made her feel like she was doing something.

Last night after the AA meeting, she had asked Mia about the building with the locked second-story access, but Mia had said they hadn't gone upstairs, just down, like into a basement or lower level. There weren't too many buildings with basements around here, but with the hilly terrain, there were certainly structures built into the sides of hills with access from different levels. She made a note to add that to the things to tell Kyle. Maybe they could pull building permits or something. But as of yet, there wasn't much on her list of things to tell Kyle. Nothing definitive, anyway.

Mia's parents had appeared at the doorway when Jessica had brought her back. She thought about the check Bruce had given her. She'd stuck it next to her terrarium while she decided what to do with it.

Crystal walked by and dropped a key chain on the desk.

"When Kendra comes back, grab the mail, will you? The box is around the side of the building."

"Sure."

She checked in the clients who had appointments and answered the phone. It all seemed so…ordinary after her weekend adventures. How was Mia adjusting to life? She hadn't said much during or after the AA meeting, but Jessica would text her tonight to see if she wanted to go to another one.

Kendra swept in the front doors, and Jessica closed the magazine she was flipping through.

"Thanks for covering for me." She put her purse in the drawer.

"No problem. I'm just going to grab the mail."

Kendra nodded.

Jessica picked up the key chain and made her way around the building, looking for the cluster mailbox set into the wall. There it was. She'd never been on this side of the building. No reason to. She found the box number that matched the one on the tag and inserted the key, opening the door then pulling out the stack of mail. Lots of catalogs and magazines. She flipped through them as she walked back, looking for anything good she might study the next time she covered the front desk. She piled the letters—bills most likely—on top of the magazines.

Something on one of the pieces of mail caught her eye as she came in the door. She set the mail on the front counter along with the key. One of the pieces was addressed to EM and Associates. Why did that sound familiar? And why was it coming here? She looked at the address. It wasn't theirs. It was for the office next door. That's probably why, even though she couldn't seem to remember any signage on that building.

"Hey, this mail was misdelivered. I'm going to run it next door."

Crystal walked through the lobby. "Where are you going?"

Jessica waved the mail. "This was put in our box by mistake. I think it goes next door. I was just going to run it over there."

Crystal snatched it out of her hand. "Stop snooping."

Jessica took a step back. "I wasn't. You told me to get the mail. I was just trying to be neighborly."

"I'll take care of it. You can go back to your station."

Jessica headed to the back. Madison had her do a blowout, and Jessica tried to shake off Crystal's attitude. She acted like Jessica was stealing the magazines or something. Maybe she'd taken a liking to Lyric and was planning on offering her the permanent position and this was her way of creating distance or something. Who knew?

When she finished with the client and shampooed the next one, she had a break. She pulled out her tiny notebook and jotted down what the woman had said about her kid's soccer team. She was a regular of Madison's, and Jessica would remember to ask her about it next time.

Sliding the book into her pocket, she headed to the front, hoping she didn't run into Crystal again. The coast was clear, so she headed outside and pulled out her phone. She opened the Google map she had saved and compared it to her surroundings until she spotted the buildings she wanted to check out.

But as she walked across the parking lot, she realized that she couldn't easily walk between the buildings. There was a retaining wall separating the two, high enough that she wouldn't want to climb it from this direction, and from the other way, it was a bit of a drop. If Brianna was being chased, she might have attempted it, but it seemed like another direction would be a better choice.

She scanned the area and compared it to Google maps. Nothing seemed like a good match. Well, she tried. As she turned and headed back toward the salon, she saw the back side. She hadn't seen it from this way before. Two service doors provided access in the back, and some glass block appeared down low where there could be some sort of lower level. She took a picture of it and texted it to Mia.

Does this look similar to a place where you could have been kept?

She didn't think it was *the* place where the girls were kept, but she was trying to get the image of what she was looking for in her mind.

It was dark, but it could be.

Huh. Okay. So a flat brick back with an alley and service doors. She'd drive home up a few back alleys and see if anything matched.

She looked at the time. She had to get back, but on her way, she skirted the building and checked out who was EM and Associates. Maybe Kyle could find a similar building through the builder of this one. There were few windows, and they all had blinds closed with no light leaking out. On the door, there was only a suite number, no company name. Weird. Probably one of those places where only a few people worked from and they didn't see clients, like a call center or something.

She slipped back into the salon, but Crystal was standing next to the front desk talking to Kendra. She glanced up at Jessica. "Where've you been?"

"I just went to get some fresh air and stretch my legs on my break." She gave a quick smile and headed back to her station, but in the mirror Crystal was staring at her.

She pulled out her little book, flipping the pages until she found a blank one to jot down notes about Madison's next client.

Crystal came up behind her and yanked the book out of her hands. "What are you doing? Are you spying on us? Taking notes?" She angrily tore through the pages.

"Uh, no, it's just things I'm learning from Madison and notes about the clients so I can remember what to talk about, to give them a personal touch."

Crystal's gaze was hard on her, and she tossed the book on the workstation counter before stalking off.

Madison touched Jessica's shoulder, causing her to jump.

"Don't take her too seriously. I think she's going through menopause. Every once in a while she turns into a real witch. And then a couple days later it's like nothing ever happened."

Jessica nodded and suppressed a shiver.

Lyric sidled up next to her and lowered her voice. "I hear you've gotten on Crystal's bad side." She gave a cocky grin.

Jessica shrugged. "I'm not sure what I did."

"Doesn't matter. It *does* help me." She shrugged. "Sorry-not-sorry. But if there's only one spot, I'd be a fool not to take every break I can get. It's nothing personal." She patted Jessica on the shoulder and moved off.

She didn't want to be like Lyric. How you treated people had to matter in the long run, even if it cost you in the present. Maybe this wasn't the place where she belonged.

The feeling that she was going to lose this job settled on her with dread. Her relationship with her folks was good but tenuous. How would they feel if she lost her first job out of school?

Eric glanced at the security camera monitor, movement catching his eye. Someone was walking around outside the building. Taking pictures. At first glance, he thought it was Mia. He studied the screen closer. No, not Mia. He took a screen shot of the girl and sent it to Gordo.

The text came back. **That's her.**

She went into the salon and disappeared from the camera's view. Was it the same girl who'd talked to Brianna?

He picked up his phone and called his wife. "Who's the girl that works for you? The blonde?"

She gave a harsh laugh. "Lots of blondes in a salon."

"She's young, probably new. I haven't seen her before. Short."

"Jessica."

"Give me her info." He reached for a piece of paper.

"Should I fire her?" His wife's voice held a note of concern.

"No. Just keep an eye on her."

He sent Gordo the info. **She's poking around. Let's warn her to stay away and mind her own business.**

If she was smart, she'd listen to the warning. If not, well, he had plans for her.

JESSICA LEFT THE SALON AND STEPPED OUT INTO THE HOT sun, thrilled she was getting off a little earlier than planned. It was exhausting avoiding Crystal.

Her steps slowed as she neared her car. Something was on the windshield. Then she remembered how Matthew had left sweet notes on Kim's car a few months ago when they were trying to get their relationship off the ground. Maybe Austin had the same idea.

She reached for the note.

IF YOU KNOW WHAT'S GOOD FOR YOU, YOU'LL STOP POKING AROUND AND MIND YOUR OWN BUSINESS. OR YOU'LL END UP LIKE MIA.

She dropped the note as her heart pounded, and her legs went weak. She leaned against the car. Then, belatedly looked around. Of course they weren't still here. Still, she couldn't shake the feeling she was being watched and goose bumps broke out on her arms. She had to get out of here.

With two fingers, she picked up the note and tossed it on the passenger seat. Locking the doors behind her, she called Kyle as she pulled out of the parking lot.

"Where are you?"

"On my way home."

"I'll meet you there."

The whole ride she wracked her brain trying to understand how she'd been found by Mia's traffickers. Had they known where Mia was staying and followed her last night? But how had they figured that out? Was Mia in danger again?

Or had the connection come through Gary somehow? Had someone discovered who all was on the camping trip? Had anyone else gotten any notes? She wasn't going to figure this out. That's what Kyle was for.

When she pulled in the driveway at home, Kyle's unmarked cruiser was parked out front. But he was standing by her front door, a scowl on his face.

She got out and hurried over.

He held a piece of paper in his gloved hand. "They know where you live too."

Austin texted Jessica to see how her day had been and if she was still planning on taking Mia to AA tonight.

Hey. Someone left a warning note on my car at the salon and at the house. Kyle's here.

What? Ice flashed through him. Was she in danger? **I'll be right over.**

Thanks.

With a shout to Matthew as to where he was going, he limped to his car and hopped in. Pushing the limit of how fast he could go between the traffic and the speed laws, he managed to get to her house quickly. He knocked on the door. He hadn't even met her parents yet, and he didn't want it to be under these circumstances.

Kyle opened the door. "Hey, Austin. Come on in." He headed down a tiled hallway to a family room.

Austin followed him.

Jessica sat on the couch, pale, arms crossed over herself. He sat next to her and took her hand.

Kyle lowered himself into the recliner. "When are your folks going to be home?"

"I'm not sure. They were going to either a museum or art gallery then meeting friends for dinner."

Kyle sighed. "These guys know where you live. They know where you work. You're not safe here. Until we find them, you have to go somewhere secure."

"I could stay with Melissa. I'll be house—" She broke off.

Austin knew what she was about to say, that she would be house-sitting for her after the wedding. The secret wedding Kyle didn't know about.

She swallowed. "I'm going to house-sit for her next time she visits Scott. So I'm sure she'd be okay with me staying there."

Kyle pursed his lips. "She has a good security system and no connection to your trip up the mountain. Can your folks go on vacation for a while?"

"I don't see why not. They're retired." She bit her lip. "Scott's coming into town Friday. They'll want to be here when he's in town. Plus there's the party Melissa's throwing him on Sunday."

Austin exchanged a glance with her.

"They don't have to go far," Kyle said.

She nodded then pulled out her phone. "I have something to show you." She swiped her screen then handed it to Kyle. "That's the back of our building. Mia said it's similar to where they were kept. And Mia told me Brianna escaped by shinnying up a pipe and out a window. On the picture there's an exhaust pipe under a small window. And there's a downspout. So I was thinking maybe you could see if the same company has built other similar projects."

He was quiet a moment. "Jessica, you need to stay out of this. These guys aren't anything to mess around with. Let us do our job."

"I know. I'm not doing anything. I just thought I'd point out a few things I'd noticed."

"I appreciate it, but no more. Okay?"

"I get it. Do you have any new leads on the case?"

"Yeah, some good ones. Knowing to look for the van was

helpful. Holcomb Springs sheriff's department found it abandoned. It had been reported stolen. They're processing it but don't expect to find anything. It's a moving target. We want to rescue the girls, and we also want to cut the head off this thing."

"Did you find the owner of the van?"

"It's a shell company, and it's taking time to track down the layers of ownership."

She leaned back against the couch cushions. "What was the name of that company again?"

"EM Import and Export. Why?"

"Next door to the salon is EM and Associates. I wonder if there's a connection."

Kyle made a note. "I'll check it out. We need to talk about your job."

"I don't want to give it up. I just got it. How's it going to look when I try to find another one?" Tears pooled in her eyes, and Austin squeezed her hand.

Kyle sighed and ran a hand through his hair. "We just have to get through these shell companies and figure out who's behind all this. We're close. I can feel it. If the paperwork and data trails don't kill us first. These guys are using technology to their advantage."

"So what's the problem with me keeping my job? They already know where I work. They're not going to do anything to me in front of all those women."

"It's them following you from work to Melissa's house."

"What if I took an Uber? They wouldn't know what car I would be in."

Kyle shook his head. "It's too risky. They still might be able to follow you. Why don't you call work and tell them you have a family emergency and can't come in the rest of the week. We should have this case wrapped up by then. We're close."

Jessica nodded. "Okay."

"Also, no seeing Mia. No taking her to AA or anything. You

can't see her or be seen with her. It's too dangerous for both of you."

Jessica nodded, but she looked miserable. Austin wished there was something more he could do for her other than sit here and hold her hand.

Kyle packed the notes in evidence bags while Jessica called Melissa.

The sound of the garage door going up was followed closely by the door from the garage opening as Jessica's parents came in. Austin guessed he was going to get to meet them now. He got to his feet.

A tall man with thick, white hair entered the family room, followed by a much shorter older woman. "Hey, Kyle. I thought that was your vehicle out there." He frowned. "Is there a problem?"

Jessica's mom came over and wrapped Kyle in a hug. "Good to see you, no matter the reason. We don't see you enough."

Jessica hung up the phone. "Mom, Dad, this is Austin Montgomery. Austin, these are my folks, Gerald and Janet Blake."

Austin shook hands with her dad and then her mom. They were older than his parents by quite a bit, but Jessica was the youngest, and they'd had her in their early forties. "It's nice to meet you."

"It's good to meet you. How's that leg of yours doing? I heard you took a nasty spill on that camping trip." Gerald pointed at his one pant leg that was bulkier than the other due to the knee brace.

"It's fine. Just a sprain."

"Well good." Gerald turned to Kyle. "What brings you by?"

"Not good news, unfortunately." He summarized what they knew about the notes and what they had decided. "You folks think you could stay at a hotel for a few days? Just until we wrap this up."

Gerald looked at Linda. "I suppose we could."

She nodded. "We should pack up. Did any of you eat? I could make some sandwiches or something."

Jessica put a hand on her mom's arm. "No, we can grab something after we leave. We need to hurry so Kyle can get home to his bride." She smiled at him. "I want to stay on Heather's good side."

Kyle laughed. "Me too."

"Okay, I need to go pack. Austin, you might as well get a tour of the house and come help." Jessica pointed out the kitchen as they passed it and then rooms down the hall until they came to hers. "Sorry, it looks like I'm still in high school. At some point, I'll paint the walls a more neutral color than purple."

She grabbed a bag from under her bed and began opening drawers.

He wandered over to her bulletin board and studied the pictures there. Then he spotted her terrarium, the rose quartz sitting in a place of prominence. It did something funny to his heart.

Jessica moved to the closet. "I don't know what I'm going to do if I'm not working. I guess I can help Melissa pack. I know she's been busy with work, trying to get things caught up before she leaves for a week." She threw a stack of clothes on the bed.

"I'm sure she'd appreciate that."

"Ooh, I've got to remember to bring my dress and shoes for the surprise wedding in case we don't get back here in time." She added a shimmery dress and a pair of sparkly sandals to the pile.

He motioned to the bed. "Ready for me to take a load to my car?"

"Sure. I'll just gather up my bathroom stuff."

Kyle was in the family room visiting with Gerald. Linda must be doing the packing. Austin motioned to the clothes. "I'm just running these out to my car."

Kyle nodded. "Yeah, Jessica needs to leave her car here." He turned to Gerald. "Can she park it in the garage?"

He nodded. "I'll move some things around."

Kyle followed Austin out, studying the street.

Austin put the clothes in the car and came back. "Do you think they're watching us?"

Kyle shook his head. "Doubtful. They're like cockroaches. They like to hide in the dark, coming out and scurrying away. But don't go directly to Melissa's, and keep an eye on your rearview mirror. They know your face too. Be careful."

Austin nodded. With one more trip, they were ready to go. Jessica wanted to bring her terrarium. Without anyone home to water it, she was afraid it would die. Austin set it on the floor in the back seat.

Jessica left her keys with her dad, and Kyle said he'd stay until they'd left.

She hugged her parents. "I'll talk to you in the morning."

Austin lifted a hand. "Good to meet you both." He touched the small of Jessica's back, and they headed down the hall. They'd just reached the front door when he heard, "Seems like a nice young man" from Jessica's mom.

Jessica smiled when they got in the car. "I do think you're a nice young man." She patted his leg. "And you must be starving. Melissa already ate, so we can just grab something for ourselves."

"In-N-Out?" He kept his eyes darting from the front to the mirrors.

"Sounds good."

After pulling into the drive-thru and taking a circuitous way to Melissa's while constantly checking that they weren't being followed, Austin was tense by the time they pulled in front of the townhome. She had the door open before they arrived and helped them bring in Jessica's bags and clothes. "You can take everything upstairs to the guest bedroom."

When all the bags were in, they sat down to eat, and Jessica filled Melissa in with more details. "I have to call the salon tomorrow. Not looking forward to that since Crystal was not happy with me today. But it means I'm available to help you pack." She put on a bright smile that Austin knew was a cover for what she was feeling.

Melissa squeezed her hand. "I appreciate it."

Once they'd eaten, there wasn't anything for him to do. Yet he didn't want to leave. Still. "I'm looking forward to our date tomorrow. I'll pick you up here instead." Duh. Could he state anything more obvious?

She nodded and touched his hand. "Thanks for the moral support. It really means a lot to me."

"Any time." He wrapped her in a hug then headed out the door.

Life had suddenly gotten a lot more complicated. He hoped Kyle was able to catch these guys quickly, because he was feeling the strain of work, keeping Jessica safe, and his feelings for her.

Chapter Twenty-One

Austin wiped his hands on his pants before knocking on Melissa's front door. This felt like a real date.

Melissa pulled the door open and smiled. "Hey, come on in."

Jessica stood in the living room. She wore some sort of long, summery dress that skimmed her sandals and tied around her neck in a floral print.

"You look nice."

"Thanks. You look pretty great yourself."

He'd opted for khakis and a button-down with the sleeves rolled up. He'd just been here yesterday. Why did he feel so nervous?

Melissa waved. "Have a good time."

"We will."

They headed out to his car. As they left the neighborhood and headed down El Toro toward the 5 freeway, Jessica asked, "So, is our destination a secret?"

He lifted a shoulder. "It won't be shortly. I thought Maggiano's for dinner and then…well, would you rather it be a surprise?" But what if she was expecting something bigger than what he had planned? He wasn't even sure if she'd like it.

"I'd like it to be whatever you want. You can tell me, or you can surprise me. I know I'll enjoy it, no matter what it is."

He figured he'd err on the side of just telling her. That way if she really hated the idea, they could think of something else. "Did you know there's a planetarium at Orange Coast College? They just put in a brand new one, state of the art. There's a show tonight." He glanced over to see her reaction as he merged onto the 405.

Her eyes widened, and she smiled. "That's fantastic. I love planetariums. What a great idea."

Heat suffused his face at her pleasure, along with relief. So he'd done something right. "I took a couple of astronomy courses in college and enjoyed them. I had kind of hoped that we'd get to look at the stars while we were up in the mountains. But that didn't happen. This seemed like a good alternative."

They arrived at Maggiano's and had a fantastic Italian dinner and dessert. As much as he'd liked the double date with Kim and Matthew, this was even better. After the camping trip, he felt closer to her, more able to open up. He thought about what Matthew suggested, about asking Jessica for help with work. He'd ask her later.

"How did your boss take your request for time off?" he asked between bites of lasagna.

Jessica lifted a shoulder. "I think she's still mad at me for some reason. She said she was fine with it, but her tone was kinda sarcastic. I don't know. I think she likes Lyric better. No one wants an employee who's got drama."

"But Madison likes your work."

"She does."

"I don't know how you work with all those emotions in the air." He shook his head.

"It's a salon. There are a lot of women. And a few men."

"Seems like a lot of wasted energy on the emotional turmoil that doesn't accomplish anything."

She laughed. "I've never thought of it that way, but yeah, it is."

"Do you want to keep working there if Crystal doesn't like you? Do you like the work?"

She poked around the remnants of her plate. "I don't want to quit the first job I got out of school. One, it wouldn't look good on my resume. Who would hire me after such a short stint? And, two, what's to say the next place will be better? I am learning a lot from Madison. Hopefully, Crystal will be in a better mood when I get back and I'll be fine."

He was just beginning to realize how much emotions were a part of the workplace. And it left him feeling unqualified.

After dinner, content and a little sleepy, they headed down to Orange Coast College. He found a parking spot, and as they headed toward the planetarium, he took her hand. They leisurely walked between the buildings to a central grassy quad which held the sleek, modern building in the center like a crown jewel. The planetarium looked a bit like something that would soar through space itself with its glass and steel resembling a swirling spiral galaxy.

Inside looked just as modern and high tech. They had some time before the show started, so they walked around and studied the various displays. The hall had many interactive science exhibits. He would have loved this as a kid. Heck, he loved it now. And he was pumped that Jessica seemed to be enjoying it too. Something they had in common.

Jessica tugged him to the railing around the Foucault pendulum. "I saw one of these at the Griffith Park Observatory on a school field trip. I could watch it all day."

A metal ball skirted just over the floor in what appeared to be a straight line, but a series of pegs around the perimeter, about a quarter of which had been knocked down, testified to the rotation of the earth under the pendulum.

As the metal sphere approached them, he saw their faces together reflected back. They looked happy and…together. With each swing, the pendulum skated closer and closer to the peg and finally knocked it down.

When the doors to the planetarium opened, they entered and settled themselves in the comfy reclined chairs. The dome above—replicating twilight—filled his vision completely.

Jessica squeezed his hand. "Thanks for thinking of this. I love how peaceful the star shows are. I almost feel like I'm floating when I look up."

"Me too."

The lights dimmed, and the show began. It was a fabulous show about space and the stars, but nothing compared to experiencing it with Jessica, holding her hand throughout.

When the show ended, they wandered through the gift shop. He wanted to give her something tangible to remember this night by, much in the same way he felt compelled to find her that perfect rose quartz.

She seemed to have almost as much fun in the gift shop, exploring the different items. She motioned to the various activity kits. "I wish I'd had something like this as a kid. Maybe I would have been more interested in science." She picked up a figurine of an astronaut. He held a flag that said REACH FOR THE STARS AND CATCH THE MOON. She laughed. "I like his attitude. He'd fit right in in my terrarium."

Austin nodded. That was it. "Let's get it." He paid for her little astronaut and handed her the bag as they walked outside. It was a warm summer night, and he didn't want the evening to end.

He led her over to a bench in the quad, and they sat. He gazed up. "Harder to see the stars here with all the light pollution." He glanced back down.

She was staring at him. Even someone as clueless as he was could read the desire in her eyes. He lowered his mouth to hers, wanting, needing her close. Pleasure twisted through his gut, and heat shot through his body. As her lips moved against his, he pulled her closer, wrapping his arms around her shoulders, hardly believing that such a woman could want a guy like him.

When her hands threaded through his hair at the base of his neck, he couldn't help the groan deep in his throat. If this is what kissing Jessica felt like, he never wanted to let her go. What had he ever done to deserve this moment?

When he broke the kiss, he touched his forehead to hers. "Wow." He had no words.

She smiled, tucking her just-kissed lip under her teeth. "Yeah, wow." She searched his eyes. "Thanks for a perfect evening, Austin."

He'd done something right. He'd made her happy, and for a moment, he'd unlocked the mystery that was Jessica.

JESSICA DIDN'T KNOW WHAT TIME IT WAS, AND SHE DIDN'T care. She didn't want this evening to end, this perfect and beautiful evening. If she thought she'd felt like she was floating in the planetarium, she was certain her feet weren't hitting the ground now. She and Austin had finally found their rhythm, and it was more powerful than anything she'd ever expected.

She leaned her head on his shoulder. "How was work this week?" A benign question, but she cared about how he spent his time. Plus, she knew there had been some stress and tension there.

He gave a husky laugh. "Funny you should ask." His hand rubbed up and down her shoulder, keeping her snugged up against him. "Matthew thinks I need your help."

She lifted his head to look at him. "What? Why me? I don't know anything about business."

"But you know about people, something I struggle with."

"I'm willing to do whatever you need, if you think it'll help. What's going on?"

He told her about his two failed presentations, about why he needed the director position instead of Randy. She listened, happy that he was opening up to her.

"Presentations have always been difficult for me. If I have something prepared, I can go through the facts and figures just fine. It's the off-the-cuff stuff and engaging the audience that I can't seem to master."

She thought for a moment. "What did you do in school?"

He gave a harsh laugh. "Prepared. Overprepared. In school there was a deadline and a rubric. I knew what was expected. And it didn't include engaging the audience. Real-life work is so much more nuanced and difficult."

She thought of her run-ins with Crystal this week and the little book she kept at work. Yeah, she'd agree with him on that.

"I think I have some trauma around presentations." His tone was light, but she knew there was something more serious under that. He let out a breath. "Gosh, I haven't thought about this in a long time. I don't know that I ever told anyone, even my parents at the time." He looked down at her. "You know, this can wait. I don't need to spoil the evening with bad memories."

"It's okay. I want you to tell me."

He nodded slowly. "It was in middle school. We had been assigned various presentations with different due dates. I don't even remember the topic. I do remember that I had prepared and done my research and had everything ready to go for when it was my turn. But the kid that was supposed to go before me was sick, so my teacher told me to come on up. I told her I was supposed to go tomorrow, that I had my presentation at home. She told me to come up anyway, that if I knew the material, I should be able to give it to the class without any crutches."

He shook his head. "I remember the same feeling coming back when Edward asked me to give a quick update without a slide deck. I just froze. Everything went out of my brain. It was like if I didn't have my tools, I couldn't even call up the information I knew was in my head. She told me I had procrastinated and hadn't prepared. When I tried to protest that I had, but I had been prepared to go tomorrow, she dismissed me. She then used me as an example to lecture the class on the importance of not leaving things to the last minute."

Anger stirred in Jessica at his words. Yeah, she knew how that felt to be judged unfairly because of someone else's perceptions of what you did and who you were.

"The next day I was prepared to give my presentation, but when I got up again, I just froze. Everything she said the day before kept playing through my head like a broken record, and I couldn't get over it. I got a D. The first and last one I'd ever gotten. And I really disliked that teacher for the rest of the year."

He paused and then looked at her. "Do I sound ridiculous or what?"

She kissed his cheek. "Not at all. I completely get it. I had a few teachers that had had my brothers. They put those expectations on me, and I could never live up to that. They never saw me for me."

"Somehow, though, I've got to get over this. If I don't, things are going to get bad. I can't work under Randy. I'd have to find another job."

"I'll help you. Tell me what's going on, and I'll give you my thoughts." She shivered a bit as the damp marine layer chilled her skin.

He pulled her in for a quick hug then stood, offering his hand. "Let's get some coffee. Sounds like we've got a lot to talk about."

Warmth spread through her that the marine layer couldn't touch. Austin wanted her help.

JESSICA ADDED ANOTHER BOX TO THE PILE ALONG THE WALL in Melissa's garage. Melissa had ordered a moving pod to be delivered when she and Scott got back from their honeymoon. Jessica had assured her that she'd keep packing while they were gone, even if she was back at work. Maybe Austin, and even Kim and Matthew, would come help in the evenings.

Melissa had conference calls throughout the day and spent a good amount of time in her home office, but the quiet gave Jessica time to reflect on the whirlwind that had been the past week.

Last night with Austin had been a fantastic date. They'd sat around drinking coffee and game planned ideas for his work around creating teams and competition with time limits and prizes. It was the best way to get engagement. If his team had fun and finished the SHIELD project ahead of time, they'd have to hire him as director.

In some ways, it helped that she didn't know much about his job. She had no preconceived ideas and no thoughts about what wouldn't work. She was able to toss out some concepts from the business books she'd been reading.

He'd seemed a bit overwhelmed, though he knew the idea had merit. It was just so out of his comfort zone and skillset. But when she asked if there was someone on his team who was gifted this way, his eyes lit up. It was like it was a foreign idea for him to use his team members to help where he was weak.

"Use them to help you brainstorm," she had told him. "And *when* you're director"—she had emphasized the when—"you can give that as an assignment to them and have regular updates on how it's going. The idea is to use the strengths of everyone around you."

"Yeah, I'm going to have to trust my team members."

"Yep."

He'd given her another toe-curling kiss when he'd walked her to the door last night. Sleep had been hard to come by, and she was paying for it today. She wanted to call him, but she was learning that he needed decompression time from his workday. He'd call when he was ready.

Her gaze landed on the little astronaut in her terrarium sitting on the kitchen counter. It made her giggle. But he was the first grown-up item in there. She spritzed the plants with the spray bottle then went about pulling items out of the fridge for dinner. It was hot, and she found the makings for a good salad with grilled chicken. Yum.

Melissa emerged from her office. "Wow, you did a lot of work today. The place is starting to look empty."

"It felt good to be useful. Salad with grilled chicken okay for dinner?"

"Sounds great. But you don't have to do that."

"I don't mind."

They ate off paper plates and chatted about the day. She had just thrown her plate in the trash when her phone buzzed. Austin. "I'm gonna head upstairs." She swiped the phone on as she plopped on her bed. Shivers chased through her body at the sound of his voice, recalling last night. They talked about everything and nothing. They made plans to go out tomorrow night, possibly with Kim and Matthew. Then Saturday was Joe's bachelor party, an all-day fishing trip with the guys. Sunday was the surprise wedding and the following Saturday the wedding everyone knew about.

Contentment settled over Jessica. She wished she could take Mia to AA meetings. It was a good reminder of how far she'd come. And how far she still had to go. But sitting here in Melissa's house, being helpful, and enjoying her company reminded her that she had indeed come a long way.

Chapter Twenty-Two

Austin's phone had been incessantly buzzing in his drawer since shortly after he got in this morning. He'd barely even started on his coffee. With a feeling of dread, he pulled it out. Five missed calls from Mom and a text.

Dad's in the hospital. Call me.

He tapped her number and cradled the phone on his shoulder while he pulled up flight times on his computer.

Fear laced Mom's voice as she told him Dad had fallen and hit his head. They were doing an MRI now.

He filled in the information on the screen to catch the next flight in an hour and a half. That would give him time to get home and throw a few things in a bag and head to the airport.

"I'm on my way. I'll see you in a couple of hours." He sent around a message to the team and grabbed his stuff. He stopped by Max's office and told him he had a family emergency. Max gave him his blessing and said he'd be praying.

Austin was on his way to see if Matthew could run him by the apartment and potentially the airport or if he would need to call an Uber. But Edward stopped him in the hallway.

"Austin. Glad I caught you. I was on my way to see you."

"I'm on my way out. I have a family emergency."

"This will just take a minute." Edward took Austin's arm and guided him to an empty room. "I wanted to let you know that, while I see how hard you're working and that you're fantastic at what you do, I don't see you as director material. It's not your skillset. I'm going to recommend to Max that he not hire you for that position."

Austin worked to keep his face neutral and his thoughts in their proper places. He could analyze all of this later on the plane. "I've actually just come up with a new plan. We started on it yesterday, and I planned on presenting it next week. I think you'll—"

"I appreciate the effort, I really do. And just so you know, I'm not recommending he hire Randy either. Randy's a jerk. But in the meantime, you have to go to his meetings, whether you want to or not." Edward gave a humorless laugh. "I gave HR the go-ahead to look for outside candidates. I wanted you to hear it from me first."

Austin gave a quick nod. "Thanks."

Edward stepped around him and strode out of the room.

Austin shook his head slightly. He was on his way to see Matthew. First things first.

Matthew had a free enough schedule that he was able to take Austin home, wait for him to pack a quick bag, and drop him off at the airport.

"Thanks, man. I'll let you know when I know something. It's too bad I have to miss Joe's bachelor party." He shook Matthew's hand then Matthew pulled him in for a bro hug.

After clearing security, Austin grabbed a sandwich and drink at Subway before heading to his gate. He was able to inhale it before it was time to board. He got one final text from Mom, saying how happy she was that he was coming, but that the doctors hadn't told her anything yet. Once he was in his seat, he let his mind click through the morning's events.

He couldn't believe Edward. Or maybe he could. If he were in Edward's shoes, would he give himself another chance after bombing two presentations? He thought maybe he would. But Max had warned him that Edward didn't have a lot of patience. The only saving grace was that Randy wasn't going to be hired either. But an outside person? Who knew what that would be like? It could be worse than Randy.

He let out a breath. No, this accident with Dad was a reminder of where his priorities should be. He was the only one available for them. His sister lived in Hawaii with her husband and two kids. She couldn't come help Mom if something happened to Dad. Austin needed to be in Phoenix.

The flight attendant gave a reminder to shut off all devices or place them in airplane mode. Without letting himself think too much about it, he sent off a quick text to Jessica.

Dad fell and I'm on a flight home. Not sure when I'll be back. I'm sorry, this isn't going to work with us. I need to be with my family. Will be looking at relocating to Phoenix.

He stared at the text, not sure if he should send it or not.

The flight attendant stopped by his seat on her way through the cabin. "Sir, you need to put your phone in airplane mode."

"Sure." He hit send and powered his phone off. But he couldn't get Jessica's face out of his mind.

Jessica had just finished scrubbing Melissa's oven—she didn't think they'd be doing much cooking over the next few days—when she saw the text on her phone from Austin. She smiled, thinking about their date tonight.

Until she read his words. Tears sprang to her eyes. She said a quick prayer for his dad. That had to be worrying him. But the rest of the text? How could he do this? They had such a great date Wednesday and a good conversation yesterday. She thought she'd really gotten through to him, and he'd gotten over his pulling away.

He had to be stressed about his dad. But she also knew that

what she had told him before was true. Ping-ponging with her feelings was a sure way to put her in a bad emotional state. And she definitely didn't want that. Even though she cared for Austin, she wasn't going to risk her sobriety over him, as much as it was breaking her heart.

And maybe the saving grace was that if he was in Phoenix, she wouldn't have to see him at Melissa and Scott's wedding. And he wasn't in danger from Gordo.

She thought of the quote from her Inspiration for Today app: "Things work out best for those who make the best of how things work out."—John Wooden. She was trying to make the best of this situation with Austin.

She scanned Melissa's townhome that was getting emptier and emptier. At least she had plenty to do, and she was helping someone else. There was some comfort in that. She thought of the verses in Isaiah 58 that talked about how helping other people was what God truly desired of us, that then her "light will break forth like the dawn, and your healing will quickly appear." It had been a section of Scripture she had clung to since Chelle had first shared it with her. Keeping her mind off herself and her problems and focusing on others had been a balm to the tender places in her soul.

And, oh, did she want quick healing.

After the Uber driver had dropped Austin off at Banner-University Medical Center in Phoenix, he tugged his carry-on behind him to the waiting room, backpack slung over his shoulder.

When Mom saw him, she jumped up. Tears spilled out of her eyes as she wrapped him in a hug. "You didn't have to come. But I'm glad you did."

When she let him go, he eased her into a chair. "Any word?"

She shook her head. "They told me it would be several hours."

"Have you eaten anything?"

She shrugged, wiping her eyes. "He fell before breakfast. With the ambulance and everything, there wasn't time. And I haven't wanted to leave here in case the doctors come out with news."

"I'll go get you something." He tucked his bags under the seat. "I'll be right back." He headed for the cafeteria, following the signs. Seeing his mom cry twisted something in him. He'd rather do something to help. So he'd get her food.

When he got back with a sandwich, fruit, and a bottle of water, she looked better.

"The doctor was here. He said there was a small brain bleed, but it wasn't too bad, better than they thought. They're going to keep him overnight for observation. As soon as they get him to a room, we can go sit with him. But he's going to have to use a walker for stability. He has one, but he forgets to use it."

Yeah, that was going to be a problem. But the news was good. And he was glad he could be here for Mom. Unfortunately, this was probably going to be the first of many hospital visits as Dad's dementia progressed.

He thought about Jessica, his job, and the life he'd begun to build in Laguna Vista. His heart squeezed at the thought of letting all of it go.

After a while, a nurse came over and told them Dad's room number. He and Mom made their way there.

Dad lay in a hospital bed, hooked up to an IV. He looked smaller and more frail than last time Austin had seen him, just a couple of months ago. Which scared him. Dad was the strongest person he knew.

Mom leaned over the bed and kissed Dad's cheek. "How are you doing?"

"I'm okay. I don't know what all the fuss is about." Then he spotted Austin. "Son? Is that you?"

Austin stepped closer to the bed, tweaking Dad's foot. "Yeah, thought I'd come out and see what was going on."

"Ah, you didn't need to." He grinned. "But I'm glad you did."

Austin pulled up chairs for Mom and him. And they visited like nothing was wrong, except that Dad was in the hospital with a bandage on his head and hooked up to monitors.

How long would Dad still remember him?

It wasn't too long before Dad dozed off. A nurse came in to check on him and told them to let her know if they needed anything. Mom turned on the TV and watched a show.

Austin grabbed his backpack. He noticed a glob of mud he hadn't cleaned off. Memories of last weekend flooded back. To stave them off, he pulled out his computer and opened it up. He scrolled through his contacts. Maybe he should start reaching out, seeing what opportunities might be here.

His stomach clenched. Phoenix was only an hour flight from Laguna Vista. Maybe he and Jessica could still make something work. But that was ridiculous. With both of their jobs, it would be hard to find time, and going out of town frequently would get tiring and expensive, cutting down on how often they'd end up seeing each other. Their relationship would die a slow and painful death. Better to cut it off now.

For once, though, his logic was of no comfort to his aching heart.

But there was something he could do. He thought about what Kyle said about the data and paperwork they were having to dig through to find the true owners of the shell companies. Data was something he knew well. He pulled up one of his data scraping programs. With a few modifications, he might get it to work helping solve the mystery of the identity of the head of the trafficking ring.

Jessica glanced up from the sink she'd been mindlessly scrubbing when Melissa came out of her office.

It was clear she immediately noticed Jessica's bloodshot eyes. "Oh, honey. What's wrong?" She came around to the kitchen and pulled her into a hug.

She poured out the story of Austin's text. She sniffed back tears, and Melissa handed her a tissue, guiding her over to the couch.

Dabbing at her eyes, Jessica leaned back against the couch. "I know he's just not ready. And normally, I'd really want a drink to make the pain go away. Nothing has hurt this bad since I've been sober."

Melissa patted her leg. "But you are staying sober." She glanced at her phone. "Come with me to get Scott. His flight gets in soon, and you shouldn't be by yourself."

"Don't you guys want some alone time?"

"We'll have plenty this week and from now on. Let's pick him up, grab some food, and then I'll drop him off at Joe's later."

"Thank you." Jessica gave her a watery smile.

An hour later they were at the arrivals area of the airport. "You go in and surprise him at baggage claim. I'll drive in circles." Jessica got out and took Melissa's place in the driver's seat. She wanted them to have a little privacy—as much as a public place allowed—for their reunion. Luckily this was the last time they'd be doing this as single people.

She was on her second loop around the airport when Melissa texted her. She began searching for them, spotting Melissa and Scott with their arms around each other, smiles on their faces. She pulled up to the curb in front of them and hopped out, giving her brother a hug. Tears unexpectedly pricked her eyes. It was good to see him.

They got his luggage loaded and soon were headed off to their favorite taco place.

Over dinner, they caught him up on what had been going

on, details of the camping trip he hadn't heard, and finally she told him about Austin.

He reached over and touched her hand. "I know a little something about running away. Remember when you found me in Monterey last year?" He gave a rueful smile.

She smiled back. "Yeah. I do. You were the first person I told about my commitment to sobriety."

"I just needed time to process how much my life was changing. We guys don't grasp our emotions as well as you women do. I bet that's what's going on with Austin right now. It's just too much all at once." He slipped his arm around Melissa's shoulders. "The changes were so much better than I knew at the time. I saw that once I got my head on straight. He will too. If he doesn't, you don't want him anyway."

She was thinking about Scott's words as they headed back to Melissa's when her phone rang. Kyle.

"Hey, Kyle. I'm in the car with Scott and Melissa. We just picked him up at the airport. Can I put you on speaker phone?"

"Yeah. You'll all want to hear this."

She tapped the speaker icon and held the phone close to the front seat.

"Go ahead," Jessica said.

"Hey, Scott. Welcome home. We'll catch up tomorrow at Joe's bachelor party. The good news is we got Gordo. He was driving in the bike lane, nearly ran a biker off the road. The biker was so mad, he called 911 and followed him, giving the dispatcher the plate and make of the car. There happened to be a patrol officer nearby who spotted him and pulled him over. He recognized him from the sketch we had put out and arrested him."

A burden fell off Jessica's shoulders. "That's fantastic news. Does Mia know?"

"I told them first. She's coming in to ID him. But here's the thing. We still don't have the head of this organization. We're close, and we don't want to tip our hand. So don't get careless."

"I'll be careful. Thanks for calling."

For a moment, she thought about texting Austin the news. No, he would need to make the next move. He was in Phoenix anyway. Gordo wasn't a concern to him. And he would be worried about his dad.

At Melissa's, she disappeared upstairs to give her brother and his bride-to-be some privacy. As she lay on her bed, she did everything she could to not think about Austin.

Chapter Twenty-Three

The next morning, Jessica was out to breakfast with Melissa, Scott, Joe, and Sarah at the Original Pancake House, her favorite place for breakfast. With any other group of couples, it might have felt weird being the only single person. But they were like family, and it was great to be included. Plus, coffee and carbs could cure almost anything. She dug into her blueberry pancakes with blueberry compote syrup and whipped cream.

Her phone buzzed, and she pulled it out of her purse, her heart hoping against hope it was Austin.

Instead it was Madison. **Hey, I know you've got a family emergency going on, but could you come to the salon for a few hours this afternoon? They moved my kid's soccer game, or maybe I wrote it down wrong. Anyhow, I can't miss the whole thing. If you can come in and help out, I'll be able to catch most of it. And Crystal won't be around :)**

With Gordo caught, there was no reason not to. **Sure. I'll be there.**

Then she remembered she didn't have a car. Kyle probably wouldn't want her driving hers. She turned to Melissa. "Do you mind dropping me off at the salon? Madison is in a bind and needs my help for a few hours this afternoon."

Melissa frowned. "Do you think it's safe?"

"Why wouldn't it be? They caught Gordo, who is the only one who knows what I look like. I won't be driving my car or coming from my house."

"But they know you work at the salon."

"I can't imagine them doing anything there. Too many people around. I promise not to leave the salon until you come to get me."

Melissa looked around the table. "What do you guys think?"

Scott shook his head. "I don't know. I'm sure it's fine, but to be on the safe side, you should stay away until Kyle and Collins can shut this ring down."

"If it were any other time, I would agree with you. But I need to keep this job, and Madison has gone to bat for me. If I have any chance at all of keeping it, I need her support. The least I can do is help her out for a few hours."

Scott let out a breath. "Okay, but let one of us know if the slightest thing seems off. Okay?"

"I will. Trust me, I don't want anything to happen to me either."

After Dad had been discharged the next morning, Austin helped Mom get him settled at home. Once Dad was in his recliner and Mom was in the kitchen making the coconut cream chicken soup Dad was craving, he turned to Austin. "Tell me what's been going on with you. How was your camping trip?"

Austin gave him the high points then slowly added in more details as Dad probed. Including, finally, about Jessica.

"She sounds like a brave young woman with lots of character."

Austin nodded. "She is, but I don't think it's going to work out."

"Why?"

Austin let out a breath. "Because I'm moving back here so I can help Mom take care of you."

Dad was quiet for a moment, his jaw working, a sure sign that he was thinking of something serious. "You need to go back home, son. I don't want you moving here. You have a life in Orange County. This disease is slowly taking away my life, and it's taking a lot of your mother's. But she pledged to stick with me for better or worse, in sickness and in health. I both hate that and love that."

He pointed at Austin. "But you, I don't want you giving up your life. You want to use your research and big brain to find fancy gadgets that make our life easier, okay. But go back and do your job. I know you. You are using your sense of duty to disguise your fear."

Austin started to protest. He wasn't afraid.

But Dad didn't let him continue. "I was so proud of you going to Laguna Vista and branching out. Make a good life there for yourself." Dad's eyes filled with tears. "Maybe when I'm gone your mom will want to come live by the ocean. Do that for her."

Austin swallowed the golf ball that had appeared in his throat, hot tears stinging his eyes. When he could finally speak, he said softly. "Okay, Dad. If you're sure that's what you want."

Dad gave him a gentle smile. "It's what I want." He held out his hand, and Austin rose and let Dad envelop him in the kind of hug he hadn't had since he was a boy.

Feeling sluggish after all those delicious carbs for breakfast, Jessica got out of the shower and proceeded to do her hair and makeup. Even on a Saturday, everything about her appearance had to be perfect for the salon. She sorted through her clothes. She hadn't planned on going into work, so she had only brought casual clothes. Still, it was only for a few hours. She picked out a turquoise flowy top and skinny jeans, pairing them with wedge sandals. It would have to do.

In the car, Melissa asked her what she wanted to do tonight when she got back. "The guys invited us to join them for dinner at Claim Jumper, but I think they should have the whole day together. After fishing at Irvine Lake and being in the sun all day, they might not smell the greatest either."

They laughed.

"Do you think Scott will regret not having a bachelor party?" Jessica asked.

Melissa shook her head. "These are all the same guys that he would have invited, other than a few that he's served with. Some of those are coming down tomorrow. Whether the other guys know it or not, they're essentially at Scott's bachelor party too."

They chatted about the wedding plans for tomorrow and what needed to be done. Melissa was going to pack for her honeymoon while Jessica was at the salon, then Kim was coming over this evening and they'd handle all the last-minute details.

"Do *you* mind not having a bachelorette party?"

Melissa shook her head. "Nope. You and Kim and I will have fun tonight. Poor Sarah is already stressed out about the bridal luncheon next Friday."

Jessica laughed. "Yeah, Sophia is planning it, insisted on it, even though Heather is the matron of honor and had planned on a spa day. Sarah decided to give in for the sake of family harmony."

"Sounds like Sarah. And with my wacky family dynamics, that's exactly what I didn't want to deal with."

"Is everyone coming in tomorrow?"

"Yeah, Larry's renting an SUV and driving Mom, Brittany, Daniel, and Nikki out. They're leaving Phoenix tomorrow morning, spending the night Sunday night and leaving early the next morning. Collins has graciously agreed to put them up at his house. I suspect they'll be disappointed when they realize I won't be around the next morning before they leave. But it is what it is."

Melissa pulled up to the salon. "I'll plan on being back here in three hours. Call me if you need me sooner or if anything feels off."

Jessica nodded as she got out of the car. "Thanks. I'll see you in a bit. Last night as a single lady." She laughed.

Austin had his flight booked and was all packed when he opened his computer and checked his data-scraping program. It turned up something in Nevada. Several of the shell companies were incorporated there. He pulled up the information on the company ownership. Eric Moritz. EM. Made sense. Though why the guy had used his own initials, he didn't know. Seemed kinda dumb. Or maybe just egotistical.

The brand on Mia's wrist popped into his mind. Just the kind of guy who would brand anything he considered his property. But hers was a WE, wasn't it? She'd never said. He sketched it out.

Then slowly turned it upside down. EM with a backwards E.

He called Kyle. He'd want to know. Even if he was at Joe's bachelor fishing trip. But he didn't answer. The cell service probably wasn't the greatest out there at the lake. But he'd keep trying. And maybe he could dig up something else.

Now that he had a name… He changed a few parameters and did a search for Eric Moritz. He'd let it run and check it again while he was waiting to board.

He packed up his computer and set his bags by the front door. He didn't want Mom to leave Dad alone to take him to the airport, so he called an Uber, which would be here any minute.

He hugged his folks goodbye.

"Let me know what she says, okay?" Dad had a twinkle in his eye.

Austin couldn't pretend to not know what he was talking about. "I will. Love you both." He kissed Mom's cheek then headed out the door.

After getting dropped off at the airport and making it through security, he grabbed some food and sat at the gate. He pulled his computer up to see what, if anything, his program had turned up. There was an article linking him to Crystal Moritz, his wife, owner of Salon Moritz.

His blood ran cold. Good thing Jessica hadn't been back to the salon. But he needed to warn her.

He got called to board, and he stowed his computer, trying to call Kyle one more time. Giving up, he sent him a text. At least he'd see it when he got to his phone.

Then he tried Jessica. She didn't answer. She might be mad at him. No *might* about it. She was mad at him, and she had every right to be. He left her a voice mail as he found his seat. "Please call me. I found out information about Mia and the salon." There, hopefully that would intrigue her enough to call him without broadcasting his business to everyone around who could hear him in the tight confines of the airplane.

Still, an uneasiness rested in his gut. It wasn't like her to pull away. She was probably helping Melissa pack, so why wasn't she answering her phone?

He sent her a text. Unlike him, she didn't withdraw from people when she was hurt or overwhelmed. Was she really that upset with him?

He typed out all the details he knew just before the flight attendant made him turn off his phone. He hoped that would be enough. But until he landed in an hour, he wouldn't know.

Jessica picked up the blow-dryer. "I can take it from here. You get to your son's soccer game."

"Thank you. You're a life saver!" Madison gave her a quick hug.

"Happy to help."

Madison grabbed her purse, said goodbye to her client, and leaned in to whisper to Jessica. "Will you be back Tuesday?"

"I should be."

Madison squeezed her shoulders. "I'll see you then."

The time had gone by quickly. This was the last client, and then Melissa would be here to pick her up. She finished the blowout, checked out the customer, and cleaned up the workstation. There was one other stylist here, she thought, but she was on the other side of the salon where Jessica couldn't see her. She'd track her down before she left to make sure she could lock up.

She grabbed her purse out of her locker and took out her phone to text Melissa. Austin had texted her. Huh. She didn't look at them. There'd be time for that later. She wasn't sure she was ready to hear whatever he might say. She shot a quick text to Melissa saying she was ready, just in case she wasn't already on her way.

Heading out to the front lobby, she could hear a blow-dryer in the background. Waiting for it to turn off or Melissa to show up, she opened Austin's text.

Oh my gosh. No. How had she missed it? EM. Eric Moritz. Crystal Moritz? Cold sweat beaded over her, and all she wanted to do was run. Where was Melissa? Should she go outside to meet her?

The front door lock *snicked* shut, and she looked up.

Crystal stood there. "Dear Jessica. You just couldn't keep your nose out of my business, could you?"

"Um." She tried for a casual pose against the desk. "I don't know what you're talking about. I just came in to—"

Crystal reached over and snatched Jessica's phone out of her hand. "You won't be needing this." She unlocked a drawer and tossed it in, locking it back up.

Do something! But what? Too many thoughts collided through her brain. She was having trouble wrapping her mind around the idea of Crystal being part of a trafficking ring. How? *Why?*

"Don't deny it. I can see it all over your face. And it was pretty well spelled out in those texts. It doesn't matter because as soon as my husband gets here, you won't be my problem anymore. It's too bad. You really had potential as a stylist. I was going to offer you the position."

"Really? I thought you liked Lyric better."

"I don't need more catty women on staff. You cared about the clients, were always trying to help out. But that propensity of yours to help others has gotten you in trouble." Crystal blocked Jessica's access to the other part of the salon where the back door was.

She could run to the back, to Madison's station, but there was no way out that direction. Though there were scissors. She couldn't imagine stabbing Crystal. It would have to be a last resort. Instead, she tried to think. How could she outwit the woman or get the keys from her somehow? Could she tackle her?

"This is an expensive place to live. I like my position of influence in society as owner of a prestigious salon. I like my designer clothes, tropical vacations, and creature comforts. I really didn't know what my husband did to make money. He was in import and export, like many businessmen. I didn't care about the details of his inventory." She let out a sigh. "But like most men, he needs a woman to come and clean up his mess."

"How can you…" Jessica couldn't even find the words. "You help women feel beautiful here. How can you participate in their destruction and abuse?"

Crystal gave a short laugh. "This isn't about beauty, my dear. It's about image. Don't confuse the two."

Jessica realized she no longer could hear the blow-dryer. But she did hear footsteps.

A man appeared behind Crystal. He must have come in through the back door. He put a hand on Crystal's shoulder. "So this is the infamous Jessica. I can't decide if you're brave or stupid. Maybe both. No matter. We need to have a talk. You've created quite a bit of work for me. But don't worry. You'll repay me for it."

Her heart pounded. Maybe he was right. She was stupid for coming here. One more bad decision in a string of many. But she wasn't brave. *Please, God. Show me a way out.* She knew what Mia had been through. Not all of it, but enough. She did not want to experience that or anything close to it.

He glanced down at Crystal. "She's a little older than our customers like, but we can make good use of her. Take care of a problem and make some money at the same time. I warned you to stay out of our business."

He took a step toward her, and she dodged behind a display, shoving it over toward him. A crash of glass and the cacophony of bottles bouncing and spilling echoed off the marble floor and walls.

She glanced over his shoulder, trying to figure out how to get past him to the back door. Buy some time until Melissa came.

Melissa! What would happen when she showed up? Would she be walking into danger too? Oh man, maybe she never should have helped Mia. She was just causing more problems for people she cared about. Scott would be devastated if something happened to Melissa because of her.

She dodged around Eric, but he grabbed her arm. She tried to wrench away.

"Not so fast." He held something in his hand. A gun.

Her legs went weak, and it was all she could do to keep from collapsing.

"We're going for a little walk."

She shot a pleading glance at Crystal, but Crystal turned and walked the other way.

Chapter Twenty-Four

Austin powered up his phone as soon as the plane landed. No calls or texts from anyone. His gut twisted. Something wasn't right. He ordered his ride then called Melissa. "Sorry to call, but Jessica's not answering my calls or texts. I found out important information. Haven't heard from Kyle either." He hoped she would infer what he meant about important information.

The plane taxied to the gate, but Austin couldn't get out of his seat fast enough. A number of people ahead of him blocked the aisle.

"Jessica's at the salon, so that's probably why she's not answering."

It took him a minute to register Melissa's words. "What do you mean she's at the salon?"

"She went in to help Madison. Kyle said they arrested Gordo, so she figured it was okay. I'm on my way to pick her up right now.

No, no, no! "Melissa, the salon's owner is married to the head of the ring," he growled into the phone. He glanced around, but nobody was paying him any attention.

"Oh, no! I'm pulling into the parking lot right now. Wait, Scott's calling."

As the silence grew in his ear, he was able to exit the plane and run up the jetway, passing people who probably thought he was rude. He didn't care.

Melissa came back on the line. "Scott was calling to see if Jessica was still at the salon. Kyle got your text and voice mail finally. They're on their way here, but Kyle is sending units ahead. Help will be here shortly." Her voice wavered.

He exited the terminal and headed to the ride share pickup area, spotting his driver. He climbed in. "I'm in a hurry. Someone's in danger."

The driver gave him a wide-eyed looked and nodded, pulling out of the parking lot.

"I'm on my way, Melissa, but I'm glad they're almost there. Can you see anything?"

"There are two cars in the parking lot, but no one has come out of the salon. Jessica had texted me earlier that she was ready to go, but I've heard nothing since. I'm going to see if the salon is open. Maybe it'll be okay." He heard her get out of the car, and her breath came quickly over the phone.

He cursed himself for not being there. Dad hadn't really needed him, though Mom had appreciated his presence. Still, if he hadn't let his feelings of overwhelm chase him and if he had controlled his knee-jerk reaction to run away, maybe things would be different.

Nothing he could do about it now.

"The doors are locked. I'm peering inside. It's all dark." A quick intake of breath. "Looks like there was some sort of a struggle." Her voice caught. "There's a display knocked over."

"Go get in your car and lock the doors until the police come. Keep the engine running in case you need to leave quickly. I'll be there soon."

"Stay on the phone with me?" He heard the car door shut, the door locks click, and the engine start.

"Yeah, I'll stay on the phone with you."

But all he could think about was that EM and Associates owned the salon and the building attached to it. He remembered the picture Jessica had showed Kyle of the back of the building. It wasn't a building *like* that one where they held the girls.

It *was* that building.

ERIC SHOVED JESSICA DOWN THE STAIRS.

She stumbled, losing her balance. Only grabbing the stair railing kept her from falling the rest of the way.

"Don't worry. Someone will come get you. Eventually." He chuckled then shut and locked the door behind him.

Jessica studied her surroundings. The room was dim. The only light came from the windows set near the ceiling. The walls were cinderblock, and this staircase and door was the only way in and out. The concrete floor had various stains on it.

Was it some sort of storage room? But there was nothing in here.

Slowly it dawned on her.

She remembered taking a picture of the back of the building and asking Kyle to look for something like this one.

Except it wasn't *like* this building. It *was* this building. This was where they had kept the girls. She saw the stains on the floor in new light.

Oh, Lord. How could people be so horrible to each other?

She lowered herself to the bottom step. Time to think. Melissa was likely here already looking for her. The salon doors were locked. Would she knock? What would she do when Jessica didn't answer any of her calls or texts? She'd call Kyle. Okay, so as long as Melissa was safe—and Jessica was going to assume she was for the moment since she hadn't been thrown down here with her—then help could be on the way.

But how would they know where she was?

And if Eric knew they were on to him, would he bug out, or would he try and take her with him as insurance? So many unknowns. She remembered Kyle's words about desperate men being dangerous.

She glanced around the area again. She didn't expect to find a weapon; they would have removed anything the girls could have used.

Then she saw it. The pipe. And the window.

But, man, she had no idea how Brianna had done it. No wonder the traffickers hadn't seen it as a threat. Who knew how to shinny up a pipe to a window fifteen feet high? Jessica was not athletic. She was wearing skinny jeans and wedges, for goodness sakes.

She walked over to the pipe, studying it. There were clamps holding the pipe to the wall at regular intervals. Maybe they could work as footholds. Nothing to do but to try it. Unless she got partway up and fell, breaking every bone in her body.

Then she wouldn't be useful to Eric at all. And she was certain that he wouldn't be charitable enough to get her medical help. No, if she wasn't useful, then there was no point in keeping her around. Or alive.

Maybe she should just wait until he came back or someone came for her. Help was on the way. No point in risking serious injury if she didn't need to.

But then…was it her imagination, or did she smell smoke?

She scanned the area. It was difficult to see in the dim light, but there were air vents near the ceiling.

And a definite haze of smoke.

If Eric thought he had been caught, why not burn the place down to hide the evidence?

She studied the pipe again. Okay. She kicked off her shoes and grabbed the pipe. She jumped, trying to wrap her legs around it, but she just slid down. How did people do this? How did Brianna do this? There had to be a way.

If she stretched up, she could reach the first clamp with her foot. She put her foot on it and then pressed down with her weight. *Ow*, that hurt. The metal cut into her toes. She hopped back down. Should she put her shoes back on?

The smoke was getting thicker. And it would get worse as she climbed higher. Assuming she could climb higher.

She slipped her shoes back on. Okay, now at least she could get to the first clamp and put weight on it. But the extra thickness of her shoes gave her very little room to balance on. She had to grip the pipe tightly with her arms.

She stepped up to the next clamp, transferred her weight, and grasped the pipe a bit higher up. She did it a few more times, getting a bit of a rhythm going.

Then her foot slipped.

Austin threw the driver a twenty as an extra tip and hopped out, running to Melissa's car. She unlocked the doors and let him in.

Sirens sounded in the distance. As soon as the police got here, they would make him and Melissa leave.

"Look, they've got security cameras around here. They could be watching us. Let's pretend to leave. As soon as they hear the sirens, who knows what's going to happen?"

"Where are we going to go?"

He opened his phone to the Google map he had of the area. "Go around to that street there."

She turned the corner just as the police pulled up, blocking the parking lot entrances.

"Are you on the phone with Kyle?" He noticed her phone sitting in its holder.

"Scott."

"Turn down this alley."

She did and eased forward until the nose of her car pointed

to a retaining wall overlooking a parking lot below them that backed up to the salon's building.

Smoke was drifting out of the eaves and windows. But the police wouldn't let the fire department get in there until it was safe for them.

"He lit the place on fire." He smacked his fist on the dashboard. "We've got to get her out of there. Scott, tell Kyle I know where she's at. At least I think I do. There's a window in the back of the building near the top of the first floor. That's how Brianna got out. If he's holding Jessica where he held the girls, maybe we can get Jessica out that way too."

Scott said something, to Kyle presumably.

"Scott, tell Kyle to pull around back in the alley and get under the window. If she comes out that way, she won't have as far to go if she can land on his truck."

More voices from Scott's end. "Okay. We're two minutes out."

It felt like the longest two minutes ever. The smoke billowed thicker, and now there were flames.

Then, not sure if he was imagining it, the window seemed to move. No, he wasn't imagining it. It was moving. He leaped out of Melissa's car, and eased himself over the retaining wall, putting his weight on his good leg, before sprinting across the parking lot and to the back of the building. He didn't even feel his knee. He heard shouting, but his single focus was on that window.

Jessica's head appeared. *Thank you, Jesus!* "Jessica, I'm here. Kyle's going to bring his truck back here so you don't have so far to go. Just wait."

"Austin! Why are you here? Never mind, I can't wait. The ceiling's on fire. I'll risk a broken ankle." She shimmied the top part of herself out the window. "Maybe I can leap for that downspout. Not sure it'll hold me."

"I'll catch you if you fall."

She got one leg over the edge, then the other.

He braced himself.

An officer ran up to him. "It's not safe for you to be here."

Austin pointed up. "Get something to help."

The officer said something, but Austin ignored him, his attention on Jessica.

She slid off the window's edge but only moved a few inches. She looked back over her shoulder. "My shirt's stuck on something. I can't see what." She let go and tried to reach it, but she couldn't. "I can't get it." Panic edged her voice.

Flames lit the back of the window. Where was Kyle? The officer could bring a unit around here, but there wasn't time.

The downspout. He didn't know if it would hold his weight, but he had to try. He braced the edges of his feet on the pipe and began climbing. When he pulled even with the window, he wrapped one arm around the pipe and leaned, hearing the metal creak. *Stay in there a bit longer.*

"Put your arms around my neck."

She leaned forward, and her weight fell on him. He didn't think anything had felt sweeter. He could see clearly where her shirt was caught on a seam in the metal of the frame. But the more he tugged, the deeper it wedged.

"I'll buy you a new shirt." He pulled against the seam, where the fabric had begun to tear, and ripped it further until the main part came loose.

The rest of her landed against him, and the drainpipe tore from its anchors in the wall, swinging them down toward the alley.

And in front of the grille of a truck.

Jessica opened her eyes. She was on top of Austin, who was laying on the asphalt. Kyle's truck stopped in front of them. Melissa hovered over them.

"Are you okay?" She touched his jaw, hardly believing he was here.

Austin's dark brown eyes stared into hers. "Never better." He grinned. "Are you hurt?"

She shook her head. Then she leaned forward and lowered her lips to his, needing to make sure he was real, that he was truly here.

He responded with the passion she felt, and it wasn't until a few cleared throats and whistles that she remembered they weren't alone. She pushed off him, and Kyle gave her a hand up.

"Let's get out of here so the fire department can get to work." Kyle motioned to his pickup truck bed, and she, Austin, and Melissa climbed in. Scott was already back there, and Joe was directing the incoming resources. Kyle pulled them around the building to the far end of the front parking lot, far enough away to be safe.

But Jessica had Austin's arms around her, and that was all she needed.

Chapter Twenty-Five

It had been a late night last night at the police station, both she and Austin answering questions about what they knew and what she had experienced. When the fire department had finally gotten the fire out, they found two bodies that were presumed to be Eric's and Crystal's. It would take some time for them to be officially identified, but Kyle said Eric had probably felt cornered when the police showed up and thought he had no way out. It would take some time to uncover and dismantle how far reaching the ring actually was.

The salon was a total loss too. So regardless, Jessica was out of a job. At least this wasn't her own doing. But other stylists relied on the salon for their income. It wasn't going to be easy to recover from the destruction the Moritzes had left in their wake.

Jessica stretched and climbed out of bed. She had a big scrape on her leg where one of the pipe clamps had gouged her when her foot slipped, and her arms hurt from so much effort.

As much as her folks had wanted her to come home, all of her things were at Melissa's. It was Melissa's wedding day, and Jessica was determined to make it special, no matter what had happened the night before.

She hadn't even had any time to talk to Austin; she wasn't

sure today would be much better. Kim would be here soon to help her with the myriad details that needed to be seen to so Melissa wouldn't be stressed and no one would guess about the surprise wedding. First of which included getting a new phone, since hers was now ashes.

Plus, she was helping Melissa with her hair and makeup, something that felt like an honor.

The surprise wedding ended up being the best thing that could have happened after yesterday with all that there was to do and look forward to.

The Salt Creek Grille had a special entrance to the patio garden from the outside sidewalk, and they had put up a chalkboard sign that said MELISSA & SCOTT'S PARTY. Nice. They'd remembered that the wedding was a surprise. Now if all the other details fell into place, it would be a fantastic evening. The staff at Salt Creek Grille had never done a surprise wedding before, but they loved the idea and got behind it.

Rectangular tables that seated ten each were set up around the perimeter of the patio with space for a dance floor in the middle. At the head was a greenery arch, and off to one side was a drink station and a buffet. A little fancy for just a going-away party, but she didn't think anyone would complain.

Melissa looked beautiful in her dress, with her hair pulled back at the top, soft curls cascading around her shoulders. Scott wore a button-down shirt and khakis. For now. They stood at the entrance and greeted people. One of Kim's friends from the design world casually took pictures of the event.

A few people commented that it looked like this space had been either just used for a wedding or was getting set up for one.

Soon, folks had filled their plates and found their seats. Soft music filled the air as the sun headed toward the sea and turned the sky peachy pink above them. The mature trees surrounding the patio gave it the air of their own private space.

Scott went to the microphone under the arch and welcomed everyone. "Thanks so much for coming. I won't be back in this area for some time, so I appreciate the chance to get to visit with you all. So let me ask the blessing and we can eat. Heavenly Father, thank you so much for all the many blessings you have bestowed on us. We are rich with your gifts of friends and family, of people to do life with. We know our futures are in your hands, and that everything is for our good and your glory. Most of all, we thank you for the gift of your Son, Jesus Christ. Bless this food and fellowship in his name, Amen."

He scanned the room. "Enjoy your dinners. They are on me tonight."

Hoots, hollers, and applause accompanied that announcement.

Jessica and Kim had come together, and Matthew and Austin had met them there. They all sat at the last table to keep an eye on things, and she and Austin hadn't been able to say more than just what was needed to pull the party off. They needed to talk, but she didn't see it happening tonight. Tonight was about Scott and Melissa.

When Scott excused himself from his table, Jessica knew it was time. She met Melissa's gaze with a grin.

Austin and Matthew moved to the back and set up a phone on a tripod, focusing it on the arch. They opened Zoom and started a meeting room. All those who couldn't come were given a link to join the party virtually.

It took a minute for the crowd to register that Scott had changed into his service dress whites. With the full medals and the sword, he looked every bit the hero Melissa deserved. He strode to the microphone and held out his hand for Melissa to join him.

"I wanted to thank you all again for coming. It means so much to Melissa and I that we've had your support. It's been hard being away from her, so I thank you all for being there for her when I couldn't be." His gaze turned to Melissa.

The love that shone between them took Jessica's breath away. Someday, maybe Austin would look at her like that.

Scott turned back to the crowd. "Since you're all here and I won't be back for a year, why don't Melissa and I just get married tonight?"

Gasps and laughter and applause ran through the group.

"You all up for that? Surprise! Welcome to our wedding!"

The volume increased as family and friends voiced their approval of the plan.

"Pastor Tom, come on up." Scott turned and took both of Melissa's hands in his.

As they exchanged their vows, Jessica glanced around the room. Sarah's eyes were bright with happy tears, Joe's arm around her shoulder. Good. Jessica had a moment of panic that Sarah might have felt upstaged, though that was so unlike Sarah. Still, it was good to see how happy she was for them.

Allie caught her gaze and mouthed, *Did you know about this?*

Jessica grinned and nodded.

Allie smiled back. Good. Jessica was glad Allie didn't feel left out.

The Ellis clan had made it from Phoenix with minimal drama. Their mom adored Collins, and she didn't seem upset about not being in on Melissa's surprise.

"I now pronounce you husband and wife. You may kiss your bride."

Scott wrapped Melissa in his arms and tenderly kissed her to the applause of everyone.

The restaurant staff brought out the wedding cake and a dessert buffet.

Austin manned the camera phone, capturing every activity for the virtual guests.

Scott and Melissa cut the cake. Joe and Kyle both rose to the occasion with spontaneous toasts, tributes to their lifelong friendships.

And then the music started. Scott swept Melissa onto the dance floor for their first dance as husband and wife to "Our Love Is Here to Stay."

At the end of the song, Scott invited everyone to the dance floor. He went to Mom and held out his hand, while Melissa approached Dad. Tears sprang to Jessica's eyes. How was it for Melissa to have these special occasions without a parent? Then again, she'd never known anything differently. Scott swept up Melissa's mom as well. He was so charming—if she did say so herself—that she couldn't help but think Melissa's mom would be endeared to him.

Dad came over and spun Jessica around the floor a bit. "Your mom and I are proud of you, Jessica. You've come a long way. You've been very brave this past week."

She was glad she'd decided to wear waterproof mascara, because her eyes kept welling up. "Thanks, Dad. That means a lot."

As the sun disappeared and stars began to twinkle in the twilight, the soft, salt-tinged breeze seemed like a blessing over the evening.

Scott and Melissa made their way to the camera phone and said hi to all their virtual guests.

Austin relayed the comments and well wishes. He was doing what he did best: solving problems with technology.

"Hey, little sis." Scott tapped her on the shoulder. "Got room on your dance card for your brother?"

She stepped into his arms. "Always for you. Besides, you're the star of the show tonight."

"Thanks to you. Melissa told me how much work you and Kim put into this. With everything that you had going on, I can't believe you had time."

"It wasn't that much. I just wanted you guys to have a special day. So are you glad you did it this way?"

"Oh yeah. I've learned this past year that life is too short not to spend it with those that you love. And in the words from *When Harry Met Sally*, when you find the person you want to spend the rest of your life with, you want the rest of your life to begin right away."

Jessica laughed. "Since when do you watch rom-coms?"

He shrugged. "They're not all that bad."

Melissa appeared over his shoulder as the song ended. "He puts up with them for my sake. It's my favorite movie. But seriously, we overcame a lot of obstacles to be together. It's not going to be easy. But it's going to be worth it."

Jessica blinked as the two moved off to talk to other guests. It had been a perfect night…for them. And that's all that mattered. The evening was winding down, and people were beginning to leave.

Kim and Matthew were giving her a ride home since she'd come with Melissa and Scott. There were a few things she needed to make sure ended up in Matthew's truck. She asked several of Melissa's close friends to be sure to take the centerpieces home.

Austin tapped her on the shoulder. "We haven't danced yet. Do you have time?"

She smiled. "I do."

His hand was warm on her back, her hand safe in his larger one. Only a few people were on the dance floor.

"Tonight went well. You and Kim did a great job pulling it off."

"You handled the technical part well. No surprise there." She smiled at him. They had danced before at Kyle and Heather's wedding. They wouldn't win any dance awards, but that wasn't the point.

"I recorded it too, so they'll have that to look back on." He paused then met her gaze. "Jessica, we need to talk—"

Kim touched her shoulder. "They're getting ready to leave."

She reluctantly stepped out of Austin's arms. "We do. But there will be time." She followed Kim, but when she looked back, Austin stood there with his hands in his pockets, staring after her.

Chapter Twenty-Six

When Austin walked into work Monday, he felt like so many things had changed since he left Friday morning. He'd changed. After setting his things at his desk, he grabbed coffee and went to Max's office. Luckily, he was already in.

"Hey, Austin. How's everything?"

"Fine." He lowered himself into Max's guest chair. He wasn't going to say anything, but then he remembered what Jessica had told him about sharing and being vulnerable. "Actually, my dad fell and hit his head. He had a small brain bleed, but he's home now."

"Wow. That must have been scary."

"It was a little." See? That wasn't so bad. "I ran into Edward before I left. He told me that he was recommending you not give me the director position. I'd like to ask you to hold off on that until you see the results from the gamified scrum we started last week to get SHIELD finished ahead of schedule."

Max leaned back in his chair. "I'm listening."

Austin opened his laptop and showed Max the leaderboard he'd created for team members to claim points as they checked off tasks on their projects. There was also a built-in chat feature. The good-natured trash talking scrolled by.

Max leaned forward. “Looks like they’re having fun.”

“They are. And they’re ahead of schedule. There are high stakes here for the team that finishes first.”

Max frowned. “What’s that?”

“Losing team has to buy the winning team ice cream.”

Max laughed. “Did you show this to Edward?”

“No, he didn’t give me the chance.”

Max nodded. “Okay. I like what you’ve done here, Austin. It’s exactly what I was looking for in a director. Let me do some thinking and talk to Edward. I’ll get back to you.”

“Fair enough.”

Austin closed his laptop, shook Max’s hand, and left the office. He had done the right thing. The outcome was in God’s hands.

Jessica spent the day packing up Melissa’s house. Melissa had said she didn’t have to, but Jessica needed to keep busy. Scott had surprised Melissa with a honeymoon at the Ritz Carlton in Laguna Niguel, and Jessica didn’t want them to worry about a thing.

In between packing boxes, she fielded calls from Madison, Lyric, and even Erika. They were stunned at the news about Eric and Crystal and that the salon was gone. It was weird to hear the admiration in their voices over what she had done.

Kyle called her and gave her an update on what he’d found out about Eric’s business dealings and the newly rescued girls.

She even talked to Sarah and Kim.

But she didn’t hear from Austin.

It was okay. Yes, it would hurt if Austin didn’t want a relationship with her, but she would be okay. God loved her. She might have made bad decisions in the past, but she wasn’t defective. She was worthy of love, and she was capable of making the right choice, the self-sacrificing one, when it mattered.

She grabbed her keys. She had somewhere she needed to go. A bit of closure would be good for her.

The traffic was heavier since it was getting close to rush hour. Kim called. "Do you want to have dinner with us? We could swing by and pick you up."

"Sure, but I'm not at home. Where are you guys going? I'll meet you there."

"California Fish Grill. But where are you?"

"I'm heading to the salon."

"You know it's not there anymore, right?" Kim gave a chuckle that sounded a bit forced.

"I know. I just need to…I don't know. See for myself that it's gone."

The line was quiet. "I understand. Just come whenever you're ready."

"I will."

A few minutes later, Jessica turned the corner to where the salon used to be. Police tape on pylons blocked off the parking lot and building. She parked along the curb and stepped out to the sidewalk. The building was a blackened pile of rubble. If she hadn't known what she was looking at, she would have never guessed it was her old place of employment, the place where she thought her career dreams were finally going to come true. And where, for the longest minutes of her life, she thought she might die.

It was this last thought that had driven her back here. She needed to see that it was defeated.

The blackened, shattered glass doors reflected the sun. She remembered seeing her reflection in them the first time she'd entered the salon, eager for the interview to go well. Now, even though they were still standing, they wouldn't be able to reflect the true changes inside Jessica.

She thought of her Inspiration for Today quote: "To be

yourself in a world that is constantly trying to make you something else is the greatest accomplishment."—Ralph Waldo Emerson. She'd been trying to be someone else for so long, and all it had done was brought her—and others—misery. Now she was discovering who she was and what her life would look like. She didn't have it all figured out yet, but that was okay. She knew Who she belonged to.

Footsteps sounded behind her on the sidewalk, and she spun.

Austin was walking toward her, a grin on his face.

"How did you know I was here?"

He lifted his phone. "Kim."

Jessica laughed. "So her invitation to dinner wasn't real, just a fact-finding mission?"

"No, it was real. But I'm hoping I can persuade you to do something else."

"What's that?"

He looked past her at the rubble. "I remember the first time I came here to pick you up. Hard to believe it wasn't that long ago."

Jessica laughed but her face heated at the memory. "You rescued me. Twice."

"I'm happy to be whatever you need, Jessica. I realized that I was holding part of myself back, trying to protect myself. I didn't believe I had enough…anything to deal with work, Dad's illness, and be what you needed." He stepped closer to her. "Dad told me to come back to you." He chuckled. "He was right. God will give me what I need when I need it. Can you forgive me for running out on you?"

She nodded, tears filling her eyes. "Of course. While you were gone, I learned something about myself. I can make good decisions, hard decisions. And I don't usually have to make them by myself. God sends us the right people when we need them. And I'm glad he sent me you."

Austin reached behind his neck and unfastened his shark-tooth necklace. "Jessica Blake, you are the strongest woman I know." He leaned forward into her space, his spicy scent surrounding her. He fastened the necklace around her, lifting her hair clear of the leather string when he was done. "Wear this to remember that I believe in you. And I want to be a part of your life."

She touched the shark's tooth. "Austin, this means a lot to you."

"You mean a lot to me. I love you." He slid his hand along her neck and pulled her close, covering her mouth with his. She tasted the sweet surrender of his heart.

Horns honked, and they got a few catcalls.

She pulled back. "Maybe we should go somewhere more private."

He tugged her close. "I don't care if the whole world knows I love you."

She ran her hand along his jaw. "I love you too, Austin Montgomery."

Chapter Twenty-Seven

Jessica had spent the whole afternoon running interference between Sophia and Sarah. She had hoped the bridal luncheon would have satisfied Sophia, the one thing she had completely her way. And it had been very nice. But today was Sarah's day, and Jessica was determined to help her have a day free from stress.

"Jessica, I know you're Sarah's wedding coordinator, but please, I need to talk to her. I want to make sure all the final details are exactly the way she wants them." Sophia tried to step around Jessica as she blocked the door to the bride's dressing room at the wedding venue.

Jessica took Sophia's arm and led her away from the door, hoping Sarah couldn't hear them. "Sophia, we've gone over this many times. Everything is exactly right, just as she wants it."

"Are you sure? Because—"

"Sophia." Jessica met her gaze. "Please. Let Sarah have her day without any stress or interference. It's the best gift you could give her."

Sophia took a step back, shock on her face. "Stress? Is that what you think I'm causing her?" Her face crumpled. "I'm going to be her sister-in-law in an hour. I'm family. I'm not *stress*." She marched around Jessica and wrenched open the door.

Oh no. The one thing she had promised Sarah she'd take care of.

Sarah looked up from where she perched on a padded bench, her wedding dress spilling out around her. She was a beautiful bride, dark hair curling around her face, veil not yet placed. "Sophia."

Sophia stood in front of Sarah. They had an audience of bridesmaids, Heather and Melissa, and Sarah's mother. "Jessica says I'm causing you stress. Is that true?"

Sarah's gaze darted over Sophia's shoulder to Jessica.

Sorry, she mouthed.

"Yes. It is. I know you mean well, but all of your suggestions have been overwhelming. That's why I asked Jessica to coordinate. She knows what I want."

Inwardly, Jessica cheered. *Yay, Sarah, for standing up for yourself.* She knew how hard that was for her. She liked peace in all her relationships.

All the fight went out of Sophia. "I never wanted to do that to you. I was trying to help you get what you wanted. When I married my husband, his mother picked out everything. I had no say in my own wedding. I didn't want that to happen to you. I wanted you to make sure you knew you had choices."

Sarah laughed. "I should have told you earlier. I'm sorry. My fear of conflict often leads to making situations worse when a simple conversation would have fixed things. Forgive me?" She reached out her hand.

"Of course. You're a beautiful bride marrying my brother. You've made him so happy. That's all I want, for the two of you to be happy."

"Thank you. Now, I think I need to get this veil on so I don't get us off schedule."

Jessica had never been more proud of Sarah.

AUSTIN WAS DETERMINED TO SPEND MORE TIME DANCING with Jessica at this wedding than the last one. He didn't even care that he wasn't a good dancer. He led her to the dance floor, much to her delight. He preferred the slow songs where he could hold her in his arms and just sway to the music, his cheek pressed to hers.

The wedding had been meaningful and the food fantastic. The garden courtyard where it was held sat on a hill. Little white lights were everywhere as the sky turned twilight and the city lights blinked on below. As the song ended, he took her hand and led her over to a particularly picturesque spot, a small alcove created by flowering plants. He thought it would be a good place to kiss her and remind her how much he loved her.

But as he leaned in, he saw a figure off in the distance. Who was that?

Jessica frowned at him. "What?"

"Is that Ryan?"

She turned to look. "Yeah. What's he doing here? I know he wasn't on the guest list. I hope he's not here to stir anything up. Let's go talk to him."

With her hand in his, they walked over to Ryan.

He gave them his movie-star grin, but Austin wasn't falling for it. "What brings you here?"

Ryan raised his hands. "I'm not here to make trouble. I just wanted to give them my best wishes and drop off a gift." He pulled a card out of his jacket pocket. "But maybe you should just give it to them for me. I was a jerk, and they both deserved better."

Jessica took the card from him.

"I heard about all the girls getting rescued." He glanced toward the festivities. "You two were instrumental in changing their lives."

Austin slid his arm around Jessica's waist. "We were in the right place at the right time."

"Yeah, about that." He scratched his forehead. "I've been talking to the church leadership about partnering with the recovery house that helps trafficked girls find their way forward."

"That's fantastic." Jessica glanced at Austin. "Austin and I have talked to them about volunteering there. He's going to teach them computer skills and online safety. I'm going to lead a Bible study, to help them see themselves the way God does."

"That sounds great. Maybe you can come talk to the leadership about the work you're doing there."

"We'd be happy to." She leaned into Austin.

He knew what she was leaving out. The check that Randy had given her she'd donated to the recovery house, and they'd put it to good use.

Ryan took a step back. "Well, I'd better be going. Pass on my best wishes, will you?"

"We will," Austin said.

Ryan walked a few steps away and then turned back. "Hey, I learned a lot from you guys that weekend. I want you to know that. I've spent some time in prayer and been doing a lot of soul searching. I think I haven't been on God's path for my life for some time now. You guys led by example. I have a feeling my life is going to look different real soon." He lifted a hand and walked off.

Jessica gazed up at Austin. "That was unexpected."

He laughed. "Almost as unexpected as Madison telling you she and Erika were opening a salon together and wanted you to join them."

She laughed with him. "Life has been full of surprises lately."

"Yes, but this isn't one of them." He leaned over and kissed her, promising her a future of following whatever adventure God had in store for them and trusting that he would provide what they needed. It was never going to be boring.

Want to know the details of what happened at Joe and Sarah's wedding?

And who is the mysterious guest that shows up?

Find out in "A Flickering New Start," an In the Shadow short story you can get by clicking here or going to https://BookHip.com/MLDCKMT

So what's in store next for the this group of friends and family? While this series is drawing to a close, a new series is coming with many of these characters making an appearance. The Holcomb Springs Small Town Romantic Suspense series will kick off with *Beneath a Star-Lit Sky.* You can order it here: https://amzn.to/3fGTVXg Keep reading for a sneak peek!

Make sure you're signed up for my Insider Updates so you can get the short story that links In the Shadows series to Holcomb Springs Small Town Romantic Suspense series.

You'll also get the prequel novella to the Hometown Heroes series, *Promise Me*— Grayson and Cait's story.

My bimonthly updates include upcoming books written by me and other authors you will enjoy, information on all my latest releases, sneak peeks of yet-to-be-released chapters, and exclusive giveaways. Your email address will never be shared, and you can unsubscribe at any time. You can sign up here: jlcrosswhite.com/promise

If you enjoyed this book, please leave a review. Reviews can be as simple as "I couldn't put it down. I can't wait for the next one" and help raise the author's visibility and lets other readers find her.

Keep reading for a sneak peek of *Beneath a Star-Lit Sky.*

Acknowledgments

This book would not be possible without the patience and willingness to read early drafts by Jennifer Lynn Cary. Jenny gets an extra dose of thanks for helping me brainstorm when I got stuck. Special thanks to Sara Benner for her expert proofreading! Many thanks to my early reviewers!

Much thanks and love to my children, Caitlyn Elizabeth and Joshua Alexander, for supporting my dream for many years and giving me time to write.

And most of all to my Lord Jesus, who makes all things possible and directs my paths.

Author's Note

When I started writing this book, I knew I wanted to talk about human trafficking. As I've been learning more and more about this version of modern-day slavery, I came to realize how prevalent it is and how vulnerable our kids especially are.

If you want more information, please check out the following websites:

rescuefreedom.org
humantraffickinghotline.org
inourbackyard.org
The human trafficking hotline is 1-888-373-7888

Both Jessica and Austin have been on quite the growth journey. We first met Jessica when she was drunk in *Special Assignment*. At the end of that book, she's made a commitment to sobriety. Then in *Out of Range*, both Jessica and Austin are part of the group that gets caught in the forest fire.

Jessica has to learn how to make her sobriety a priority even as her support system shifts and her world gets crazier. But she also learns that her risk-taking personality can be used for good.

Austin has to learn how to let people into his world, to open up and trust Jessica with his heart, knowing that people are flawed and imperfect and that's okay.

We've all had times when it felt like the sands of our world were shifting underneath us and we weren't sure how to make good choices going forward. Jessica and Austin show us how we can reach out to those around us to help us on this journey called life.

I hope you come away from reading *Over Her Head* with a little clearer understanding of how we are all created in God's image and how dearly he loves us and wants to rescue us.

About the Author

My favorite thing is discovering how much there is to love about America the Beautiful and the great outdoors. I'm an Amazon bestselling author, a mom to two navigating the young adult years while battling my daughter's juvenile arthritis, exploring the delights of my son's autism, and keeping gluten free.

A California native who's spent significant time in the Midwest, I'm thrilled to be back in the Golden State. Follow me on social media to see all my adventures and how I get inspired for my books!

www.JLCrosswhite.com
Twitter: @jenlcross
Facebook: Author Jennifer Crosswhite

Instagram: jencrosswhite
Pinterest: Jennifer Crosswhite

facebook.com/authorjennifercrosswhite
twitter.com/jenlcross
instagram.com/jencrosswhite
pinterest.com/tandemservices

Sneak Peek of Beneath a Star-Lit Sky

Leading inexperienced people in the wilderness, even by someone with the skills Reese Vega had, was a recipe for disaster. The only person he would do this gig for was his brother. Even then, he was starting to regret it.

Reese stood to the side of the trail, the vanilla scent of ponderosa pines wafting around him, and wished he was hiking alone. The trip had originally been booked by Holcomb Springs Outfitters as a snowshoe tour, but the snow had melted to slushy piles on the trail and only remained in the shadows of the trees. Still, it was a beautiful day, if only he could enjoy it. Alone.

As the group of several girlfriends who had come up for a weekend away passed him, one of the women screamed and jumped, grabbing her friend's arm. "What was that? I heard something in the bushes. Is it a bear? Or a mountain lion?" She shot Reese a wide-eyed look.

He resisted the urge to roll his eyes. "Probably just a squirrel."

With all the noise they'd made, most wildlife was long gone. Even the chattering blue jays had left the area. The squirrel was probably hoping for a handout. Reese craved the quiet of the outdoors. It soothed him in a way nothing else could, especially after his injury. But this… this was not the kind of outdoors he liked.

But it was a peace offering for his brother who ran Holcomb Springs Outfitters. Maybe it would help mend the fences Reese's enlisting in the military had broken in his pacifist family. He could only hope. They had wanted him to be someone different than who he was. They hadn't exactly been in his corner.

He pointed for the group to continue on the trail while he remained behind to check on the stragglers. There were always stragglers. It gave him a chance to grab a minute of quiet. His headache had worsened from the chatter of the women. That and their endless flirting. He'd almost take another tour of duty compared to more tourists.

But due to his traumatic brain injury, that was no longer an option. And he'd told his brother, Raul, that he'd help run his outfitters shop until Raul got back on his feet. Literally. He'd had knee surgery and couldn't lead the hikes and camping trips. And being as the outfitter shop was the family's main source of income, Reese couldn't say no.

It was only temporary. He'd do his family duty and make an attempt to improve relations. And then he could figure out what he was going to do next. And it wouldn't be escorting tourists through the wilderness.

Reese stepped toward the guest who had fallen behind. The man wasn't wearing proper hiking boots. His tennis shoes were soaked from the slush, and he was breathing hard, his face red. Many people had no idea how the seven-thousand-foot altitude could affect them.

"Not too much farther. The lookout point is just ahead. Great view of the lake. It'll be worth it." Reese tried to infuse his voice with an enthusiasm he didn't feel but Raul would expect. Raul was so much better with people than he was.

The man glanced up, nodded, and then went back to staring at the trail. Not enjoying the beauty around him, missing the whole point of a hike in the woods.

Reese shrugged as the man plodded past him. Not his problem. He rubbed his temples, hoping to ease the pain. Reaching into his pack, he grabbed a bottle of Aleve and popped a couple into his mouth, washing them down with water from his bottle.

A yelp went up from the area of the lookout, and Reese sprinted up the trail. One of the women on the girlfriends' trip was sitting on her bottom a little way down the slope of the lookout, just before the sharp drop-off.

Her friend rushed over to him. "We were trying to take a selfie with the lake in the background. I think she stepped off, and then she just fell."

He nodded and knelt beside the woman. Another two steps, and she would have been over the drop-off. People didn't have common sense. He should have been up here to keep an eye on them. But then what about the straggler? He didn't know how Raul did it.

"Are you hurt anywhere?" He scanned the woman, looking for any obvious sign of injury.

"My ankle. I think I twisted it when I stepped back and tried to catch my balance." She glanced up at him and gave him a small smile.

He tugged her jeans up above her ankle. At least she had boots on. He palpated the area. "Does that hurt?"

She winced. "A little."

It wasn't swollen, but that could change quickly. "What's your name?"

"Andrea." She looked up at him and bit her lip.

He should have remembered. Raul would have remembered. He never did live up to his family's expectations. He reached in his pack for an Ace elastic wrap from the first aid kit. He eased off her boot, wrapped her ankle, then slipped the boot back on with the laces loosened. "That should stabilize it to get you down the hill. Do you think you can put any weight on it?"

"Maybe. If you help me."

A glance shot among her friends, smiles they didn't try to hide.

Great. Was this a set up? "Okay, everyone get your final pictures, and we'll head back." He slipped his arm under the woman's shoulders. "On three, we're going to stand together. Just put your weight on your good foot and lean on me."

Her "okay" came out breathy.

"One, two, three." He pushed to his feet and pulled the woman up with him.

She gingerly put weight on her foot then immediately retracted it. "It hurts to stand on it."

He should have her friends help her back down the trail. "Let's get one of your friends on the other side."

Another woman stepped to the side of Andrea, and between the two of them, she hobbled down the trail.

"It's a good thing we have a strong guy like you to help us out of trouble," the friend said, someone else whose name he couldn't remember.

And there it was. Raul was married, so maybe he didn't have women hitting on him all the time, but there was almost always one on every tour he'd done so far. "Best not to get into trouble in the first place."

He got them back down to the van and loaded up. "Do you want me to take you to the urgent care clinic? It's not big, but we have a doc who can check out your ankle."

Andrea shook her head. "No, it's not as sore as it was at first."

Her cheeks tinged pink, and he wondered if it hurt at all.

"Besides," she quickly added, "my friends can take me later if I need to go. I'll just put some ice on it back in our room."

They pulled into Holcomb Springs Outfitters parking lot. Raul came out in his knee brace to help the guests with their gear and thank them for coming.

Reese closed the van door as the last guest left.

Raul laid a hand on his shoulder. "You should thank the

guests and ask them to come back. Let them know we enjoy serving them."

"Even if we don't?" Reese brushed past him and carried the gear into the back of the shop. He'd have to repack the first-aid kit. "I don't lie." He opened the kit and rummaged through the supplies.

"It's not lying. It's good business."

Reese grunted. He never was going to see eye to eye with his family on things. Important things.

"How'd it go?"

"Fine." He told Raul about Andrea's injury. "I'm not convinced it wasn't an elaborate setup by her and her friends to flirt with me."

Raul grinned. "It's all part of the game. I should keep you around, put your face on the brochures and ads. It'd be good for business."

"I'm only here until you are well enough to lead the tours again."

The grin disappeared from Raul's face, and his whole body deflated as if more than his knee was injured.

Reese almost wished he could take the words back, but what was the point? Raul needed to know the score. Reese repacked the bag and made sure everything was ready to go for the next trip. Military preparedness had been ingrained in him.

Raul put his hand on the door leading from the back of the shop to the main floor. "Want to come over for dinner?"

Reese recognized the olive branch. "Tell Marissa I appreciate the offer." He knew it'd come from Raul's wife. "But I wouldn't be good company. My head's killing me. I'm going to go lie down."

Raul's brow furrowed, but they'd been down this road enough that he knew not to baby Reese. Instead, he gave a short nod. "Come on over if you change your mind."

Reese lifted his chin, hefted his backpack, and headed out to his classic 1978 red-and-white Bronco. In a few minutes, he was on the road heading toward Holcomb Lake and the garage apartment on Raul and Marissa's lake house, looking forward to staring at the water and appreciating the quiet, hoping it would calm his pounding head.

He should give Raul more credit. He was trying. But in the end, would anything change? He'd trusted his family to have his back and they'd let him down. Letting himself get too close, too trusting again, would only end in heartache.

Ella Sommer's neatly ordered world meant that on Saturday nights, while Mom was bowling with her friends, Ella had dinner with Amanda. Ella liked nothing better than ending the week with a good meal shared with a good friend. She parked her Subaru in front of the restaurant in downtown Holcomb Springs. This time of year was her favorite, between holidays when it was just the locals and not full of tourists, when she knew practically everyone she saw.

By the end of February, her fifth-grade classes always got restless. Christmas break was too far in the rearview mirror and spring break was around the corner, just not close enough. Winter had kept them cooped up for too long. So dinner at Bella Sorgenti with her co-teacher and best friend, Amanda Elliot, was the break she needed. And they hadn't even had the opportunity to dish about the Spread the Love dinner dance last weekend, an event Ella had purposely chosen to serve at from the kitchen, where she heard some gossip but couldn't see who all had attended. It was long past time for a girlfriend sesh.

She climbed out and headed for the wooden sidewalk. Downtown tried to maintain a Western theme in a nod to its gold-rush roots. Watching that she didn't step in a pile of slush, she barely noticed that someone was holding the door to Bella Sorgenti for her.

"Thanks," she mumbled and then looked up. Her feet froze

in place. "Oh, hi, Lucas." She had avoided her ex-fiancé and coworker at school as much as possible since their relationship ended over Christmas break.

"Hi, Ella. How are you?" His brown eyes were warm, and for a moment, she thought he genuinely wanted to know. Maybe they'd moved from the avoidance stage to the cordial stage.

But before she could speak, she noticed a woman with him. A beautiful woman she had never seen before. Who had her hand threaded through Lucas's. So, not a cousin or visiting family member. Well, of course Lucas was dating again. Why not?

"Uh, good. Meeting, ah, someone for dinner, actually." He didn't need to know it was Amanda.

Lucas tugged the woman closer. "I'd like you to meet Sophie Graff, my fiancée."

Sophie took a half step forward. "So nice to meet you. You teach with Lucas, right?"

Ella didn't know what she was expecting, but it wasn't that. Too many competing thoughts and emotions flooded her, and it took all of her self-control to keep them from showing. At least, she hoped that's what she was doing.

She nodded, hoping she didn't look like a bobblehead doll. "Yep, I work with Lucas." But before she could politely extricate herself from this mess and get inside and drown her emotions in carbs, Sophie stuck out her left hand. Was she supposed to shake it? Did she not want to let go of Lucas's hand that much? Then the dazzling diamond caught Ella's eye. The ring.

She barely gave it a glance. "That's very lovely. Well, have a great evening. I'd best get inside." Sidling around Sophie, she let the warmth and comforting scents of Bella Sorgenti envelop her. Scanning the room, she didn't see Amanda. She stepped up to the podium. "Hi, Selena. It'll be Ms. Elliot and me tonight. She's not here yet, is she?" Ella had Selena in her classroom the first year she'd taught.

"No, but your favorite table is open. I'll bring her back when she comes."

"Thanks." Ella made a beeline for the private booth and slid inside, avoiding making eye contact with others in the restaurant. She just couldn't deal with being polite to anyone at this moment. Selena followed with a basket of warm, buttery garlic bread and a bottle of sparkling Italian mineral water. Ella took a bite of the bliss and closed her eyes.

So Lucas hadn't wasted any time moving on. Dating, she had suspected. After all, he was a catch. Thin, with a close-cropped beard, always dressed well, had a good job. But engaged? They hadn't been broken up three months yet. And Sophie clearly wasn't a local girl.

Amanda slid in the booth across from her. "Sorry I'm late."

"If you'd been here a few minutes earlier, you could have witnessed one of the more awkward moments of my life."

Amanda reached for the garlic bread. "Which was?"

Ella gave her the rundown, watching Amanda's face. "You knew, didn't you? That's why some of the conversations in the teachers' lounge stop when I come in. I thought it was just about our breakup."

Amanda shook her head. "I didn't know for sure. But I'd heard some snippets that made me wonder. I didn't think he'd be engaged though."

Miranda came over and took their orders, which were always the same. Spinach lasagna for Ella and whatever seasonal ravioli there was for Amanda. And a piece of tiramisu to split for dessert. The routine was as comforting as the food and company. And after the shock Ella had, she needed some comforting.

After Miranda left, Amanda leaned her forearms on the table. "How are you feeling?"

Ella shrugged. "Shocked mostly. Maybe numb, I don't know. I'm actually not sad. I don't want Lucas back. I wasn't even that sad when we broke up. What's wrong with me?"

"There's nothing wrong with you. Lucas is one of those guys

who looks good on paper, but there really wasn't that magical chemistry between the two of you that great couples have."

Ella waved that away. "That's only on the Hallmark channel or romance novels. Relationships need more than chemistry."

"I know, but they need chemistry too."

Amanda was an inveterate romantic, so Ella wasn't going to argue with her. Ella's nature was more practical. It was why, she supposed, they worked so well together. Their styles complemented each other. The best tactic was to change the subject.

"Any news from the Spread the Love dance since I was stuck in the kitchen the whole time?"

Amanda thought for a moment. "Wally and Stan put everyone to shame with their dancing, as usual. For a couple of old guys, they sure can move. You'd never guess, the way they plant themselves at the booth at the Jitter Bug Too or the hardware store."

"And we raised enough money to upgrade some of the equipment at the community center. Not every kid wants to play basketball after school in the winter." Since she volunteered there a lot helping with tutoring, she had a sense of what the kids wanted. "I'm hoping we can install a climbing wall."

Amanda pointed a piece of bread at her. "Maybe we could get Reese or Raul Vega to teach the kids."

Ella's lovely dinner turned to lead in her stomach. "Reese? He's back? On leave, or is he out of the military?"

"Yeah. Didn't you know? He was at the Spread the Love dinner with Raul and Marissa. I guess he's helping out while Raul's knee is healing." Amanda's gaze narrowed at her. "What's going on? You look pale. You didn't even react that strongly to Lucas."

Ella shook her head. "Oh, it's nothing. We just went to high school together, that's all, and not even that long. He was a senior when I was a freshman."

"Uh huh." Amanda's gaze didn't waver. "Spill."

Ella's face heated. Why? She'd had so little interaction with him, she had no idea why her body was betraying her. She shrugged. "I might have had a crush on him, but he was the high school bad boy. It was a long time ago. He couldn't wait to leave town. I'm surprised he's back."

That was the problem with letting someone get to know you. They knew you too well. Amanda still studied her. "Maybe he has strong family ties."

Ella shook her head. "I didn't get that impression. Raul is quite a bit older. I don't even remember his parents."

Amanda grinned. "I didn't think you knew him all that well."

"I didn't. It's a small town. Everyone knew everyone." They desperately needed to change the subject. It was suddenly way too hot in here. "Back to Spread the Love. Was Lucas there with Sophie?"

Amanda opened her mouth then closed it. "Yeah."

"I wonder if she had her bling and if everyone already knows what I didn't." Ella poured more sparkling water and sucked it down.

Amanda reached over and touched her hand.

Ella shook her head. "It's not that I'm upset that he's engaged. I don't want him back. I just don't want people pitying me and talking about me behind my back. That's all."

Amanda leaned back as Miranda set the tiramisu between them along with two coffees and to-go boxes.

Forking a bite of the chocolate, espresso, and creamy confection into her mouth, Ella moaned. "This is the cure for everything."

Amanda nodded, eyes closed with her own bite. After she had taken a sip of coffee, she said, "That still leaves your problem."

"I don't have a problem."

Amanda laughed. "I think you have two: Lucas and Reese. What is your plan? And I know you always have a plan."

"Eat a lot of this?" She wiggled her eyebrows as she scooped up more dessert. "How can anything be bad when this tastes so good." She leaned her head back against the booth. "Seriously, though, I can just avoid both of them. If I've managed to do it while working with Lucas, I can certainly avoid Reese until he leaves again. I doubt he'd even remember me." A flash of memory flicked through her brain, but she pushed it away before Amanda could discern something and grill her about it. "Speaking of plans, what are yours for spring break?"

"My parents are using a time share in Palm Springs, and they invited me down. At least it'll be warm, even if I'll be surrounded by old people."

"And college students."

Amanda conceded that. "Just nobody my age. What about you? Please tell me you are making plans beyond organizing your book collection or spices."

"Hey! An organized house runs smoothly and saves everyone time. Since Mom and I take turns cooking, it's important that we both are on the same page where everything is kept." She pointed her fork at Amanda. "You have benefited firsthand from my organization skills."

"Point taken. But it's not an acceptable activity for spring break. You need to get out of here and do something."

Ella sipped her coffee. "I know. I've been thinking about it. You know, Lucas accused me once of being incredibly predictable. That was one of the reasons for our breakup, even. Not that he's Mr. Adventure. I actually thought being predictable was an asset. But it's gotten me to thinking; what could I do that would be unpredictable, that I would enjoy?"

"What did you like to do as a kid? Did your family go anywhere special, do anything? You, your mom, and Evan," she quickly corrected. "Sorry."

She'd stumbled onto a sore spot in Ella's life. Her dad had left them when she was ten and then faded out of their lives. "We went camping a few times, usually with another family from church, and we borrowed equipment. It was fun. I remember running around, climbing on things, getting dirty, and none of it mattered." She put her coffee cup down and smiled. "It was like we were one big family. Mom's burden was lightened, and it was like Evan and I had a bunch of cousins. I haven't thought about that in a long time." She took a sip and tilted her head. "That actually kind of sounds like fun. Not the getting dirty part but being outdoors, not having a schedule. But I can't camp alone. Ooh, maybe I could go to one of those campgrounds that has trailers already set up. Some of them are retro, really cute. That could be fun."

Amanda scooped up the last of the tiramisu. "Talk to Anne. She knows everything and will have all the best info, saving you googling time."

"Good point. I'll swing by the library Monday after school. I need to meet with her anyway to set up the spring break reading program for the kids."

"Promise me something." Amanda turned to her as they left the restaurant. "Do something fun and unexpected, okay? If you don't have a solid plan, I'm dragging you to Palm Springs with me. Friends don't let friends organize their spices on spring break."

Ella laughed and gave her a hug. "I promise. I'll have fun, and it'll be unexpected."

BUY *BENEATH A STAR-LIT SKY* HERE. HTTPS://WWW.jlcrosswhite.com/books/beneath-a-star-lit-sky/

Books by JL Crosswhite

Sign up for my latest updates at www.JLCrosswhite.com and be the first to know when my next series is releasing.

Romantic Suspense

The Hometown Heroes Series

Promise Me

Cait can't catch a break. What she witnessed could cost her job and her beloved farmhouse. Will Greyson help her or only make things worse?

Protective Custody

She's a key witness in a crime shaking the roots of the town's power brokers. He's protecting a woman he'll risk everything for. Doing the right thing may cost her everything. Including her life.

Flash Point

She's a directionally-challenged architect who stumbled on a crime that could destroy her life's work. He's a firefighter protecting his hometown… and the woman he loves.

Special Assignment

A brain-injured Navy pilot must work with the woman in charge of the program he blames for his injury. As they both grasp to save their careers, will their growing attraction hinder them as they attempt solve the mystery of who's really at fault before someone else dies?

In the Shadow Series

Off the Map

For her, it's a road trip adventure. For him, it's his best shot to win her back. But for the stalker after her, it's revenge.

Out of Range

It's her chance to prove she's good enough. It's his chance to prove he's more than just a fun guy. Is it their time to find love, or is her secret admirer his deadly competition?

Over Her Head

On a church singles' camping trip that no one wants to be on, a weekend away to renew and refresh becomes anything but. A group of friends trying to find their footing do a good deed and get much more than they bargained for.

Writing as Jennifer Crosswhite

Contemporary Romance

The Inn at Cherry Blossom Lane

Can the summer magic of Lake Michigan bring first loves back together? Or will the secret they discover threaten everything they love?

Historical Romance

The Route Home Series

Be Mine

A woman searching for independence. A man searching for education. Can a simple thank you note turn into something more?

Coming Home

He was why she left. Now she's falling for him. Can a woman who turned her back on her hometown come home to find justice for her brother without falling in love with his best friend?

The Road Home

He is a stagecoach driver just trying to do his job. She is returning to her suitor only to find he has died. When a stack of stolen money shows up in her bag, she thinks the past she has desperately tried to hide has come back to haunt her.

Finally Home

The son of a wealthy banker poses as a lumberjack to carve out his own identity. But in a stagecoach robbery gone wrong, he meets the soon-to-be schoolteacher with a vivid imagination, a gift for making things grow, and an obsession with dime novels. As the town is threatened by a past enemy, can he help without revealing who he is? And will she love him when she learns the truth?

Made in the USA
Middletown, DE
18 August 2025

12510552R00182